"You okay? What's going on?"

Joe asked.

Annie laughed. "I'm fine. I was just getting dressed."

When she stopped and pressed a hand to the smile that kept turning up the corners of her mouth, he arched a brow. "And?"

"And I can't snap my jeans," she admitted, grinning broadly. "Look."

She held up her blouse, revealing her slim hips and barely zipped, unsnapped jeans. His gaze drawn like a magnet, all Joe could think about was wrapping her close in his arms so that nothing and no one could ever hurt her or the baby again. She was his. *They* were his—

Even as he tried to convince himself, his mind taunted him with images of Annie in the arms of another man. No! he wanted to roar. She wouldn't have done that to him, to *them*. She couldn't have.

But then again, he'd never thought she'd leave, either.

Dear Reader,

It's summer. The days are long…hot…just right for romance. And we've got six great romances right here, just waiting for you to settle back and enjoy them. Linda Turner has long been one of your favorite authors. Now, in *I'm Having Your Baby?!* she begins a great new miniseries, THE LONE STAR SOCIAL CLUB. Seems you may rent an apartment in this building single, but you'll be part of a couple before too long. It certainly works that way for Annie and Joe, anyway!

Actually, this is a really great month for miniseries. Ruth Wind continues THE LAST ROUNDUP with *Her Ideal Man,* all about a ranching single dad who's not looking for love but somehow ends up with a pregnant bride. In the next installment of THE WEDDING RING, *Marrying Jake*, Beverly Bird matches a tough cop with a gentle rural woman—and four irresistible kids.

Then there's multi-award-winning Kathleen Creighton's newest, *Never Trust a Lady.* Who would have thought small-town mom Jane Carlysle would end up involved in high-level intrigue—and in love with one very sexy Interpol agent? Maura Seger's back with *Heaven in His Arms,* about how one of life's unluckiest moments—a car crash—somehow got turned into one of life's best, and all because of the gorgeous guy driving the other car. Finally, welcome debut author Raina Lynn. In *A Marriage To Fight For,* she creates a wonderful second-chance story that will leave you hungry for more of this fine new writer's work.

Enjoy them all, and come back next month for more terrific romance—right here in Silhouette Intimate Moments.

Leslie J. Wainger
Senior Editor and Editorial Coordinator

Please address questions and book requests to:
Silhouette Reader Service
U.S.: 3010 Walden Ave., P.O. Box 1325, Buffalo, NY 14269
Canadian: P.O. Box 609, Fort Erie, Ont. L2A 5X3

Linda Turner

I'm Having Your Baby?!

Silhouette®
INTIMATE™ MOMENTS®

Published by Silhouette Books
America's Publisher of Contemporary Romance

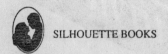 SILHOUETTE BOOKS

ISBN 0-373-07799-8

I'M HAVING YOUR BABY?!

Copyright © 1997 by Linda Turner

Printed in U.S.A.

LINDA TURNER

began reading romances in high school and began writing them one night when she had nothing else to read. She's been writing ever since. Single and living in Texas, she travels every chance she gets, scouting locales for her books.

Prologue

Gasping, her lungs straining, she ran through the dark, deserted alleys of downtown like a wild thing, her face as colorless as the pale moon that played hide-and-seek with the clouds overhead. The night was chilly, the black asphalt of the streets damp from the recent rain, but she never noticed the cold or the still-dripping eaves and dirty puddles that had collected in potholes. Blindly, she ran on, granting herself no mercy despite the stitch that burned like a fire in her side. Only one thought hammered in her brain. Home. She had to get home. She would be safe there.

Somewhere in the stygian darkness behind her, the terror she couldn't put a name to hunted her. She'd lost him for now, but she knew he was back there somewhere in the maze of shadowy streets and alleys, cursing her, damning her, chasing her. She could feel him, smell him on her skin. If he got his hands on her again, he wouldn't make the mistake of letting her fight free a second time. Sobbing, she cut through another dark passageway, her long hair streaming out behind her.

Suddenly, a large Victorian house loomed before her, looking as out of place among the towering buildings of downtown as a well-preserved but shrunken old woman among giants. Frantic, she tried to punch in the security code that opened the front door, but her fingers were trembling so badly she couldn't manage it. Her blue eyes wide with fright, she dared to look over her shoulder. It was three in the morning and the street behind her was empty and still. Too still. Whimpering, she whirled back to the keypad and wildly stabbed in numbers. When she finally hit the right combination three tries later, she was through the door in a flash.

She didn't remember running through the deserted foyer or darting up the central staircase that looked like it had come straight out of *Gone with the Wind*. Suddenly, she was stumbling to a stop in front of her own apartment, and somewhere deep inside, the control that had gotten her this far started to crack.

Shaking with reaction, she fumbled for the spare key on the ledge above the door and practically fell inside. The second the door shut behind her, darkness engulfed her. Then the tears started. Hot, endless, racking tears that slid soundlessly down her cheeks. Wrapping her arms around herself, she wanted to collapse boneless to the floor, but she couldn't. Not yet. Not when she could still smell the monster's sweat on her, still feel his hands on her, hurting her, marking her skin. Bile rising in her throat, she tore at her clothes and stumbled to the bathroom without bothering to turn on a light.

Dazed, aching, desperate to be clean again, she stood under the shower lathering herself with hands that felt like they would never be steady again. Her arms grew heavy, her movements stiff and jerky. The hot water turned lukewarm, then finally cold. Roused from the numbness that engulfed her like a fog, she blindly shut off the shower and grabbed a towel. Tired. God, she was so tired! Exhaustion pulling at her, she made her way down the dark hall to the bedroom and slipped into bed. Before her head hit the pillow, her mind shut down and she was spiraling down into the black, protective folds of sleep.

Chapter 1

It rained again just after dawn, the slow, soaking, drizzly kind of rain that made it impossible to crawl out of bed in the morning. Snuggling deeper under the covers, she buried her face in her pillow and fought wakefulness with everything she had in her. It was early yet, she thought drowsily, refusing to open her eyes to check the clock. And she was still so tired—she felt like she'd just gone to bed. Just two more hours. That was all she needed. Maybe then she'd wake up with enough energy to get her through the day.

But even as her mind drifted and sleep beckoned, the murmur of the rain called softly, insistently, to her. Outside the bedroom window, the city was beginning to wake up. Traffic was already starting to pick up, and somewhere nearby, the steady warning beep of a delivery truck backing up shattered the peace of the morning. Groaning, she gave up in defeat and pushed up on her elbows to check the clock on the nightstand. Her eyes never made it past the dark head on the pillow next to her.

A man. There was a man in bed with her.

Horrified, she stared at him in confusion. She was hallucinating. She had to be. Who was he? What did he want? The answers her dazed mind supplied sent sick panic skittering through her. Dear God, what had he done to her? With bile rising in her throat, she searched her blurred memory for answers, but before she could come up with any, he stirred, and her heart stopped in midbeat. Scrambling backward on the bed, her only thought to get away, she screamed.

Sound asleep, Joe Taylor jerked awake. "What the hell!"

Bolting up and still groggy, he instinctively grabbed for the gun he kept in the nightstand drawer. It wasn't until his fingers closed around the cold, hard butt of the revolver that he recognized the sharp, feminine cry and realized that the only threat was the unexpected visitor in his bed.

And just as quickly, he was furious. What the hell was she doing here? Did she think she could leave him for two months without a word, then crawl back into his bed whenever the mood struck her? Like hell!

Shoving the gun back in the drawer, he turned toward her, angry words already rising to his tongue, only to freeze, shocked, at the sight of her. With her stubborn chin, wide mouth, and too large eyes, she'd never fit the traditional definition of beauty, but there had always been something about her that had stolen the breath right out of his lungs. This time was no different, but not for the usual reasons. Looking thinner, more petite than he remembered, she was pale as a ghost, her oval face scratched and bruised, her sapphire eyes wide and terrified.

"What the hell happened to you?" he demanded. "You look like you've been in a fight."

When she cringed like a trapped animal, Joe scowled.

What the devil was wrong with her? Why was she looking at him like that? He started to ask her, but she never gave him a chance. Her eyes darting around the room, she felt blindly behind her for the edge of the mattress. When she found it, she whirled and flew from the bed...only to take two steps and suddenly seem to realize she was naked.

"Oh, God!" she gasped.

Blushing scarlet, she swallowed a sob and looked frantically around for something to cover herself with. All she found was a towel on the floor. In the time it took to blink, she had it wrapped around her and was running for the door.

There'd been a time when Joe would have laughed at her modesty, snatched the towel from her, and dragged her back into bed for some serious loving. But not now. Not after she'd completely cut herself off from him for two months. And not after he'd caught sight of the bruises covering her. Spitting out a curse, he rolled from the bed and moved, lightning-quick, to cut her off.

"Dammit, quit running from me!" he snapped, uncaring that he was standing stark naked before her. "You're hurt. Let me see."

"No!" Her eyes wide and desperate and dark with terror, she backed away from him as if he was a rapist. "Stay a-away from m-me!" she stuttered in rising hysteria. "You even think about hurting me, and I swear I'll claw your eyes out! If you don't believe me, you just try it!"

Shocked, Joe stopped in his tracks. "Hurt you?" he repeated incredulously. "You think I would *hurt* you?"

"I don't know!" she cried, looking anywhere but at him. "How am I supposed to know what you're capable of? I've never seen you before in my life!"

Unable to believe he'd heard her correctly, Joe blinked in confusion. Was this some kind of joke, or what? She had to be pulling his leg. But Annie had never been much of an actress—her feelings were always right there on her face for the whole world to read. And right now, there was nothing but terror there. And a total lack of recognition in her eyes.

Dear God, she wasn't faking. She really didn't know who he was!

Staggered, he frowned at her in bewilderment. What the hell was going on here? How could she not know him? He was her husband, for God's sake!

Not thinking—needing some answers, dammit!—he started to reach for her, only to have her shrink back in horror. He stiffened, a muscle clenching in his jaw. He'd thought she no longer had the power to hurt him. He was wrong. His expression grim, he carefully reached past her for the robe hanging on the hook on the back of the bedroom door.

Any hope that she would feel less threatened when he was decently covered died the second he belted the robe and lifted his eyes to hers. Her arms crossed protectively across her breasts to hold the thick bath sheet in place, she bumped up against the door, wariness etched in every line of her slender body.

"I'm Joe Taylor," he said quietly. "Your husband."

Whatever reaction he had been expecting, it wasn't the sudden flash of temper in her sapphire eyes. "Don't be ridiculous. If you were my husband, don't you think I'd remember you?"

For an answer, he strode over to the dresser, snatched up a silver-framed photo, and thrust it into her hands. "Then how do you explain this?"

The smiling man and woman who stared up at her from the picture were decked out in their wedding finery and obviously very much in love. And while there was no doubt that the groom had the same square-jawed, rugged good looks, brown eyes, and coal-black hair as the man standing before her wearing nothing but a robe, the woman was a total stranger to her.

Puzzled, she tried to shove the picture back into his hand, but he wouldn't take it. "If this is supposed to prove something, I missed the point. That's not me."

"The hell it isn't! If you don't believe me, look in the mirror."

She should have, but something held her back. Something that gripped at her heart with cold fingers. "No."

"Why?" he asked softly. "Because you're afraid I'm right? Then tell me what you look like."

Goaded, she opened her mouth to do just that, but no words came out. Nothing. She didn't have a clue if she was a redhead or a bleached blonde, pretty or plain. Fear, like a snake slithering through high grass, slipped through her blood, and the only way she could fight it was to look in the mirror. Without a word, she jerked around to face the dresser.

And came face-to-face with the woman in the picture. "No!"

She thought she screamed, but her cry was hardly more than a hoarse, strangled whisper. The reflected image was bruised and scratched, but there was no question that the woman in the mirror and the one in the wedding picture were one and the same. They were both her, and she didn't recognize either one of them.

"No!" she cried again, her voice strong with fear as she shoved the picture back into the hands of the tall, lean man who watched her like a hawk. Her husband. Oh, God! "This is some kind of a trick," she said desperately. "I don't know who you are or how you managed to make that picture, but I want you out of here. Do you hear me? Get out!"

Joe had no intention of going anywhere, but he knew if he made one wrong move, she was going to shatter. "Calm down,'' he said soothingly, taking a step back and giving her room. ''Nobody's going to hurt you, especially me. Just take it easy. There's nothing to worry about—people have trouble with their memories all the time. Just relax and it'll probably all come back to you. Do you remember your name?''

She automatically opened her mouth to answer, only to hesitate, the arrested look of surprise that washed over her face changing abruptly to horror. Stricken, she stared up at him helplessly.

She couldn't remember her own name.

Something twisted in Joe's heart. ''It's Annie,'' he told her gruffly. ''Annie Taylor. Sit down, honey, and let's talk about this. Tell me what you do remember. What'd you do yesterday?''

Hot tears slowly gathering in her eyes, she just looked at him blankly. ''I don't know. I—I don't remember.''

''Then how about last night?'' he tried. ''You weren't here when I went to bed, so you must have come in sometime after that. How did you get in? Did you have your key with you? Where's your purse?''

He kept the questions simple, but she didn't have any answers. She couldn't even tell him what day it was, and she was scared out of her mind. He couldn't say he blamed her. More worried than he dared let her see, he said, ''Maybe you left it in the living room. Let's check it out.''

With her trailing behind him, he strode out of the bedroom and looked around for her purse. But there was no purse, no luggage, nothing but a single key lying on the table in the entrance hall. ''Well, this explains how you got in,'' he said, holding up the key. ''You used the spare that's usually kept over the doorjamb. Now, what about your clothes?''

They found them in a heap on the bathroom floor, torn, dirty and bloody. Joe swore at the sight of them and turned to find her staring at them without the slightest sign of recognition. Her face was expressionless, as if the bloody clothes themselves had nothing to do with her, and it was that, more than anything, that told him something was very, very wrong.

"I think you need to see a doctor," he told her. "Today."

"No!"

The panic was back in her eyes, and she looked ready to bolt.

Moving to reassure her, he said quickly, "I'm not talking about going to a hospital or anything like that. Just to a friend. Grant Alexander. I know you don't remember him, but he was best man at our wedding, and he's a damn good internist. All I have to do is give him a call and he'll fit you in this morning."

"But I don't have any clothes—"

"There are some things in the closet in the bedroom," he cut in, his mouth flattening as he thought of the things she'd left behind in her haste to leave. "Why don't you get dressed while I give Grant a call?"

She didn't want to—he could see the doubts clearly in her eyes—but she couldn't seem to come up with another excuse. Nodding reluctantly, she headed for the bedroom.

"What do you mean, you woke up and she was in bed with you?" Grant demanded the second Joe called him and told him Annie was back. "Just like that? After she disappeared for months?"

"I always knew where she was, Grant. She called me the day after she left and gave me the address of the apartment she'd rented," Joe reminded him. "And Phoebe kept in touch." In fact, if it hadn't been for Annie's best friend and partner in the real estate office they ran together, he wouldn't have known if his wife was alive or dead.

"But Annie was the one who should have been talking to you. Not that I'm criticizing," he added quickly. "You know I'm crazy about her, buddy. I think you two were made for each other—I just don't know how you kept from going after her. I know, I know—you promised her you wouldn't, but I'd have been over there ten minutes after she told you where she was. So is she back for good or what?"

"I wish to God I knew," Joe said flatly. "There's a problem. I think she's got amnesia."

"Yeah, right. Tell me another one."

"I'm serious, Grant." He told him everything then, from the second he'd awakened to find her naked in his bed to the moment he found her bloody clothes on the bathroom floor. "I'm telling you, something's seriously wrong. She didn't even remember her name until I told her what it was."

"That sounds pretty damn convenient, don't you think?"

Joe stared at the locked bathroom door that Annie was hiding behind and had to admit that there was a cynical side of him that had wondered the same thing. But the look of panic on her face when she'd looked at their wedding picture was something that would go with him to his grave. Not even an Academy Award–winning actress could fake that kind of fear.

"You wouldn't ask that if you could see her," he said. "She's got some nasty bruises on her. In fact, she's banged up pretty bad. I don't know if she's been in an accident or car wreck or what, but every time I get anywhere near her, she starts shaking like a leaf."

"Then what was she doing in bed with you this morning?"

"To tell you the truth, I don't even think she knew I was there. And I was dead to the world. It seems like I've been putting in twenty-hour days ever since she left, and last night I guess it just caught up with me. I never heard her come in. Then, this morning, she woke up screaming. I'm telling you, Grant, she's really got me worried.''

He didn't ask his friend if he could take a look at her, but he didn't have to. All business, he said, ''I'll meet you at the office within the hour.''

''We'll be there,'' Joe said with a quiet sigh of relief. ''Thanks, pal. I owe you one.''

Dressed in a faded yellow blouse and old jeans that apparently should have been familiar to her but weren't, Annie followed the grim-faced, enigmatic man who claimed to be her husband into the parking garage where he kept his car. He, too, had changed, and looked much less threatening in black slacks and a white shirt than he had naked. Still, as she walked from the sunny street into the darkened interior of the garage, she felt as if someone had stepped on her grave. Shivering, she stopped cold, unable to make herself go any farther.

Don't be a ninny, an irritated voice muttered in her head. *You can do this.*

She had to. Her past, her very identity, had somehow been stolen from her, and the cold black hole in her memory scared her to death. She didn't know who she was or what she was, and if she was ever going to find out, she had to go with him to his doctor friend and find out what was wrong with her.

But when Joe stopped next to a green Regal that was apparently his, then unlocked and opened the passenger door for her, a soul-destroying fear came out of nowhere to clutch her by the throat. ''No!'' she said hoarsely. ''I can't do it!''

Surprised, Joe glanced over his shoulder to find that she'd stopped six feet back. ''Can't do what? You said you'd go to the doctor.''

"I know. I'm sorry. I thought I could, but I can't." Her gaze slipped from him to the car, and right before his eyes, she turned a sickly shade of green. "I can't," she choked. "I can't get in that car with you."

A muscle bunched in his jaw. "So it's me."

"No. Yes! I don't know!" she cried.

In the dark, quiet shadows that surrounded them, she thought she heard him swear, but she couldn't be sure. He was so quick at hiding what he was thinking—she couldn't read his eyes at all. Was he going to insist she get in his car? The coppery taste of fear pooled on her tongue. What if he tried to force her? Was he the type of man who would do that? God, why couldn't she remember?

Frustrated, furious with herself for not remembering, she knew she'd fight him if he so much as laid a finger on her. But the struggle she braced for never materialized. Instead, even as she watched, the tension slowly drained out of him. "Okay," he sighed, "if you can't, you can't. It's no big deal. The important thing is to get you to the doctor. Would you feel more comfortable if I called a cab? *I'll* follow you in my car," he quickly assured her, "so you don't have to worry about anyone crowding you. How's that sound?"

Grateful, she nodded stiffly. "I think that might be better."

Joe had the foresight to request a woman driver when he called for a cab, and forty minutes later they reached the medical complex Grant Alexander shared with five other doctors. His office was on the second floor, and Joe gently nudged Annie in the direction of the stairs without sparing a glance at the elevator. If she panicked at the thought of getting in a car with him, he didn't even want to think about what she would do if he followed her into the close confines of an elevator.

The reception area was fairly crowded, but they didn't have to wait. Within seconds, they were shown into Grant's private office, and moments later, the doctor himself was rushing in. As tall as Joe, but stockier, with Ivy League good looks, he greeted Joe, then turned to Annie, his sharp, intelligent eyes narrowing slightly at the sight of her battered face.

"Hello, Annie," he said. "It's been a while. How are you?"

He didn't rush her, didn't try to touch her or do anything that would spook her. Relieved, Annie smiled weakly. "I'd like to think I've been better, but I can't be sure of that. I'm sorry. I know I should know you, but I don't."

"There's no need to apologize," he said easily. "You look like you've had a rough time of it lately."

She shrugged, unable to tell him any more than she'd been able to tell Joe. "I guess so. I don't remember."

"Anything?"

Mutely, she shook her head. His gaze, missing nothing, traveled over the vivid bruises that marred her tender skin. Frowning, he said, "Let me get my nurse to show you into an examining room, and I'll see if I can find out what the problem is. Okay?"

Logically, she knew she had no reason to fear him. He was a friend of Joe's and a doctor, no less. Still, her heart lurched with a panic that was becoming all too familiar. "Your nurse will be there?" she blurted, before she could stop herself.

Surprised, he couldn't miss her sudden wariness or the defensive way she wrapped her arms around herself. Exchanging a look with Joe, he nodded. "She'll be right there the entire time. Even then, if you feel uncomfortable or scared at any time, I want you to tell me. Would you feel more at ease if Joe sat in on the exam?"

Her eyes flew to Joe's, the pounding of her heart turning erratic. It wasn't a completely unexpected question. Although she still found it hard to believe that the dark, silent man at her side was her husband, he apparently had been for some time and it was perfectly natural for the doctor to assume that she would feel safer with him at her side.

Nothing, however, could have been further from the truth. She had no reason to believe that he'd hurt her, but there was something about him that made her knees weak and her pulse jump. Something that made her want to trust him, yet run from him at one and the same time. And God help her, she didn't know why.

"N-no, that's not necessary," she said shakily, and missed the sudden tightening of her husband's granite jaw as she forced herself to drop her arms from around herself. "I know I'm being paranoid, but I can't seem to help it. I feel like someone dropped me into an episode of 'The Twilight Zone' when my back was turned. Nothing makes sense."

"So you remember 'The Twilight Zone,'" Grant said with a smile as he opened the door at his nurse's knock. "That's a start, anyway. Let's go take a look at you, then see what else you remember."

It didn't take Annie long to discover why Grant Alexander's waiting room was full. He was a kind man with a gentle touch who took the time to talk to his patients. He didn't rush her into the exam once his nurse had helped her change into a gown, telling her instead about his friendship with Joe and the wild times they had had together over the years. He made her laugh...and relax. Then the examination started.

Because she didn't know exactly what had happened to her, Grant recommended a complete physical, and she endured it as best she could. But it wasn't easy. Dressed in a gown that tied in the back, she felt horribly naked and vulnerable. She tried to convince herself that there was no reason to tense up, but the knotting muscles of her stomach didn't seem to get the message. When he touched her, it took all her self-control not to cringe.

She thought she'd hidden her distaste for the whole procedure pretty well, but when he finished the pelvic exam and his nurse helped her sit up, she quickly discovered she wasn't fooling anyone, least of all him. Taking a step back, he gave her some space and said quietly, "You don't have to hide what you're feeling, Annie. It's okay to be scared."

Flushed, she looked away. "And I thought I was hiding it so well. How'd you know?"

"Your breath catches in your throat every time I start to touch you." His gray eyes discerning, he examined the bruises on her face. "Why do you think that is?" he asked. "Because you don't remember me, or because I'm a man and some man hurt you?"

She wanted to say that it was because he was a stranger, but everyone she'd encountered today—from her husband to the taxi driver to Grant and his nurse—were strangers. It was only the men who sent fear backing up in her throat.

"I d-don't know," she stuttered. "Just the thought of being touched by a man—*any* man—makes me... I can't explain it.... I just—" Unable to find the words, she shrugged, tears welling in her eyes. "I'm sorry," she choked. "This is so *stupid!*"

He handed her a tissue, his eyes kind as they met hers. "Don't be so hard on yourself. You've obviously suffered some kind of a trauma. You have a bruise on your temple, but no concussion, so I don't think it's a head injury that's causing your amnesia." Patting her hand, he pulled up a stool and sat. "Tell me what you do remember."

Despite his full waiting room, he looked as if he was prepared to hear her life story—if she could recall it, but in the end, there was nothing to tell. She had a vague memory of taking a shower the previous night, then going to bed. Before that, her mind was a blank.

"What about last week? Last year? Your childhood? Where did you go to high school?"

She couldn't tell him how many brothers or sisters she had, her favorite color, if her parents were even alive. Nothing. For all practical purposes, her mind was as empty as a newborn baby's. Except for the fear that had lingered there like a black shadow ever since she looked in the mirror, saw a stranger's face, and realized that something terrible must have happened to her.

Suddenly cold all the way to the bone, she asked bluntly, "Was I raped?"

He opened his mouth, then hesitated, and she went pale. "Oh, God!"

"No, no," he said quickly, swearing. "There's no evidence that you were molested recently—"

"Recently?"

Cursing himself, he nodded for his nurse to leave them alone. As soon as the door shut, he turned back to her. "Annie, I think Joe should be in on this conversation."

"If I wasn't raped, then something else must be wrong. What is it?"

"Annie—"

"Tell me!"

"You're pregnant, okay? Dammit, you're pregnant!"

The news hit her hard, like a freight train that came out of nowhere. Pregnant, she thought, dazed. She was pregnant, and her husband's best friend was waiting expectantly for a response from her. Hysterical laughter threatened to choke her. How was she supposed to know how to react when she didn't remember anything? Had she planned this pregnancy? Did she even want a baby? How would Joe, a husband she didn't know, feel about becoming a father?

Instinctively, her hand slid down to the faint bulge of her stomach. "When?"

"I was hoping you could tell me that. You don't remember getting pregnant?"

Something in his tone warned her that the question was a loaded one. "No," she said cautiously, "but Joe should. Shouldn't he?"

He winced, then quietly dropped the bomb she unconsciously braced for. "It's hard to pinpoint how far along you are since you're barely showing and you can't remember when you had your last period. And Joe might not be much help. You left him two months ago, and he hasn't seen you since. Which means the baby might or might not be his."

Each word hit her like a blow, sucking the air from her lungs. Stunned, she heard a roaring in her ears and realized it must be the rush of her blood. This couldn't be happening, she thought. It was all just some horrible nightmare that would be over any second.

But the sympathy in his gray eyes was too real, the regret he couldn't hide too personal, and she knew he wouldn't lie to her. Not about something like this.

"Oh, God," she whispered, "he didn't tell me. I woke up screaming in his bed and he never once told me that I had no right to be there. Why? Why didn't he tell me?"

"I can't speak for him," Grant said, "but my guess is that there wasn't time. You were hysterical and scared to death of him, and getting you to a doctor was more important than giving you a play-by-play of your marriage. He's a good man, Annie. Seeing you like this couldn't have been easy for him."

"But I left him. Why?"

"That's something you'll have to discuss with him," he said, patting her hand as he pushed to his feet. "Why don't you get dressed now, then come back to my office when you're ready? I'm going to talk to Joe, then see about getting you in to see someone else about your amnesia."

He left before she could call him back, shutting the door quietly behind him. Alone with the questions that stumbled around in her head in search of answers that weren't there, Annie didn't move for a long time. What kind of woman could be pregnant and not know who the father of her baby was? Dear God, what had she done?

Restless, Joe prowled around Grant's office like a man who had just missed the last bus out of town. What the hell was taking so long? Had Grant found something? Something serious? Dammit, he should have insisted on sitting in on the examination! Whether she remembered it or not, Annie was still his wife, and he had a right to know if something was seriously wrong with her.

The door behind him opened then, and he whirled to see Grant step across the threshold, his aristocratic face set in grim lines. "What is it?" he asked sharply. "And don't try to put me off by claiming nothing's wrong," he warned his friend tersely. "I can see by your face there's a problem."

"Not one I was expecting," Grant retorted somberly, as he moved to the tufted leather chair behind his desk and sank into it. "Sit down, Joe. We need to talk, and I don't think you're going to like what I have to say."

He didn't want to sit, but something in his friend's expression had him reaching for a chair. "I don't see how it could be any worse than what I've been imagining for the last thirty minutes, so just lay it on the line. I can take it."

From the hard, searching look Grant gave him, it was obvious that he wasn't so sure of that, but he finally nodded. "First off, I could find no physical cause of Annie's amnesia, so I've got to believe that it's a result of some trauma she suffered and doesn't want to remember. She's terrified of men, and while I was examining her, she voiced a fear that she'd been raped. She wasn't," he said quickly, when Joe seemed to turn to stone. "But deep down in her subconscious, she was aware of the possibility that she could have been. I think it's safe to say she was attacked."

Joe had come to the same conclusion, but hearing his own fears put into words turned his stomach. A muscle jumped along his tight jaw. "That might explain why she refused to remember what happened to her, but why would she block out the rest of her memory?"

"The mind is a funny thing," Grant replied, "and we're a long way from understanding it. Just to be sure, I'd like you to take her to Preston Ziggler for a second opinion. Amnesia is not something you run into every day of the week, and he's had more experience with it than anyone else in the city. I'll give him a call and see if he can fit her in sometime this afternoon."

Joe nodded. "Fine. Whatever you say. Whatever it takes to get her memory back. She might hate my guts, but I'd rather see recognition and hate in her eyes than this god-awful wariness. You are saying that she'll get her memory back, aren't you?"

"Probably," Grant agreed, "though there's no saying how long it will take." He hated like hell to tell him the rest, but there was no way to avoid the truth. "There's something else you should know. God knows, I wish I didn't have to be the one to tell you this, but you're going to have to know eventually anyway. And I'll tell you right now, there's no use asking Annie about it because she can't tell you a damn thing—at least not yet. So don't hassle her for answers she can't give you. That's the last thing she needs right now."

"Hassle her about what?" Joe growled, scowling. "Dammit, what the devil are you talking about?"

It wasn't the kind of news you wanted to tell your best friend, but the Fates hadn't given him a choice. Cursing the powers that be, he sighed heavily and gave it to him straight, with no sugarcoating. "She's pregnant, man. And she hasn't got a clue who the daddy is."

Chapter 2

Annie was pregnant.

Nothing else registered. Caught off guard, Joe stared at Grant like a man who suddenly didn't understand English. How? When? Questions slapped at him, stunning him. A baby. They were going to have a baby, ready or not. From out of nowhere, a laugh bubbled up in his chest and almost choked him. Of all the things he'd imagined, this was the last. Lord, how was a man supposed to react when he found out he was going to be a father for the first time? A crooked grin started to tilt up the corner of his mouth.

Then the rest of Grant's announcement slapped him in the face.

She hasn't got a clue who the daddy is.

He stiffened even as he told himself not to be a fool. This was Annie they were talking about. She'd been a virgin when he met her. He'd courted her for months, wooing her and earning her trust and love before she'd allowed him any kind of true intimacy. There was no way she'd have let a stranger touch her, let alone get her pregnant, just weeks after she'd left him. She just wasn't capable of that kind of behavior. The baby had to be his.

If you won't give me a baby, then I'll find someone who will.

From the cold ashes of their last bitter argument, the threat she'd made right before she left him echoed cruelly in his mind, taunting him. Things hadn't been good between them for a while—mainly because of work. In the months before she left him, he'd had nothing but one problem after another with the staff at Joe's Place, the restaurant he owned on the Riverwalk. He was losing money and customers, and all his attention had been focused on finding new people to replace the troublemakers, then getting the business back on its feet financially. At the same time, Annie and Phoebe had just opened their real estate office the previous spring and were having to hustle just to break even.

In all the chaos, Annie had wanted to have a baby. Her timing couldn't have been worse.

He'd tried to reason with her, to convince her to wait, but every discussion had ended in an argument. She'd accused him of not wanting children at all when nothing could have been further from the truth. Six months to a year—that's all he'd wanted. Six months to get their lives back on track. Then they could start talking about babies.

But Annie hadn't been willing to wait. She'd given him an ultimatum, and they'd both said some things they shouldn't have. She'd ended up sleeping in the guest room, and when he woke up in the morning, she was gone. When she'd called later, it was to announce that she needed some serious time to herself to think about their future—*if* they had one. So she'd rented an apartment on the north side. She'd contact him when she was ready to talk.

Respecting her wishes and giving her the time she wanted was the hardest thing he'd ever done, but he hadn't had much choice. She'd been so upset that if he'd come after her, he would have lost her for sure.

And now she was back. And expecting a baby. There was a possibility that she could have been pregnant when she left him and not known it. But if that was the case, why hadn't she let him know when she discovered her condition? She'd been gone for two months, for God's sake! Surely sometime during that time, she could have found a few minutes to pick up the phone and let him know he was going to be a father.

Unless the baby wasn't his.

The thought slipped like a dagger between his ribs. He immediately tried to reject the idea. But she'd been hurt and furious and in a reckless mood when she'd left him, desperate for a baby. And as much as he hated to admit it, she hadn't been the same Annie he'd married for some time. She'd been on edge, unhappy, and nothing he'd done had seemed to please her. She'd complained about the hours he worked and the attention she claimed he didn't give her. She might very well have gotten that attention from another man.

"Joe?" Grant said worriedly, when he just sat there. "I know this has to be a shock—"

"Shock?" he laughed harshly, his face set in bitter lines as he looked up from his grim thoughts. "Yeah, it's a shock, all right, when you find out your wife might be carrying another man's baby. And the hell of the thing about it is that she doesn't have any more of a clue how she got in that condition than I do. Dammit, Grant, I need some answers, and I need them now! When is she going to get her memory back?"

Helpless, the other man could only shrug. "There's no way to predict that."

"Then try narrowing it down. Are we talking about a couple of days? A week? What?"

"It all hinges on the severity of the trauma she suffered," he replied. "If I were you, I'd take her home, take care of her, and make her feel safe. She'll remember when she's ready."

"And if the baby's not mine?"

"Then you've got some decisions to make," his friend said somberly. "Either way, that's something you can't discuss with her now. The less pressure she has to deal with, the faster her memory should come back."

"What do you mean...her memory *should* come back? Is there a possibility that it won't?"

Grant hesitated. "I don't like to say never, especially when this isn't my field of expertise. I think that with time, she will remember her past. Recalling whatever or whoever terrorized her, however, is another matter. Something scared her enough to make her forget her own name, and she may block that for the rest of her life."

All too easily, Joe could see the stark terror in her eyes when she'd thought he was going to hurt her. He wasn't a violent man, but at that moment he would have given everything he had to put his hands around the throat of the man who had put that look in Annie's eyes. "That may be for the best," he said grimly. "Some things are better off forgotten."

Grant agreed. "Whatever happened, at least she followed her instincts and came home. I know it's not much consolation, but deep down inside, she has to trust you, man, or she never would have run to you."

Long after they left his friend's office, Joe tried to find some comfort in that thought, but trust was the last thing he saw in Annie's eyes when she looked at him. The sapphire blue depths that had once gazed up at him with such love were leery and full of apprehension. As cautious as a lone woman on a deserted highway who had no choice but to accept the help of the first stranger who came along, she finally let him talk her into his car, but she clung to the passenger door, ready to bolt if he so much as looked at her wrong.

And as much as he hated to admit it, it hurt. The Annie he knew, the only woman he'd ever loved, had been full of fun and sass and unafraid of the devil himself. Seeing her like this—pale and nervous and clearly frightened—of him, dammit!—tore him apart. What the hell had happened to her? Who had hurt her and why?

As Grant had predicted, it was determined after a battery of tests that Annie's amnesia was psychological rather than physical. She would remember her past when she was ready and not until then. As for her pregnancy, Annie's gynecologist, Dr. Sawyer, couldn't tell them. When she was further along, a sonogram would help determine how developed the baby was, but at this stage, it was impossible to pinpoint exactly how far along she was. Yes, Dr. Sawyer admitted, Annie could be less than two months pregnant. But then again, the doctor had seen women who were three or four months along and didn't look much bigger than Annie. Joe was told to take her home, make sure she took her prenatal vitamins, and let her rest. For now, there was nothing anyone else could do.

So eight hours after they left the old Victorian house where they lived, they returned, knowing no more than they had when they'd set out...except that Annie was carrying Joe's or somebody else's baby. Every time he thought about it, it was all he could do not to grab her and demand some answers. Answers that she couldn't give him, he reminded himself bitterly as she gazed up at the house like a first-time visitor.

Anticipating her questions, he said, "It's called the Lone Star Social Club. Back in the trail-riding days, cowboys used to come here on Saturday nights to meet decent women."

Earlier, Annie had been too upset to even notice where she was, let alone appreciate the old mansion's turrets and gingerbread architecture, but now she couldn't help smiling. Painted cream and trimmed in rose and robin's-egg blue, with stained glass in every window and wide porches upstairs and down that wrapped all the way around it, it looked like something out of a fairy tale. "It's gorgeous! How in the world did it survive all these years?"

"Actually, it almost didn't. Ten years ago, the city was on the verge on condemning it when somebody stepped in and saved it. It was divided into apartments and restored, and it's been the talk of the Riverwalk ever since. In case you don't know, it's located on pretty prime property, so whoever saved it must have had some major bucks."

Surprised, she said, "What do you mean, *whoever saved it?* Don't you know? Whoever owns it is your landlord."

"Technically," he agreed. "But he must be some kind of recluse because he's never revealed his identity to anyone."

Trailing her hand along the porch railing, Annie marveled at the wonder of the workmanship. "If I owned this, I think I'd tell the whole world. It's beautiful. Is it haunted?"

He smiled, not surprised by the question. She might not know who she was, but she was still the same romantic she'd always been. "That depends on who you talk to. Some say that on still summer nights, you can hear the sound of music coming from the old ballroom in the attic.

But it could just be coming from the nightclubs farther upriver.''

Her eyes wistful, Annie shook her head. ''No, I like the ballroom version better.''

''I know,'' he said ruefully, and punched in the security code on the keypad to the left of the mansion's front door.

There was no elevator, only the grand staircase that led to the second floor. As they started up it and Annie marveled over the wainscoting and sweep of the stairs, it suddenly hit Joe that while she might be home again, he was a long way from having his wife back. If he even wanted her back. He was a stranger to her, and she was scared of men. To make matters worse, she had not only walked out on their marriage without trying to save it, she might have also betrayed him in the worst way a woman can betray a man. And she didn't even remember it. How were they supposed to live together under those circumstances?

Wishing he could feel nothing but indifference when he looked at her, he couldn't help noticing as they stepped into their apartment that whatever hell had sent her running blindly back there for protection was beginning to exact its toll. The bruises on her face stood out in sharp relief against her colorless skin, and she'd looked as if she had hardly enough energy to put one foot in front of the other.

Something shifted in his heart then, a damnable tenderness he seemed to have no control over. Silently cursing himself for the weakness, he said tersely, ''You look bushed. Why don't you go lie down while I fix us something to eat? I'll call you when it's ready.''

She wanted to argue—except for the brief history he'd given her about the house, he'd barely said two words to her since they'd left Grant Alexander's office that morning. And over the course of the afternoon, his expression had grown more and more forbidding. They needed to talk, but she was so tired she could barely see straight.

"Maybe you're right," she admitted. "I am a little wiped out. Just give me a few minutes to put my feet up and I'll be good as new."

Five minutes. That was all she thought she needed, but the second she sank down on the couch and stretched out, what was left of her energy drained out of her. Her eyelids grew heavy, and within ten seconds flat she was out like a light. Forty minutes later, when Joe came into the living room to wake her, she hadn't a clue that he was there until his hand settled lightly on her shoulder and he called her name.

Her eyes flew open, and before she was even awake, she found herself staring up into the face of a man as he bent over her, his dark, shuttered brown eyes much too close for comfort. Her breath lodged painfully in her throat, and for a split second, she was caught in the claws of a nightmare. The feel of a stranger's hands on her, hurting her, was all too real.

A blind man couldn't have missed the terror in her eyes. Swallowing a curse, Joe jerked his hand back. "I didn't mean to startle you. Are you all right?"

A scream already working its way up her throat, she blinked, and just as quickly, recognition rushed through her. Limp, she pressed a shaking hand to her pounding heart. "J-Joe!"

"I called your name," he said in that rough voice she knew would follow her into her dreams. "I thought you heard me."

"No. I must have died away—"

"The food's ready when you are—"

They both spoke at once, their words tumbling over each other as they sought to bridge the sudden awkwardness between them. Quickly sitting up, Annie swung her legs over the side of the couch. "I'll be right there. Just give me a second to wash my face."

"Take your time," he said stiffly as he turned toward the door. "Just come on in the kitchen when you're ready." He was gone before she could say another word and never saw her wrap her arms around herself as the door swung shut behind him.

When she left the bathroom a few minutes later, her face was freshly washed and she was sure she was ready to face her husband. After all, he wasn't a threat to her. She didn't know why she had left him, but every instinct she had told her it wasn't because he'd physically or mentally abused her. He just didn't seem the type, so there was no reason to jump when he touched her. She was home. And safe.

Yet nothing seemed familiar. Not the antique iron bed in the master bedroom where she'd slept last night, or the living room with its rose-colored camelback sofa, or the gourmet kitchen, complete with a commercial stove large enough to feed an army. And most especially not the man she'd apparently shared the apartment with for the past five years.

Stopping in the kitchen doorway, she watched as Joe turned from the stove, two heaping plates of something that smelled wonderful in his hands. He'd been personable and charming with everyone they'd encountered over the course of the day, everyone, that is, except her. With her, he'd been reserved, watchful, his thoughts and feelings well hidden behind those dark brown eyes of his. He hadn't said a word about the baby other than to inquire about how she was feeling, and she didn't have a clue if he was glad or mad that she was back in his life. Which was something she could definitely identify with. She didn't know why she'd come back to him when she was scared or where, if anywhere, they were going from here. Questions. God, she had so many questions!

"There you are," he said, spying her in the doorway. "You want to eat outside or in? There's a harvest moon tonight, and it's not too cold."

Confused, she followed his gaze from the dining alcove, where a Duncan Phyfe table large enough to easily accommodate eight sat, to the French doors at the far end of the kitchen that opened onto an outdoor balcony that overlooked the San Antonio River two stories below. There, in the gathering twilight, an antique wicker table and two chairs offered an enticing view of the Riverwalk.

"Oh, outside," she said, a delighted smile spreading across her face. "I had no idea we had a view of the river. It's beautiful!"

If Joe had needed any further proof that she had blocked out everything about their life together, she'd just given it to him. She loved that balcony—in happier times, they'd eaten every meal out there when the weather permitted— yet there was no doubting her surprise at the sight of it. She honestly didn't remember it.

"That balcony and this apartment is why we haven't bought a house yet," he informed her as he crossed to the patio table and set their plates on it. "You loved this old place from the moment you moved in and refused to even consider leaving it unless we found something similar. So far, we haven't. I'm beginning to think it doesn't exist. Have a seat and I'll get us something to drink."

Joe wasn't surprised when she didn't have to be told twice. Captivated, she stepped onto the balcony, which was hardly big enough to hold the table and two matching chairs, and stared down at the sights below. Framed on both sides by a forest of tropical plants and flowers, the river lazily meandered through skyscrapers and under arched bridges, creating a colorful, inviting oasis right in the middle of downtown.

She was still there, watching the activity below like a tourist, when he returned a few minutes later with glasses of iced tea. Taking the seat across from her, he couldn't help smiling when she hardly spared him a glance. "Your food's getting cold," he pointed out dryly. "And it's one of your favorites."

That got her attention. Glancing down at the concoction on her plate, she frowned and lifted a doubtful eyebrow at him. "Are you sure? It doesn't look like something I would like."

Considering the fact that she didn't remember her middle name, let alone her favorite brand of soda, he wondered how she could possibly know what she did and didn't like. But he only said, "Trust me. You'll love it."

"What is it?"

"Fajita chicken spaghetti. You helped me come up with it on a rainy Saturday afternoon, and I've been serving it at the restaurant ever since. It's one of the most popular items on the menu."

"Restaurant?" she echoed, surprised. "You own a restaurant?"

"Right down there, around the bend," he said, nodding downstream. Watching her closely, he said, "It's called Joe's Place. Don't you remember?"

Mutely, she shook her head and took a bite of the spaghetti. "Oh, this is delicious! And this is something we came up with together? When? How?"

She was full of questions, and as they both dug into their food, she asked about everything from the restaurant to how they'd met. "Actually, you have the house to thank for that," he told her ruefully. "I tempted fate the day I moved in here."

"How?"

"Apparently, a lot of cowboys met their downfall here when this place was still a social club. I don't know if the ghost of the lady who ran the place is still wandering around working her magic or what, but according to legend, when anyone single moves in here, they end up falling in love within one year."

"And you lived here when you met me? How long?"

"Two weeks."

Her eyes dancing, Annie clearly didn't believe him. "You're kidding."

"Ask Mrs. Truelove if you don't believe me. The old lady who manages the place," he explained when she looked at him inquiringly. "I don't know if it's true or not, but supposedly she's the granddaughter of the lady who originally ran the place after the Civil War. I'll introduce you to her tomorrow."

Remembering the doctor's suggestion that she be allowed to remember in her own way at her own speed, Joe turned the conversation to their neighbors and life on the river, avoiding more personal topics...like how she'd turned his bachelor pad into a home soon after he'd married her and brought her home with him for good. They'd been so happy then, neither one of them had thought anything could ever come between them.

Then she asked about their separation. Leaning back in her chair, she frowned. "Why did I leave you? What happened? Was there another woman or what?"

She could have been asking about the marriage of a stranger on the street for all the emotion she showed. "No," he said flatly. "It was nothing like that. I never cheated on you, Annie. When I make a vow, I stand by it. I thought you were the same way.''

He didn't make any accusations, but he didn't have to. She was the one who'd left him and come back pregnant, without a clue as to who the father of her baby was. And there wasn't a single thing she could say to defend herself.

The easy, lighthearted mood shattered, and what was left of her appetite evaporated. Suddenly she found herself fighting the need to cry and was horrified. It was just the baby, she rationalized. Pregnant women cried over everything, didn't they? Especially when they were tired. She needed sleep, some time to herself to think, to try to figure out who she was. Tomorrow, she promised herself dispiritedly, would be better. It had to be. How could it get any worse?

Carefully setting down her fork, she dropped her napkin next to her half-full plate. "I wish I could tell you that my vows were just as important to me," she said with quiet dignity. "Obviously, I can't. No one regrets that more than I do. Now if you'll excuse me, I think I'll go to bed. It's been a long day."

She pushed to her feet, but he was there, blocking her path, before she could step back into the kitchen. "I know you're exhausted and I promise I'll let you go to bed in just a second, but first there's someone I need you to talk to—"

The doorbell rang then, cutting him off, and there was something in his sudden inability to quite meet her eye that set Annie's heart thumping in her chest. Warily, she looked past his broad shoulders toward the entrance hall. "What have you done, Joe? Who is that?"

"It's just Sam Kelly. I called him while you were sleeping and asked him to come over after supper. He's a friend, Annie. He won't hurt you."

"If he's another doctor—"

"He's not. He's a detective with the San Antonio Police Department."

Alarmed, she took a quick step back and came up hard against the patio table. "He's a cop? No! I don't care if he is a friend of yours, I won't speak to him. I haven't done anything wrong."

Cursing himself for not telling her sooner and giving her time to prepare herself, he tried to calm her without touching her, as he instinctively wanted to. He might as well have asked himself not to breathe. He could do it for a while, but not forever.

"It isn't a question of you doing anything wrong," he told her, hooking his thumbs in the back pockets of his jeans to keep from reaching for her. "Something happened to you, and we need to find out what it was. Sam can help. He's not just a friend—he's our neighbor. He lives right next door. I called him because I thought you'd be more comfortable talking to him than some rookie you don't know from Adam."

If panic hadn't been churning in her stomach like boiling acid, she might have been amused. How did she make him understand that she didn't know *anyone* from Adam? "There's nothing to talk about," she argued. "I don't remember anything."

"He still needs to be aware of the situation. Sam's a damn good detective. If anyone can find out what happened to you, it's him." When the doorbell rang again, he lifted an eyebrow at her. "It's your call. If you really don't want to talk to him, I'll explain the situation to him. Considering the circumstances, I'm sure he'll understand."

She hesitated, wanting nothing so much as to escape to the bedroom. But whatever she was, she didn't like to think that she might be a coward. She needed to know what she was running from. If this Sam character could help, then she had to talk to him. Even if her knees did shake at the thought.

Straightening her spine, she sighed. "No. You're right. Maybe he can help me find some answers."

The man Joe let into the apartment was tall and lean, with an angular face and dark brown hair that was cropped close and still somehow managed to curl. His smile appeared the second he spied Annie sitting on the couch, his eyes kind but watchful as he approached her. He looked like someone she could trust, but that didn't do a lot to settle her nerves.

"You don't remember me, do you?"

His tone was wry, his stance nonthreatening, and Annie found herself liking him. "No, I'm sorry, I don't. But don't take it personally. I don't remember me, either."

"Or me," Joe added as he shut the front door and joined them in the living room. "Since there's no sign of any head injuries, the doctors think she's suffering from some sort of trauma-induced amnesia. She showed up here last night, took a shower, and went to bed. That's all she remembers."

"So you have no memory of how you got here?" Sam asked, turning to Annie, his forehead knit in a frown. "Did you drive?"

She shrugged. "If I did, I don't know where I left the car. What kind of car do I have, anyway?"

"A '62 Volvo sedan," Joe said, rattling off the license plate number for Sam. "It's your pride and joy. There's no way you'd voluntarily walk off and leave it even if you ran the damn thing into a tree."

Pulling a small notebook from his pocket, Sam noted the information in his own particular brand of shorthand. "I'll call it in and see if there're any reports on it." Watching every nuance of Annie's expression, he said, "How do you feel when you try to remember? Or do you feel anything at all? What's going on in your head, Annie?''

That was something she didn't even have to think about. Her arms stealing around herself, she stared off into the blackness that had once been her past and felt again that sinister wickedness that lingered just out of sight in the shadows, stalking her every waking moment. "Fear," she said hoarsely. "I'm scared to death and I don't know why."

"Did someone hurt you?"

"I don't know."

"How do you think you got the bruises?"

Her gaze dropped to the sickly yellow discolorations that marred her wrists below the sleeves of her blouse. There were others under her clothes, on her throat and breasts and thighs. She didn't have to remember how she had gotten them to know that they weren't the result of any kind of accident. The outline of gripping fingers was clearly visible on her skin.

Rubbing at them as if she could rub them away, she could only shrug. "I can't imagine."

His jaw rigid, Joe retrieved a brown grocery sack from the entrance-hall closet and gave it to Sam. "Those are the clothes she was wearing when she came home. I found them on the bathroom floor this morning. You'd better take a look at them."

The long-sleeved white blouse, black slacks and tapestry vest that Sam dumped out on the coffee table were caked with dried mud. One sleeve of the blouse was nearly torn off, but it was the large rust-brown stains on the garments that drew both men's eyes.

Careful not to touch them any more than necessary, Sam scowled. "Someone lost a hell of a lot of blood, and it obviously wasn't Annie. I'm going to take these into the lab and have them analyzed."

Annie hardly heard him. She'd seen the clothes before. She knew how terrible they looked. But seeing them now, in the old-fashioned prettiness of the living room, she just felt sick. "I think I-I need t-to lie down. I d-don't feel..." she swallowed thickly and jerked to her feet "...very well."

Joe swore and hastily moved to her side, cursing himself for his thoughtlessness. "C'mon, honey, why don't you go to bed? It's been a rough day, and you're worn out. Excuse us a second, Sam. I'll be right back."

He didn't give her time to protest but simply ushered her into the master bedroom and quickly found her one of his old T-shirts to sleep in. He would have helped her change, but one look at her face and he knew that was never going to happen. Which was probably for the best.

"Can I get you anything else?" he asked stiffly. "Something to drink? Another pillow?"

"No, nothing. I'll be fine. Really."

If she was fine, he was Rip van Winkle. With his T-shirt clutched to her breast and her blue eyes large and haunted, she looked small and vulnerable and needed somebody to hold her. But it wasn't going to be him or any other man. Turning away, he headed for the door before he gave in to the temptation to reach for her anyway. "Then I'll leave you alone. Good night."

Her soft, husky good-night followed him across the room, but he didn't look back. He didn't dare.

"Is she okay?" Sam asked worriedly as soon as he rejoined him in the living room. "I know amnesia must be a hell of a shock to the system, and she didn't get those bruises from a walk in the park, but I don't think I've ever seen her look so breakable."

"She's pregnant," Joe said, and saw by the quickly concealed surprise on the other man's face that he didn't need to elaborate. Sam, like most of their friends, knew that Annie had left him months ago. It didn't take an Einstein to figure out that her condition, in all likelihood, had nothing to do with her husband. "She's scared to death of being touched. She wasn't raped, but it might not have been from lack of trying on some bastard's part. Until she regains her memory—which could be months, if ever—the only clue we've got to what happened to her is her clothes. I want whoever hurt her caught, Sam."

Sam nodded, understanding perfectly the need for revenge. Whatever their problems were, Annie was still Joe's wife, and Joe was the type of man who protected what was his. "I'll get back to you as soon as I get a report from the lab. If nothing else, we should be able to find out something about the blood on her clothes and where she might have picked up that mud. Unfortunately, that's not a hell of a lot to go on. Finding her car would help. Do you know where she's been living since she left here?"

"In an apartment on Mockingbird Lane," Joe replied tersely and gave him the address.

Wishing he didn't have to ask the next few questions, Sam knew there was no way around them. "I hate like hell to ask you this, Joe, but I've got to. Was she living by herself? Dating anyone? What about her neighbors? Do you know anything about them?"

His mouth pressed flat into a thin white line, he shook his head. "No. Nothing. She's been working with Phoebe at their real estate office, but other than that, she could have taken up with the Dalai Lama and been living with a lover from a past life for all I know. She wanted privacy and I gave it to her."

Surprised, Sam glanced up from his note-taking. "Do you really think she'd do something like that?"

"I don't know," he replied, and silently cursed the bitterness he heard in his voice. "At this point, I don't know anything except that she's not going to be able to handle any more questions. You saw the way she reacted to the sight of her clothes. She can't take the stress right now."

"Then my best bet would probably be to start at the real estate office," Sam said as he pushed to his feet and headed for the door with the bag that held Annie's ruined clothes in his hand. "I'll nose around her apartment, too, and see what I can find out. I'll get back to you when I have something to report."

With Sam's leaving, silence descended over the apartment, but it was a far from peaceful quiet. Left alone with his thoughts, Joe found his gaze drifting down the hall to the closed door of their bedroom. Was she asleep? he wondered broodingly. Or staring up at the ceiling and dreading the moment he came to bed? Dammit, what was he going to do with her? They were still married, but in her mind, she'd known him all of one day. Considering the circumstances, only a monster would insist on his marital right.

Not that he was looking for or expecting sex with the lady, he hastily assured himself. They made a fine pair. She didn't want him to touch her, and he, dear God, didn't trust her as far as he could throw her. Even if her memory came sweeping back tomorrow, what possible chance at a future did they have?

Long after the rest of the world was asleep, he was still pondering the question, the answer as elusive as ever.

He didn't sleep with her.

The thought hit Annie the moment she opened her eyes the following morning. Staring at the empty side of the bed, she didn't have to see the unrumpled pillow to know that she had had the bed to herself all night. She seemed to have a sixth sense where Joe Taylor was concerned, and if he'd been anywhere within touching distance over the course of the last eight hours, the thumping of her heart would have awakened her immediately. Instead, he'd chosen to sleep elsewhere rather than share a bed with her.

She should have been relieved. The last thing she needed right now was a husband she didn't remember crowding her. He'd done the gentlemanly thing and given her space, and she should have been thanking him for it. Instead, something that felt an awful lot like hurt wrapped around her heart, confusing her. Had she actually *wanted* him to sleep with her?

You're pregnant, Annie, a voice in her head snapped, *and you can't even assure the man that the baby is his. How else do you expect him to react? A lesser man might have told you to come back when you had the answers he was entitled to. Be thankful he's letting you stay because you've got nowhere else to go.*

Flinching at the lonely thought, she threw back the covers and rolled out of bed, only to be presented with another problem when her eyes fell on the jeans and faded shirt she'd worn yesterday. She had no other clothes. What was she supposed to wear?

"Annie? You awake?"

The tap that followed the hushed whisper was the only warning she got. The door flew open and she was caught flat-footed in her panties and the T-shirt she'd borrowed from Joe as he swept into the room. His arms loaded with clothes, he hardly spared her a glance. "Good, you're awake. I brought you some things—"

In the act of dumping the clothes on the bed, he looked up...and stopped short. In one all-encompassing look, he took in her bare legs, her tousled hair and the shadowy nipples that she knew were barely concealed by the thin material of his T-shirt. He didn't move so much as a muscle, but he didn't have to. His eyes turned hot and molten, and she would have sworn he touched her. Her breath hitched in her throat, her body quickened, confusing her.

She wanted to run, to bolt for the door, but she couldn't and didn't know why. He was her husband; he must have seen her like this a thousand times before. There was no reason to act like a virgin caught stepping from her bath. She was safe.

But the look in his brown eyes was dark and dangerous and intimate, touching her deep inside. She felt heat bloom in her cheeks and wanted to hide. All she could do was wrap her arms around herself to cover her breasts and drag her eyes away from his to the colorful garments that slid from his hands to the bed. "You went shopping this early in the morning?"

"Actually, I went over to your apartment and bullied the manager into letting me in," he replied stiffly. "I thought you'd feel more comfortable in your own things, and there was no use buying anything since you had a whole closet full of clothes right across town. I hope you don't mind."

Touched, Annie didn't know what to say. Going to her apartment, seeing where she'd lived when she'd left him, where she'd possibly betrayed him with another man, couldn't have been easy for him. But he'd done it for her…to help her feel more like herself. Did he have any idea what that did to her? She wanted to cross to him, to touch him, to ease the rigidity of his jaw and assure him that he had no reason to doubt her. But how could she know that for sure?

So she stayed where she was and said, "No, of course I don't mind. In fact, I was just wondering what I was going to wear. I'll have to buy maternity clothes eventually, but for now, I can wear my old clothes. Thanks."

It was the wrong thing to say. At the first reminder of her pregnancy, the heat in his eyes cooled. "I'll leave you to sort through them," he said curtly. "We usually eat breakfast at the restaurant, so come on out when you're ready."

Striding out of the bedroom that they'd once shared as man and wife, he shut the door behind him with a snap that made her wince. Was this the way he was going to react every time the baby was mentioned? she wondered, staring after him. If he did, it was going to be an awfully long pregnancy.

Chapter 3

Annie expected Joe's Place to be one of those elegant, high-dollar restaurants where the local in-crowd could be seen sipping champagne over brunch on the river. The second she stepped through the river-level entrance, however, she saw that it was anything but that. Instead of crystal, white tablecloths and fancy chandeliers, it was strictly blue-collar. The decor was straight out of the fifties, complete with black-and-white linoleum floors, red chrome tables and chairs, and a soda bar, in perfect condition, that looked as if it had been salvaged from an old drugstore. Annie took one look and loved it.

The Saturday-morning breakfast crowd was loud, relaxed and boisterous, and when customers called out to Joe—and to her, too—she couldn't help smiling. Fascinated, she watched waitresses in old-fashioned uniforms wind their way through the crowded tables with hurried grace, trays loaded with plates of ham and eggs and hash browns balanced one-handed over their heads. Cholesterol was obviously not a major concern here, and no one seemed to care. The place was packed.

The tantalizing smell of coffee filled the air, as well as that of freshly baked cinnamon rolls, and Annie felt her mouth water. It seemed like days since she had eaten. Closing her eyes, she dragged in a deep breath, savoring the combination of scents. Pancakes and sausage, she thought, smiling. She'd get a short stack and all the coffee she could drink.

The nausea came out of nowhere. One second she was anticipating the sweetness of syrup on her tongue, and the next, her stomach roiled sickeningly. Caught off guard, she stiffened, horrified. No! This couldn't be happening! Not here. But even as she told herself that she probably just needed to eat, her stomach had other ideas. Nausea rose with sickening swiftness in her throat, and she knew that if she didn't do something fast, she was going to disgrace herself right there in front of a restaurant full of people. Her hand pressed to her mouth, she looked frantically around for a rest room.

She didn't remember making a sound, but Joe was suddenly there, immediately taking charge as he slipped an arm around her waist. "Hang on, honey," he said quietly, and quickly urged her to the rear of the restaurant, where the rest rooms were concealed by a large screen painted with palm trees. Without batting an eye, he whisked her into the ladies' room.

Before Annie realized that he had followed her inside, she ran out of time. Groaning, she lost the meager contents of her stomach while Joe held her head. Mortified, she wanted to crawl in a hole. "Just shoot me right here and get it over with," she moaned. "Then I can die in peace. I can't believe I did that!"

A smile tugging at the corners of his mouth, he chided,

"Don't be ridiculous. You don't remember it, but right after our honeymoon, I got the flu and was sick as a dog for twelve hours straight. You never left my side." His hands incredibly gentle, he brushed her hair back from her colorless face, gave her a cup of water to rinse her mouth, then helped her over to a chair in front of the vanity mirrors that lined one wall. "Just sit here a minute and get your breath. You'll be good as new in no time."

If she'd had the energy, Annie would have laughed at that. He couldn't be serious! She was a whipped puppy, so embarrassed she didn't think she'd ever be able to look him in the eye again. "You shouldn't be in here," she murmured, turning her face away. "What if someone came in and saw you?"

"They'd just see a man taking care of his nauseated wife," he said simply, wiping her hot face with a paper towel he wet at the sink. "How's that feel? Better?"

It felt like heaven. He had big, strong hands, the kind that could, no doubt, break a man in two if he was angry enough. But he was so gentle with her, so careful, she found herself fighting the need to lean into him and give herself over to his caring.

Disturbed, she caught his hand before it could make another cooling swipe down her face. "If this is an example of what the mornings are going to be like for the next couple of months, I'd better not go out in public for a while," she said with a rueful grimace. "Why don't you go get us a table and I'll be out as soon as I wash up? I just need a few moments to get myself together."

His fingers trapped in hers, Joe stared down at her and felt as if he'd just been kicked in the head by a mule. Morning sickness. When he'd seen the blood drain from her face and her hand flutter to her mouth, his only thought had been that she was in trouble. She'd looked up at him with desperation in her eyes, and he hadn't known if she was scared of the crowd or what—he'd just known he had to help her. And all the time, the baby was just making its presence known, refusing to be ignored even though it would be months before it would be here. Like it or not, he was going to have to deal with that. But how, dammit? How the hell could he?

Pulling his hand from hers, he straightened, the agitation churning in his gut locked inside where no one could see. "Take your time—there's no hurry. I have a table by the kitchen reserved for our use at all times."

No one so much as lifted an eyebrow when he walked out of the women's rest room, but Joe knew his staff. The second he'd walked through the front door with Annie, the news had spread like wildfire. By the time he took a seat at his table, he wasn't surprised to see Drake Gallagher, his manager, striding toward him with a frown etching his chiseled face.

He and Drake went way back, back to the days they'd first worked together as busboys when they were just sixteen. Drake had eventually gone on to manage a place in Austin, but when Joe's Place had been in trouble, he'd ditched that job to come back to San Antonio and help Joe get the restaurant back on its feet. Annie had always been a favorite with him and, like the rest of the crew, he'd had a hard time accepting her leaving.

Never one to mince words or worry about taking advantage of their friendship, Drake signaled a waitress to bring them both a cup of coffee, grabbed a chair across the table from him, and said without preamble, "It's about time you two came to your senses. I'd about given up hope on you. So what's wrong with Annie? She looked a little green around the gills."

Joe opened his mouth to tell him that she was pregnant, only to shut it with a snap. The news would be out soon enough—there was no sense fueling speculation any sooner than he had to, and he didn't want to talk about it in front of half the restaurant. "Her stomach's kind of jittery this morning. We've got a problem, Drake."

"Oh, God. What is it this time?"

His lips twitching at his groan, Joe understood how he felt. In the last few months, they'd done nothing but put out fires. Pouring cream into his coffee, he told him of Annie's return home and amnesia. "She's not going to know you or any of the rest of the staff, so spread the word, okay? And make sure none of the guys corner her. She's pretty skittish right now."

Stunned, Drake nodded. "Of course. She's probably scared to death. What do you think happened to her?"

"I don't know, and neither does she. The police are checking into the situation, but unless she remembers something or the lab finds something on her clothes, they won't even know where to start an investigation. In the meantime, I don't want to leave her alone, so you're going to have to take over most of the load here until things get back to normal."

"Hey, no problem," Drake assured him. "You just take care of Annie and don't worry about this place. I can handle things for as long as you need me to. It's not like I've got a family to rush home to, and Annie needs you. Maybe you should get her out of town for a while, take a vacation or something. A complete change of scene might do you both good."

If they'd really been back together, Joe would have jumped at the chance to be alone with her on some secluded beach a million miles from their nearest neighbor. But although she was back, they weren't even close to being reconciled and there was a possibility that they never would be. Regretfully, he shook his head. "The doctors said she has a better shot at remembering if she has the security of familiar things around her. And I don't think we should be away from town right now. The builders are coming along fine on the new place, but I want to be here if there're any glitches. And Annie needs to be near her doctors just in case she starts to remember."

The conversation turned to business then—a booking for a private party, problems with a supplier, the previous day's receipts, which were up—and neither man noticed the woman who rushed across the restaurant until she was practically upon them. "Joe! Thank God, I found you! I'm sorry to interrupt, but I've really got to talk to you."

Surprised, Joe lifted a brow at Phoebe Duncan, Annie's best friend and partner. A small woman with a shock of red hair and impish green eyes, she was one of those unflappable women who usually roll with the punches. She almost always kept her head when everyone else was losing theirs. But not today. Her freckles stood out in sharp relief across her pale cheeks, her eyes were wild, her curly hair disheveled. She'd been maid of honor at his and Annie's wedding, and in all the years since, Joe didn't think he'd ever seen her so frazzled.

Quickly rising to his feet, as Drake excused himself to check things in the kitchen, Joe pulled a chair out for her. "Sit down, Phoeb. You look like you're stuck on fast-forward. What's going on?"

She sat, but only to pop up again like a jack-in-the-box. "It's Annie. God, you must think I'm some kind of nutcase to come rushing in here like this, but I didn't know what else to do. Have you heard from her? I know you guys haven't been talking, but I was hoping she called you. No one's seen her at the office—"

"She's okay, Phoeb—"

"She didn't even check in yesterday to let me know she wasn't coming in," she continued, not even hearing him. "Of course, she could have gone to Kerrville. She mentioned she had to meet with a lady there who wanted to list her property with us, but she didn't say when she was going. And I don't know the woman's name, so I can't check with her." Chewing on her bottom lip, she said, "Something's wrong, Joe. I can feel it in my bones. She's not answering her phone and her car's gone. Maybe you should call the police."

"She's fine, Phoebe," he tried again, smiling. "She showed up at—"

That was as far as he got. Annie stepped out of the rest room then, drawing her friend's gaze, and with a cry of relief, Phoebe was out of her chair and hugging her as if she hadn't seen her in years. "Thank God! Do you know how worried I've been? Where have you been? I've been going crazy picturing you in all sorts of trouble and all the while you were with Joe. You dog, why didn't you call me and tell me you were back together?"

Taken aback, Annie looked wildly to Joe for help. "I'm sorry, but I don't know who—"

"How did the renter turn out the other night?" Phoebe asked eagerly as she released her and sank back into her chair at the table. "Did he take the entire tenth floor? At the price he was getting, he would have been a fool not to. So did he sign the contract? Tell me everything."

"What night?" Joe demanded sharply before Annie could so much as open her mouth. "You're not talking about Thursday night, are you?"

"Yeah. Why?"

"Annie had a meeting that night? With who? Where?"

He threw the questions at her like darts, not giving her

time to answer one before he thought of another. Surprised, she started to tease him about his fierceness, only to notice just then that Annie was waiting for her to answer as expectantly as Joe was.

Her brows drawing together in a frown, Phoebe glanced back and forth between the two of them in confusion. "Is someone going to tell me what's going on here or do I have to guess? Annie?" she asked when her friend hesitated and looked to Joe for an answer. "Why are you looking at Joe like that? What's wrong?"

"She has amnesia," Joe answered for her. "That's why she didn't call in yesterday—she didn't even know you existed."

"Oh, c'mon!"

Amused, she clearly didn't believe him, but Joe was dead serious. "I talked to Sam Kelly about it last night, and if you'd waited a little while, he would have showed up at your office some time today to tell you all about it. Annie came home Thursday night after I'd gone to bed and I didn't know she was there until the next morning. I should have called you myself, but yesterday was so wild, frankly, I didn't even think about it. We spent the day going from one doctor to the next trying to find out what happened to her."

The blood slowly draining from her face, Phoebe glanced uncertainly at Annie. "This is a joke, isn't it? Like that time you tried to convince me that George Strait listed his house with us?"

Liking her immediately, Annie wished she could have given her the answer she wanted, but she had no memory of that or any other joke she might have played on her. "I'm sorry, but it's true. I know we must be friends, but I don't even know your name. Have we known each other long?"

The other woman winced as if she'd struck her, tears welling in her eyes. "Oh, God, Annie, you really don't remember! I'm Phoebe. Phoebe Duncan. We've been best friends since first grade. How can you not know me?"

"That's what we're trying to find out," Joe interjected. "Let's order breakfast, then you can tell us about this meeting Thursday night."

After her earlier bout of nausea, Annie was sure she was crazy to even think about eating breakfast, but the second the waitress set her order of pancakes and sausage in front of her, her mouth watered hungrily. Suddenly starving, she dug into her food like a field hand who'd been hard at work for hours and immediately discovered why Joe's Place was packed to the gills with customers. The food was out of this world.

While they were eating, Phoebe told Annie about how they had met in first grade, their instant friendship, and the mischief they'd just naturally fallen into over the years. Unable to stop grinning, Annie was sure her friend was stretching the truth, but Joe assured her she wasn't. When she and Phoebe got together, there was no telling what would happen.

Polishing off the last of her French toast, Phoebe sighed in contentment and pushed her plate away. "Well, there's another inch to the hips, but it was worth it. I don't know how you do it, Joe. Every time I eat here, the food gets better. So when are you going to give me some of your recipes?"

"I'm not," he retorted, chuckling as he leaned back in his chair. "Flattery will get you nowhere, Phoeb. You know that."

Undaunted, she only shrugged, her green eyes twinkling.

"You can't blame a girl for trying. Nothing ventured, nothing gained."

"True enough. Now what about Annie's meeting Thursday night? Who was it with and where?"

"A Mr. Sal Larkin," she answered, abruptly somber, "at the Transit Tower. He was coming from Houston and wouldn't be able to meet with her until around eight o'clock. Normally, I would have gone with her, but it was my grandfather's eighty-fifth birthday and the family was having a party I couldn't get out of."

"So you went to the party, and Annie met the renter alone. And that's the last time you saw or heard from her?"

She nodded miserably. "I had no idea she was in any kind of trouble. By the time I got in Thursday night, it was too late to call her, so I figured I'd check in with her the next morning before I left for a seminar in Austin for the day. But I missed her again. She never showed up at the office at all yesterday, and when I couldn't reach her at home this morning, I really started to worry."

"What about this Sal Larkin character?" Joe asked with a frown. "What do you know about him? Is he someone you've dealt with before?"

"No. We got the leasing contract with the Transit Tower and ran our first ad at the beginning of the week. Mr. Larkin called on Wednesday and spoke to Annie about needing an entire floor of the building. Apparently he wanted to get out of Houston and move his telecommunications company to San Antonio."

"Have you heard from him? Did he actually show up for the appointment?"

"I don't know. He didn't call, so I assume he showed up." Glancing at Annie, she said, "Does any of this ring a bell, girlfriend? What happened after you left the office that night?"

Annie would have given anything to remember, but her mind was a clean slate. "No, nothing. I can't even tell you where our office is, let alone what happened after I left it."

"You can't, but maybe someone can at the Transit Tower," Joe said. "I'm going to check it out. Phoebe, will you stay with Annie until I get back? I don't like leaving her alone."

Annie, already rising to her feet, had no intention of being baby-sat like a two-year-old. "I'm going with you. If something happened there, I have a right to know what it was."

"I'll tell you everything when I get back," Joe promised. "Here are the keys to the apartment—"

"I'm going, Joe," she cut in firmly. "Just because I lost my memory doesn't mean you have to treat me like a little girl. I can handle this."

Exasperated, he demanded, "How do you know? You don't even know what *this* is!"

"Then I'll find out at the same time you do," she said stubbornly, lifting her chin. "You're coming, aren't you, Phoebe? I'd like for you to be there."

"You're damn right I'm coming! Somebody hurt you, and I want to find him as much as you do. Besides," she added, grinning, "after watching you two avoid each other like the plague for months, just seeing you talk to each other again is the best surprise I've had all year. I wouldn't miss this for the world. Let's go."

Mumbling under his breath about stubborn women, Joe knew when he was beaten. Giving in, he escorted them both outside.

The Transit Tower was one of the city's oldest office buildings and one of the most distinctive landmarks on the San Antonio skyline. With its steep pointed roof and radio antennae that seemed to climb straight up into the clouds, it stood out among the other skyscrapers like an old oak among saplings.

Circling the building and the surrounding blocks twice, Joe finally gave up the idea of parking on the street and headed for the large parking garage next door. With all his attention focused on the traffic, which was surprisingly thick for a Saturday morning, he never noticed Annie's agitation until he started to turn into the garage's entrance bay. Still leery of getting in a car with him, she'd chosen to sit in the back seat, leaving the front for Phoebe, but her comfort zone ran out before he even knew anything was wrong. He'd barely stopped to take the ticket at the automatic entrance gate when she fumbled for her door handle.

Startled, he glanced over his shoulder at her and frowned at the sight of her ashen cheeks. "Annie? What is it? What's wrong? Dammit, honey, you can't get out here! Let me park first."

In a panic, she hardly heard him as she clawed at her seat belt and finally found the release. "No! I can't go in there! I just can't. Please…"

She had the same look of terror on her face that she'd had when she woke up and found herself in bed with him the previous morning, the one that ripped his heart right out of his chest. Alarmed, cursing the fact that she was out of reach in the back seat, Joe turned and stretched out his arm to her, needing to touch her. "Calm down, sweetheart. It's all right. There's nothing to be afraid of—I'm not going to let anyone hurt you—"

The impatient blaring of a horn sounded from right behind them, cutting him off. Swearing, Joe shot the other driver a furious glare in his rearview mirror and saw that three other cars had lined up behind him and were waiting to enter the garage. "Damn! I'm holding up traffic—"

"Annie and I don't need to go into the garage with you," Phoebe said quickly, as she released her own seat belt. "Why don't we get out here and wait for you at the front door? C'mon, Annie, let's take a walk."

Annie didn't have to be told twice. She was out of the car as if the devil himself was after her, hurrying away from the garage entrance just as fast as her legs would carry her.

Frowning after her in concern, Joe almost got out to follow her. Then the driver behind him blared his horn again. "Take care of her," he told Phoebe as she hurriedly climbed out of the car. "I'll just be a second." Pushing the button for a gate ticket, he drove into the garage, but not before he caught a last glimpse of Annie standing on the sidewalk with Phoebe, her eyes huge in her pale face as she stared in revulsion at the building.

What was going on inside that head of hers? he wondered as he cruised the first floor, then the second, for an available parking spot. She wasn't a woman who scared easily. In fact, she didn't blink an eye at showing property in parts of the city that most people wouldn't be caught dead in. But she'd definitely been in a panic the second he approached the garage. Had something happened to her here?

Anxious to get back to her, he shot up the ramp to the third floor and sighed in relief when he saw that there were plenty of spaces there. Finally! Turning into the first empty spot, he quickly parked and locked the car and was halfway to the elevators when he stopped short at the sight of the car parked all by itself at the far end of the floor. Even in the shadows that engulfed the garage, there was no mistaking that it was Annie's. As far as he knew, there wasn't another '62 Volvo that distinctive shade of yellow in the city.

He reached it in ten long strides, his brow furrowed as

he tried the door. It was locked. Peering in the driver's-side window, he could see her day planner lying on the front seat, apparently right where she'd left it. Nothing looked out of place or the least unusual.

"Dammit, why would she just walk off and leave her car here?" he muttered to himself. "She loves the damn thing. She wouldn't just leave it."

Scowling, he walked completely around the vehicle, looking for something, *anything,* that might tell him what had happened there two nights ago. But if she'd run into any kind of trouble there, there was no sign of it. The car was untouched, everything just as it should be.

Then he saw it. A brownish stain on the pavement a few spaces over from the one where her car was parked. Even as he started toward it, he tried to convince himself it was probably just an oil stain. But as he drew closer and went down on one knee to examine it, a sick feeling spilled into his stomach. Unless he was mistaken, it was dried blood.

For a long time, he didn't move. He was going to have to tell Annie. Clenching his teeth on an oath, he would have given just about anything to keep it from her, but she had a right to know. First, he had to call the police. Returning to his car for his cellular, he quickly called Sam Kelly.

Watching her friend pace restlessly as they waited for Joe, Phoebe said, "Maybe this wasn't such a good idea, Annie. Are you sure you're okay? You're as white as a sheet. Why don't you wait here and I'll go back inside and get Joe and tell him you've changed your mind? We can do this another day."

As her gaze darted to the garage entrance, Annie would have liked nothing better than to jump at the suggestion, but she couldn't. Not when the fear gripping her threatened to render her powerless. It was a feeling, she was discovering, that she hated.

Glancing at the other woman, wishing she could remember her and the good times they'd had over the years, she asked quizzically, "What kind of woman was I before? You've known me all my life. Right now, you know me better than I do. What was I like? Was I a wimp or what? I can't believe I was one of those women who looked over her shoulder every time she went out of the house, but I can't deny that I'm scared. And I don't know why. God, this is so hard!"

Tears welled in Phoebe's green eyes. Impulsively, she reached over to give her a fierce hug. "You, a wimp?" she laughed shakily. "Are you kidding? You're the gutsiest person I ever knew. Why do you think we've been friends for so long? We're partners in crime, kid. We always have been. So you quit worrying about what kind of person you are. You've got amnesia, for God's sake! Who wouldn't be scared?"

She would have said more, but Joe stepped out of the parking garage then. Annie took one look at the granite set of his jaw and braced for bad news. "What is it? What's wrong?"

"I found your car," he told her.

"And?" Phoebe asked, obviously waiting for the other shoe to drop.

"And it's fine. It's on the third floor and appears to be untouched."

His tone was matter-of-fact and not the least bit alarming. Annie should have been relieved, but she was starting to figure Joe Taylor out. When his eyes were shuttered, his face blank, he was hiding something. Her eyes searching his, she said, "But there's something else, isn't there? Something you're holding back because of me. Just spit it out, Joe. If it concerns whatever happened to me, I have a right to know.''

She was right, but that didn't make telling her any easier. He'd seen her fear yesterday morning when she thought he was going to hurt her, and then again just moments ago. He didn't need to know what she'd been through to know that it must have been pure hell. Given the opportunity, he would have made sure she never remembered it at all, but there were some things he couldn't protect her from. This was one of them.

''There's a stain two spaces over from your car,'' he said flatly. ''I can't be sure what it is, but it looks like dried blood, so I called Sam. He should be here any moment.''

''Show me. Maybe it'll jog my memory.''

''The hell I will!'' he growled. ''The doctor said you'd remember when you were ready, and not until then. Forcing the issue won't do you or the baby any good.''

Watching the interplay between the two of them, Phoebe sucked in a sharp breath. ''Baby? What baby?''

''She's pregnant,'' Joe said curtly. ''She didn't tell you?''

''No! My God, a baby! That's wonderful!'' Joy lighting her face, she turned to Annie to hug her, only to freeze at the despair in her eyes. ''What is it? What's wrong? You've been wanting a baby for years—''

Realization hit her then, widening her eyes. ''Oh, my God, you don't remember!''

Miserable, Annie shook her head. ''No. Nothing.'' At her side, she could feel Joe growing colder and colder, but there was nothing she could do about the awkward situation. If anyone knew what she'd been doing the last few months, it was Phoebe, and there were questions that needed to be asked. Joe was entitled to hear the answers.

"Did I..." She glanced away, heat climbing in her cheeks. "Was I seeing anyone that you know of?"

Phoebe, clearly as uncomfortable as she, cast a quick look at Joe's stony face and could do nothing but shrug. "I don't know. I'm sorry, but the only time we ever argued in our lives was when you left Joe. I thought you were making a big mistake and told you so. You didn't want to hear that, of course, so we made a pact not to discuss your love life. If you were dating anyone, I didn't know about it, but then again, I made it clear I didn't want to. And you never whispered a word about possibly being pregnant."

Annie wanted desperately to believe that she hadn't said anything about the baby because she'd been so stressed about the possible breakup of her marriage that she hadn't even realized that she was pregnant. But she only had to look at Joe's set face to know that he'd jumped to a completely different conclusion—if she hadn't even told her best friend about the pregnancy, it was probably because the baby wasn't her husband's.

No! she wanted to cry. She wasn't that kind of woman! But even as the words hovered on her tongue, she couldn't say them. Not when she didn't know for sure who or what Annie Taylor was.

Silence fell after that, a thick, uncomfortable silence that no one seemed inclined to break. Then Sam Kelly arrived with an evidence team. "I'm going in with you," she told Sam, and shot Joe a challenging look that just dared him to try and stop her. "I need to see whatever's in there."

The tension in the air was thick enough to cut with a knife, and Sam obviously didn't have to be hit in the head to know that he had just stepped into the middle of a disagreement. Glancing from Annie to Joe and back again, he didn't take sides either way. "That's your choice," he said diplomatically. "I can't tell you if that's wise or not—

you'll have to use your own judgment. Joe said when he called that your car looked untouched, but we're going to dust it for prints anyway, so don't touch it until we've had a chance to go over it."

They all headed for the two parking-garage elevators, where they split up, with the evidence team taking one and Annie, Joe, Phoebe and Sam the other. At the most, it was a forty-second ride to the third floor—it should have been easy. But the second the doors slid shut, closing them in, Annie knew she wanted nothing to do with whatever was on the third floor.

Trapped at the back of the elevator, however, she had left it too late to change her mind. Breaking out in a cold sweat in spite of the fact that it was a warm autumn day, she rubbed her chilled arms and tried to focus on positive thoughts as they rose slowly toward the third floor. She was perfectly safe. Joe and the police were here, and there was no reason to be afraid.

But when the elevator doors finally slid open and everyone else filed out, she stood flat-footed where she was.

Her gaze trained on the shadowy confines of the garage that stretched out in front of the open doors, she didn't see Joe stop when she didn't follow. "Annie?"

He didn't say anything else, just her name, but he told her without words that she didn't have to do this. All she had to do was push the button for the first floor and turn her back on whatever was out there waiting to terrify her. He and Sam would handle this for her, and no one would condemn her for it.

No one but herself. She could turn tail and run and all it would cost her was her self-respect.

Dragging her tortured eyes from the shadows, she lifted them to Joe. "When you were a kid, were you ever afraid of monsters under your bed at night?"

He nodded. "Sometimes."

"Everyone told you there was no such thing and there was no reason to be afraid, and you wanted to believe them more than anything. But every time you got anywhere near that bed once the sun went down, you got this big lump in your throat. Do you remember?"

"I remember, honey."

"This garage is where my monsters live." She couldn't tell him how she knew—she didn't know. She just knew she had a lump in her throat the size of the Alamo and she wanted out of there. But running wouldn't accomplish anything. The nightmare went with her wherever she went.

"I have to face this monster, Joe." She barely spoke above a whisper, but she was already stepping out from the corner of the elevator, her shoulders square and the glint of determination in her eyes.

From his scowl, he clearly didn't agree, but all he said was, "Just remember, you don't have to prove anything to anyone."

She didn't agree, but she only nodded and forced herself to walk to his side. At the far end of the floor, the bright yellow Volvo drew her like a magnet.

This was her car? she wondered in surprise as she slowly walked toward it. According to Joe, it was her baby, her pride and joy, a member of the family that she'd polished and waxed and changed the oil in as often as you wiped an infant's bottom. It had been beautifully restored and no doubt drew looks from everyone who passed it on the street. And it didn't look the least bit familiar to her.

Watching her carefully, Joe asked, "Do you remember it?"

She shook her head numbly. "No. How long have I owned it?"

"Eight years. You bought it right after your twenty-first birthday."

He could have told her she'd bought it last week, and she wouldn't have known any different. Joe handed Sam his set of keys, then joined her and Phoebe off to the side as the evidence team dusted the vehicle for fingerprints inside and out. And she felt nothing, absolutely nothing.

"There are quite a few prints," Sam told them a few minutes later. "But considering the condition of the car, I don't think we're going to find anything out of the ordinary. It looks like Annie just locked it up and walked away."

Squatting down on his haunches, he examined the rust-brown stain on the concrete fifteen feet from the car. "It's blood, all right," he said curtly as he pushed to his feet and stepped out of the way so his men could collect what evidence they could. "And a hell of a lot of it." His sharp eyes meeting Annie's, he arched a brow at her. "Are you getting any flashbacks? Anything that might tell you what happened here?"

"Besides fear?" she replied, shivering. "No. Nothing."

She was trembling and from the looks of the green cast to her complexion, on the verge of nausea. Wanting to take her in his arms and reassure her, Joe reminded himself that he couldn't lose his head over her just because she was in trouble. "Why don't you and Phoebe wait for us downstairs, then?" he suggested. "There's nothing more you can do, and you're only torturing yourself by hanging around here."

"I agree," Phoebe said, adding her two cents. "This place gives me the willies. Let's get out of here."

This time, Annie didn't have to be told twice. Leaving the men to finish investigating the scene, she hurried toward the elevator with Phoebe on her heels.

As soon as they were out of earshot, Sam said, "I didn't

want to say anything in front of Annie, Joe, but I wouldn't be surprised if these bloodstains turn out to match the ones on her clothes. What the hell was she doing here?''

Joe explained about Annie's meeting with the potential renter from Houston. ''We don't know if the guy ever showed or not. Phoebe's going to call him as soon as she gets back to the office and find out.''

''I'll get his name and number from her and do it for her,'' he said. ''If I can't get him, I've got a friend on the Houston force who owes me a favor. He'll track him down and see what he knows about what went down here on Thursday night.''

If he was still alive.

Sam didn't say the words, but they were both thinking them. If the dried blood on the floor matched that on Annie's torn clothes, someone had lost an awful lot of blood. And if that someone was the renter from Houston, he could not only be missing and hurting right now. He could be dead.

Chapter 4

From the garage, they walked over to the Transit Tower and checked out the tenth floor. To Annie's relief, the enervating fear that had gripped her in the parking garage was noticeably absent in the office building, and she was able to look around with interest. The rental space was empty of furniture and similar to that found all over the city. If she'd ever been there before, she had no memory of it.

Sam, however, was taking no chances. He had the evidence team check for fingerprints while he questioned the building security guard. The place was covered with hundreds of different prints that could have belonged to anyone, however, and the security guard was little help. He recognized Annie from a previous visit but didn't remember seeing her or anyone else on Thursday night.

At a dead end, there was little more anyone could do for now. One after the other, they drove out of the parking garage, with Joe following Sam in the Regal and Annie and Phoebe bringing up the rear in the Volvo. Since Annie's purse and driver's license were still missing, Phoebe drove, cracking jokes all the while to tease Annie out of the somber mood she'd fallen into.

They didn't see him. But he saw them. Especially *her*. Sitting in the passenger seat of the familiar yellow Volvo, she looked him right in the eye and didn't even blink. Stunned, he almost ran off the road.

Had she seen him? She must have—she couldn't have missed him! But if she'd seen him, she sure as hell hadn't acted like she'd known him, which didn't make any sense. The lighting had been poor the other night, but he wasn't stupid enough to think that she hadn't gotten a good look at him. He'd been right in her face, for God's sake! Given the chance, she should have been able to pick him out of a lineup at fifty yards.

If it hadn't been for her, he'd have been in Mexico by now, damn her to hell! It was what he'd worked and planned and risked everything for. But after she'd gotten away from him, he'd been afraid to chance it. He was well known to the police, and once the tricky little bitch went to them with a description of him and his van, his butt was fried. So he'd laid low and waited for them to come for him, sweating like a pig. But there'd been no knock at his door, nothing.

He'd waited for a day and a half, wasting precious time, and with every passing hour his fury had grown until he'd known he couldn't afford to wait any longer. She was a loose end, one that he'd left dangling long enough. She knew more than enough to send him to the chair, and unless he found a way to shut her up for good, he'd spend the rest of his life looking over his shoulder.

So he'd come back to the parking garage in the hopes that in the struggle between them, she might have dropped something that would tell him who she was. Instead, there she was, driving right past him. God, he had to be living right! She might as well have delivered herself to him on a platter. All he had to do was follow her, find out where she lived, and take care of her when the timing was right. She'd never know what hit her.

A feral gleam burning in his close-set blue eyes, he executed a quick U-turn and threw a rude hand gesture at the other drivers who dared to honk at him. Seconds later, he was a half block behind the Volvo and slowly closing.

A derisive smile curling his thin lips, he marveled at the stupidity of his quarry as the two women in the Volvo drove ten blocks to a parking garage on the river without ever realizing that they were being followed. Talk about a bunch of dumb idiots, he thought. He boldly drove into the garage behind them and found a space just five spaces away from theirs on the first floor, and they never noticed.

He didn't intend to let them out of his sight, but he'd hardly climbed out of his van and started after them when they were joined by a tall, lean, dark-haired dude who looked like trouble. Swearing under his breath, he quickly stepped back behind his van and reached for the knife hidden in his boot. But he didn't need it. The trio headed for the stairs that led to the Riverwalk and never glanced back.

Following them after that was a piece of cake. Blending in with weekend tourists, he drew nearer without them being aware of it. Then, before he quite realized where they were headed, they stepped through the doors of Joe's Place. By the time he followed them inside, the three of them were stepping through the swinging doors of the kitchen like they owned the place.

"Damn!"

Muttering a curse, he hesitated and was wondering what to do next when the restaurant hostess approached and shot him a friendly smile. "A table for one, sir? Smoking or non?"

He should have split right then and gotten out while he still could without being recognized. But he was desperate. Unless he found out who the curly-haired chick was, he was a condemned man. Glancing around, he spied an empty table that gave a clear view of the kitchen door and nodded toward it. "I'll take that one. You sell beer in this joint?"

"Yes, sir, we do." If she thought it was too early to be hitting the bottle, she kept the thought to herself. Her smile firmly in place, she handed him a menu. "I'll send your waitress right over. Enjoy your meal."

Not sparing the menu a glance, he kept his eyes on the kitchen door and waited for the waitress. Ten minutes later, she still hadn't showed and he was getting impatient. He started to grab a busboy and demand some service, but just then, a fresh-faced waitress hurried over to him, her cheeks flushed with excitement.

All smiles, she said charmingly, "I'm *so* sorry! I didn't mean to keep you waiting, but the place is a madhouse today. The owner's wife came in today after being gone for months and everybody's talking about her. She's got amnesia! Can you believe it? At first I thought she was just playing around, but it's true. Every time she sees me, she usually asks about my baby, but this time, she didn't even know who I was. It was the strangest thing. What are you supposed to say to a person who hasn't got a clue who you are?"

Stunned, the man just looked at her. Was she for real? Had the bitch really lost her memory? Was that why she'd looked right through him? Elated, it was all he could do not to grin like an idiot. All this time, he'd been worrying for nothing. She wasn't going to send the cops after him— she wasn't going to do jack squat. Because she didn't have a clue about what happened to her Thursday night. If he was lucky, she never would.

"Amnesia, hmm?" he said, schooling his features to casual interest. "I never knew anyone who had that before. And you say this is the owner's wife?"

"Yeah. Annie Taylor. Joe—that's the owner—" she explained helpfully, "was hoping that she might remember the restaurant since they used to eat most of their meals here, but so far, nothing's clicked. It's like she was just born yesterday or something."

"She doesn't know *anybody?*"

"No, not even Joe. Isn't that the wildest thing you ever heard?"

"Yeah, wild," he muttered. Trying not to look too excited, he leaned casually back in his chair. "So is this permanent or what? There must be something the doctors can do."

"You'd think so, wouldn't you?" the girl said chattily. "But apparently she has to remember on her own. And poor Joe can't push her too much or she might never get her memory back."

"No kidding? Man, that's rough." An idea already forming in his head, he had to fight back a smug smile of anticipation. So he'd scared her witless, had he? If the little witch thought she was terrified now, wait till she found out that he was just warming up. By the time he got through with her, she'd be lucky if he didn't turn her into a blubbering idiot.

Suddenly realizing how much she'd been talking, the waitress laughed. "I didn't mean to talk your ear off—I just find this kind of stuff so interesting. So what can I get you?"

He almost told her to forget it—she'd just given him everything he needed, including the broad's husband's name—but what the hell? He felt like celebrating. "How 'bout your biggest chicken-fried steak and a beer?" he suggested. "I just got some good news."

"I'm going with Phoebe for a couple of hours," Annie announced as she and Phoebe followed Joe into his office. "She's showing a house at two and I'd like to see it."

Phoebe had made the suggestion as they'd followed Joe through the downtown traffic, and Annie had jumped at the chance to do something that would get her mind off what might have happened to her Thursday night. She'd expected Joe to agree that it would be better for her to get out for a while than sit around worrying about what Sam's lab tests were going to turn up, but now, seeing his sudden scowl, she wasn't so sure.

"You want to go back to work? I don't think so."

Taken aback, she blinked. "Excuse me?"

"You're in no condition to even think about working yet," he said in the patient voice a father might use with a young daughter when explaining why she couldn't go out and play on the road. "As soon as I get some work together to take home with me, we'll go back to the apartment."

A meek, obedient wife might have taken that sitting down, but Annie had a feeling that was something she'd never been. Amusement warring with the first faint stirrings of temper in her eyes, she cocked her head and openly studied him. "I'll be the first to admit that I don't remember a thing about our marriage," she said dryly, "but I can't believe that I married a dictator. It just doesn't feel like something I'd do. Are you sure you're my husband?"

Watching the beginning of the fireworks from well out of the line of fire, Phoebe laughed. "He's all yours, girlfriend. I know—I was a witness."

Joe's lips twitched, but his jaw remained as unyielding

as the Rock of Gibraltar. "Grant said you were supposed to rest," he told Annie. "And so did Dr. Sawyer."

"I did," she argued. "I slept ten hours last night. And it wasn't like I was planning to run a marathon or anything," she added. "Phoebe's going to be doing all the work. I'm just going along for the ride. Maybe I'll remember something."

Unmoved, he shook his head. "Forget it. You're not supposed to force your memory."

Exasperated, Annie turned to her friend for help. "Is he always this stubborn?"

"From where I'm sitting, I'd say you two were pretty even," Phoebe said with a grin. "God help the baby."

Annie gave her a withering look. "That's not quite the endorsement I was hoping for, Phoeb. I'm trying to win an argument here, in case you hadn't noticed."

"Just for the record," Joe pointed out, "you were the one who always had the tenacity of a bulldog. So I'd watch who I was calling stubborn if I were you."

"But this is ridiculous! You can't expect me to sit around here and the apartment for the next six to eight months and twiddle my thumbs waiting to have the baby. I'll go crazy."

She had a point. She had amnesia, not a deadly disease, and he couldn't keep her pinned up for the entire length of her pregnancy. But just the thought of letting her go anywhere without him made him want to bar the door. Because he was concerned, he told himself. That was all. Right now, she was as vulnerable as a child and had no one to protect her but him.

Yeah, you keep on telling yourself that and you just might start to believe it in another hundred years or so, a caustic voice drawled in his head. *You know you never got over her. Why don't you just admit it and put yourself out of your misery?*

Muttering a curse under his breath, he growled, "I have no intention of keeping you locked up like some kind of prisoner. I was concerned about you being stressed out from this morning, but you know better than I do how you feel. Go ahead and go if you want. Just call if you're going to be late getting back. Okay?"

When her face lit up like a Christmas tree and she nodded, he tried not to take it personally. She wasn't thrilled at the thought of getting away from him—she just needed a break. Considering the circumstances, he supposed he couldn't really blame her.

"We'll only be gone a couple of hours," Phoebe assured him. "After the showing, I thought I'd take her by the office and see if anything looks familiar. I'll have her back by two-thirty or three, tops."

He nodded, resigned to the inevitable. He didn't have to worry that Phoebe would let anything happen to her. She was as protective as an older sister and wouldn't let her out of her sight. Still, he knew he would be watching the clock every second that they would be gone, and there wasn't a damn thing he could do about it. Pushing to his feet, he forced a smile. "Then you'd better get out of here or you'll be late for your appointment."

Within ten minutes of leaving with Phoebe, Annie knew why they had been friends for most of their lives. Carefree and irreverent, Phoebe told one outrageous story after another, swearing they were all true, not stopping until Annie cried with laughter. And for the first time since she'd awakened naked in a strange man's bed, Annie was able to forget the horror of not remembering who or what she was. With Phoebe, it didn't matter that she couldn't remember having been maid of honor at her wedding when she married right out of college, or being there for her when her husband beat her and she kicked him out. The bond between them was deeper than memories, and they seemed to have a zillion things to talk and laugh about. It was wonderful.

Wiping at her streaming eyes as they headed for the Dominion, an exclusive gated community on the outskirts of town where the rich and beautiful lived, she laughed, "Stop it! You're killing me. You're making that up!"

Her eyes twinkling, Phoebe held up her hand and swore solemnly, "As God as my witness, I'm not. We were on our way to Dallas and had *three* flats in one day! And not one man stopped to help us. You changed the last one, and when a carful of college boys flew by and honked, you threw the tire iron after them."

"I did not!"

"Yes, you did. I swear! It took us twenty minutes to find it in the tall grass on the side of the road."

Grinning, Annie said, "God, I wish I could remember that. We must have had some fun times together."

"Oh, we did! Lord, we were something. Do you remember the time we…"

She didn't remember anything, of course, but that didn't stop Phoebe from reminiscing. Listening, Annie felt as if she was eavesdropping on another woman's life, a woman she still didn't know but was beginning to realize she liked a great deal. Was she really that daring? That adventurous? She and Phoebe must have given their parents fits growing up…and a lot of reasons to laugh.

Soaking up the stories like a sponge, she couldn't seem to stop smiling. "It's a wonder we didn't spend all our time in detention when we were in school. I bet the principal was crazy about us."

"Old Cue Ball?" she retorted with a chuckle. "Why do you think he lost all his hair?"

They were still chuckling when they met with the prospective buyer at the entrance to the Dominion and showed him a mansion that overlooked the golf course. It was a breathtaking place, and watching Phoebe in action, Annie could see why she'd gone into business with her. She was good. Damn good. All joking forgotten once the buyer showed up, she was gracious and professional and able to answer all the man's questions without once consulting her notes. Singing the property's praises without being too pushy, she dropped subtle hints that the place wouldn't be on the market for long considering how reasonable the asking price was.

Listening to her, Annie almost choked on a laugh at that. How could Phoebe say that with a straight face, when the asking price was nearly a million dollars?

Behind the man's back, Phoebe winked at her. "We've got a live one here," she whispered when the buyer stepped out onto the patio to inspect the pool. "What do you want to bet he doesn't walk away from here without signing a contract?"

"Are you kidding?" she hissed, casting a quick look toward the open patio doors. "All he's done since we got here is point out everything that's wrong with the place."

Practically rubbing her hands with glee, Phoebe grinned. "Don't you just love it when a man plays hard to get?"

Annie laughed—she couldn't help it—and before it was all said and done, she had to give Phoebe credit. The man followed them back to their office, filled out the necessary paperwork, and signed on the dotted line. Annie would never have believed it if she hadn't seen it with her own two eyes.

Laughing, Phoebe gave her a high five as soon as they

had the office to themselves. "God, I love this business! It's days like this that make it all worthwhile. C'mon, let's celebrate!"

Considering the size of the commission she'd just made, Annie expected her to suggest they go out for champagne or something, but her friend reached into the bottom drawer of her desk and drew out a cookie tin instead. Popping the lid, she held it out to Annie with a smile. "It doesn't get any better than this, girlfriend. Try one."

Amused, Annie reached into the tin and pulled out something that seemed to be a combination of a cookie and a brownie and was dark with rich chocolate. Taking a bite, she groaned with pleasure. "Oh, that's wonderful! Did you make these?"

Phoebe nodded. "It's your mother's recipe. When we were kids, we used to drive her crazy eating the dough before she could bake it. I was hoping you'd remember."

Her smile fading, Annie tried, but as before, all she came up with was a black wall that blocked her memory and wouldn't let anything through. "I want to," she said huskily, "but I can't. There's just nothing there. Tell me about my mother…my parents. Where are they? Do I see them often?"

"They died in a car accident when you were twenty," her friend said softly. "Your father was never around much when we were growing up—he was always working—but your mom was great. She taught us both to drive a stick shift and water-ski. And man, could she cook! She was always trying something new. It's too bad she didn't live long enough to meet Joe. She would have loved talking shop with him."

She sounded like a wonderful mother, but nothing Phoebe said stirred a memory. Regret darkening her eyes and squeezing her heart, she said, "I wish I remembered her. Maybe then I wouldn't feel so alone."

"You have Joe, Annie. I know he still seems like a stranger to you, but you can count on him," she said earnestly. "Just give it some time."

Since time was all she had, Annie could do nothing else. But no one seemed to realize how difficult that was. She was living with a man she didn't know, sleeping in his bed at night, while the two of them circled each other during the day like two adversaries in some kind of contest. She could see the emotions in his eyes every time he looked at her, feel the jerky beat of her heart whenever he inadvertently touched her, and couldn't for the life of her explain any of it.

"Tell me about him," she said impulsively. "I have so many questions that I can't ask him to his face."

For a minute, Phoebe almost told her, but then she shook her head, a crooked smile tilting up one corner of her mouth. "Oh, no, you don't. The doctor wants you to remember on your own. If you want to talk about Joe, you tell me about him. For all practical purposes, he was a stranger to you until a couple of days ago. Now that you've spent some time with him, what do you think of him?"

That was something she didn't even have to think about. "He's strong and protective—the kind of man who naturally takes charge in a crisis. And gentle," she added, remembering the way he had taken care of her when she was sick. "He's a good man."

"Yes, he is," Phoebe agreed. "Make sure you remember that in the days and weeks to come."

The opening of the second Joe's Place was still two months away, but Joe knew he was quickly running out of time. The entire staff, including a chef and manager, had to be hired, the menu had to be decided on and the work on the building itself wrapped up. While Annie was out with Phoebe, he spent the afternoon going over résumés for potential managers. Determined to avoid the type of problems he'd had before he brought Drake into the operation, he went over one after another.

Nothing, however, registered, and he had no one to blame but himself. Every time he let his guard down, his thoughts wandered to Annie. What was she doing? Had the office she shared with Phoebe brought back any memories? And if it had, were they good ones or bad ones? How long would it take her to remember their marriage?

He had to believe that eventually it would all come back to her. It had to. She needed her past, needed the security of knowing who and what she was, and he wouldn't deny her that even though he knew those selfsame memories would cause problems for them. He *was* the workaholic she'd accused him of being before she'd walked out—he couldn't deny it. But he had to draw the line when she compared him to her father, who, according to both Annie and Phoebe, had loved making money more than he'd ever loved his wife and child.

The money had never been an issue, dammit! He hadn't come from an upper-middle-class background like hers. His father had never kept a job for longer than a month or two without finding an excuse to quit. While her mother had stayed home with her when she was a child, his mother worked just to keep food on the table. He didn't want that for his wife and child if something happened to him. He'd tried to explain to her how important it was to him to build a nest egg so that when they did have children, their future would be secure, but she hadn't listened. She'd wanted a baby and nothing else mattered, least of all his own hopes and dreams for her and his children.

And he still resented that, he discovered as he stared blankly down at the résumé of a wanna-be manager. She tore his life up when she left him, and now she'd torn it up again by coming back the way she had. If, God help them, she didn't get her memory back, only a blood test would tell them if the baby was his when it was born. How the hell was a man supposed to concentrate when he had a thing like that hanging over his head for months to come?

Frustrated, angry with her and himself and the entire situation, he reached for the next résumé. It went without saying that he might as well have saved himself the trouble. His eyes kept drifting to his watch. Where the devil was she?

Finally giving up in defeat, he abruptly pushed to his feet, put the résumés away, then wandered out into the restaurant to greet customers and make sure they were enjoying their meals. It was that personal touch and his true interest in the customers' wants and needs that had made Joe's Place a success over the years. But when his eyes kept drifting to the restaurant's front doors, he knew he wasn't fooling anyone, least of all himself. Keeping the customers happy was important, but he was prowling around for only one reason. He was waiting for Annie.

It wasn't, however, until she stepped through the main doors an hour later that he realized that he hadn't really expected her to come back to him at all. Relief hit him then, the force of it stunning him, infuriating him. What the hell was wrong with him? He had no problem with watching over her, protecting her, seeing to her needs until she got her memory back. But he wouldn't, by God, care. Because if he did and she left him a second time, he didn't think he could endure it.

The restaurant was packed that night, the crowd lively. Deciding that he wasn't ready for another intimate dinner on the balcony like the one they'd shared the night before in their apartment, Joe suggested they eat supper at the restaurant instead, and Annie readily agreed. He thought he'd be able to keep his distance more easily in a crowd, but he hadn't reckoned on Annie. She'd had a wonderful afternoon with Phoebe and was thankful to have made a new friend, even though it was one she'd had for years. Her eyes sparkling, her smile as quick as her laughter as they waited for their food to be brought to their table, she retold some of the stories that Phoebe had told her and had no idea that Joe had heard them all before. And he didn't tell her. This was the Annie he had first met and fallen in love with, the one who had been gone for too long.

Watching her, captivated in spite of all his best intentions, he fought the pull of her smile and the sparkle in her eyes, but she didn't make it easy for him. In spite of the other diners who sat at tables all around them, the world was reduced to just their table. And Annie. He couldn't take his eyes off her.

She ate her steak and baked potato and part of his, eating with a ladylike grace and truck-driver appetite that he couldn't help but appreciate. Amused in spite of himself, he said, "How about dessert?"

"Oh, I shouldn't," she protested, then made him laugh when she said wistfully, "but strawberry shortcake does sound good."

"Hey, don't stop on my account," he said dryly, and signaled for the waiter.

Afterward, when she laughingly claimed she was starting to waddle, he walked her home. There were two ways home—they could walk along the river or take the stairs to street level and cut through the next block—but with no conscious decision on his part, Joe took the Riverwalk.

It was a mistake—he realized it immediately. The moon was out, music spilled from the nearby restaurants and clubs, and lovers strolled hand in hand everywhere he looked. Keeping his hands strictly to himself, he should have looked for the nearest flight of stairs and gotten the hell out of there, but he didn't. Memories played in his head, haunting him, seducing him. How many times had he and Annie walked this same way, touching each other all the way home, teasing each other until they were both hot and breathless and couldn't wait to fall into bed? They'd driven each other crazy more nights than he could remember, and he'd loved it.

If she hadn't left him, if she hadn't come back to him just because she was pregnant and in trouble, they could even now be going home to bed.

But she had, and he'd never been one to play what if. His mouth compressed in a flat line, he hurried her along. "C'mon, it's getting late. You must be tired."

Annie opened her mouth to tell him she was fine, but he didn't give her a chance. Jostling through the festive crowd, he pulled her after him and extended his stride, until she almost had to run to keep up with him. Then they reached the arched gate that opened onto the private back gardens of the Lone Star Social Club. Quickly unlocking it, he hustled her inside, into the house, and up the stairs before she could even think about catching her breath.

"Joe! What in the world! What's wrong?"

"I've got some paperwork to catch up on," he retorted as he unlocked their apartment door and pushed it open. "Will you be okay here by yourself if I go back to the office for a while?"

He didn't step into the apartment, but waited in the hall like a man who had a train to catch. Confused, she stared up at him searchingly. The charming man she'd just had dinner with was gone, and in his place was the cold stranger who kept his emotions safely hidden and treated her like an unwanted relative who had suddenly turned up on his doorstep without warning. He had to deal with her, but he really didn't want to, and for that, she felt the constant need to apologize.

She told herself she had no right to feel hurt—you had to care about someone before you gave them the power to hurt you. And in spite of the fact that they'd been married for five years, Joe Taylor was a virtual stranger to her. But still, there was an ache deep within her chest that was as raw as an open wound, and he had put it there. She would have died, however, before she let him know it.

Forcing a smile that never reached her eyes, she said airily, "Of course. I probably should go to bed anyway— it's been a long day. So go on. I'll be fine."

Her tone was just right, her smile breezy. She gave every appearance of being strong and independent, and there was no reason to linger. He stayed, however, right where he was and frowned down at her. "Are you sure? Maybe you shouldn't be alone right now—"

"I'll be fine," she insisted. "Will you just go? If I need you, I'll call. Okay?"

He should have gone then—he told himself he wanted to. But the memories that had dogged his quickened footsteps all the way home were there in the dark depths of her sapphire eyes, and he couldn't look away, couldn't turn away. He saw his hands settle heavily on her shoulders and would have sworn they belonged to someone else. Then he was dragging her up on her toes and he couldn't stop. He just couldn't stop.

He crushed his mouth to hers, his tongue already plundering, savoring. He didn't give her time to think, to object, but took like a man who hadn't tasted any kind of sweetness in ages. Hungry, greedy for more, he couldn't get his breath, couldn't get a handle on his self-control and didn't care. His blood was hot, boiling, his head spinning. And still he wanted more.

Lost to everything but the fury of his own needs, he didn't realize that she'd stiffened like a poker until he wrapped his arms around her and tried to draw her flush against him. Her arms wedged between them, she didn't give so much as an inch. Between one frantic heartbeat and the next, his head cleared.

He'd damn near taken her right there in the hall like a madman!

Swearing, cursing himself, he released her, but it was too late. The second he stepped back, he saw her eyes were wide with shock, her cheeks bright with color. "I'm sorry! That was a stupid thing to do! I know you didn't want that—I don't know what came over me." Stumbling for an acceptable explanation when there wasn't one, he backed away. "It won't happen again," he promised. "You don't have to be afraid."

Desperate for a way out, he finally remembered why they were standing in the hall. "I'm going back to the restaurant now. The number's in the book by the phone. I'll be back by eleven. Lock the door."

Dazed, she stumbled across the threshold and shut the door, only to lean weakly against it, conflicting emotions hitting her from all sides. He'd kissed her. Why? What did he want from her? She'd been so sure that he was only tolerating her presence because of the possibility that she was carrying his baby, but the hot emotions she'd seen in his eyes when he reached for her had nothing to do with anything as bland as tolerance. Lord, who would have thought the man could kiss like that? She must have kissed him a million times before, but this was the only time she remembered, and she couldn't seem to get her breath.

It won't happen again. You don't have to be afraid.

Wincing, she hugged herself. She hadn't been afraid... exactly. If her life had depended on it, she couldn't have said what she was. Except confused. And restless. He, on the other hand, hadn't been able to get away from her fast enough.

Pressing her ear against the door, she listened to the dying sound of his footsteps as he headed for the stairs halfway down the hall and told herself that he wasn't running from her, only the situation. She wasn't the Annie Taylor he'd married and separated from. It wasn't *her* he was rejecting.

An hour ago, she might have taken comfort from that, but it didn't help now. Because *she* was the Annie Taylor he'd kissed.

When the phone rang ten minutes later, she was in the master bedroom turning down the bedspread. Figuring it was Joe, checking to make sure she was okay, she stretched out on the bed and reached for the extension. He must have called the second he got back to the restaurant. "You don't have to worry about me," she said huskily, by way of a greeting. "I'm fine. Really."

She wouldn't have been surprised if he'd apologized again, but her only answer was silence. Frowning, she unconsciously tightened her fingers around the receiver. "Joe? Is that you?"

There was no answer, just a silence that hummed in her ear, and for no reason she could explain, her heart started to knock against her ribs. It was just a wrong number, she told herself. Just some ignorant person who didn't know how rude it was to not admit that he'd dialed wrong, then apologize. There was no reason to be afraid.

But when she hung up, she was shaking.

Five seconds later, she was in the living room, fumbling with Joe's address book for the number to the restaurant. It had to be here somewhere, she told herself frantically. He'd told her it was. All she had to do was calm down and think. *Think*, Annie! What would he list it under?

She was near tears when she found it and quickly reached for the phone. She had three numbers punched in when she suddenly froze. What was she doing?

Disgusted with herself, she slammed down the phone. "Don't be such a baby!" she muttered. "It's just a stupid wrong number, for heaven's sake! There's no reason to get all bent out of shape. Or call Joe! He's busy and won't appreciate you calling him away from work just because you're paranoid."

There was absolutely nothing to be afraid of. In her head, she knew that, but her body wasn't listening. Her pulse was pounding, her palms damp, her mouth dry as dust. She wanted to hide, which was ridiculous. This was her home. Closing her eyes, she dragged in a shuddering breath and willed herself to calm down.

How long she sat there, she couldn't have said. Her breathing gradually returned to normal, her heart rate steadied. Finally thinking more clearly, she double-checked the lock on the front door and found it secure. Her tight nerves eased, but she knew there was no way she was going to be able to sleep. Not now. The apartment was too quiet, too empty.

For the sake of her sanity, she switched on the TV just to break the heavy silence that engulfed her, then went looking for a book to read. She was just reaching for one on the top shelf of the bookcase in the living room when the phone rang again.

She froze, she couldn't help it, her heart in her throat.

She wouldn't answer it. It was probably just another wrong number, anyway. She'd just let it ring and whoever was on the other end would eventually get disgusted and hang up. All she had to do was wait him out.

But it could be Joe.

The thought slipped up on her from behind, nagging at her. He'd been reluctant to leave her there alone—he could be calling to make sure she was all right. If she didn't answer, he'd be worried....

She made no conscious decision to move, but suddenly she was across the living room and reaching for the phone. "Hello?"

For a split second, she thought it was going to be another wrong number. Then a rough, male voice on the other end of the line said, "Annie."

That was it—just her name in a matter-of-fact voice that was more of a statement than an inquiry. There was nothing threatening about it, nothing the least bit sinister. But between one heartbeat and the next, she was terrified, and she couldn't explain why. Sobbing, her skin crawling, she slammed down the receiver. Feeling dirty, she ran for the bathroom.

Chapter 5

The water pounding down on her head had long since grown cold, but Annie never noticed. Huddled in the corner of the shower stall, her brow furrowed with fierce concentration, she soaped a washcloth, then ran it over her breasts, hips, legs and arms, missing nothing in between. Then she numbly repeated the process. Once, then twice, then again. In the bedroom, the phone rang, but she didn't hear it. Time, the world, ceased to exist. There was just her, the water and the soap.

Clean, she thought dully. She had to get clean. She had to get the dirt out from under her skin.

Down in the restaurant, Joe frowned and hung up the phone in his office. There was nothing wrong, he assured himself. Annie had probably unplugged the phone in the bedroom when she'd gone to bed. And once she was asleep, she'd never hear the one in the living room. There was no reason to go running up to the apartment, as if she was some sort of maiden in distress. He'd heard her lock the dead bolt himself, and she'd promised to call if she needed him. The fact that she hadn't could only mean one thing—she was perfectly safe and he was being paranoid.

Deliberately, he tried to bring his attention back to his paperwork, but he couldn't shake Annie from his thoughts. Just because she hadn't called didn't mean she wasn't in trouble. What if she hadn't been able to get to the phone?

"Damn!" Pushing back his chair from his desk, he muttered curses, chastising himself for worrying like an old woman. But there was no getting around it—he wasn't going to get any more work done tonight until he knew for sure that she was all right. Gathering up his paperwork, he headed for the door.

"I'm going to check on Annie," he told Drake. "I probably won't be back tonight."

"Sure thing, boss," Drake responded, with a mock salute. "Don't worry about anything here. I'll hold down the fort."

It normally took him five minutes to walk home, but this time he made it in two. Worry etching his brow, he unlocked the front door to the apartment and stepped inside. The TV was on in the living room, tuned to an old John Wayne movie. Annie had always been crazy about the Duke—the sound of his familiar drawl should have been comforting, but wasn't. A quick glance around assured him that everything was as it should be, but he couldn't shake the feeling that something wasn't right. Then he heard it. The shower.

Relief flooded him, and he groaned aloud at his own stupidity. He'd had this image of her struggling with some unknown intruder and all the time she'd just been taking a shower. With the water pounding down on her head, she couldn't possibly have heard the phone ringing. God, what an idiot he was! Thankfully, he hadn't called Sam like he'd wanted to. He'd never have heard the end of it.

Promising himself that he'd have a phone installed in the damn shower stall tomorrow, he sank down on the couch to watch the end of *True Grit*. Ten minutes passed, then another five, and the water continued to run in the bathroom. Wondering what was taking Annie so long, he glanced at his watch and frowned. Nearly twenty minutes had passed since he'd stepped into the apartment, and he didn't know how long she'd been in there before that. What the hell was she doing?

His frown deepening with concern, he crossed to the bathroom door and knocked sharply. "Annie? What's going on in there? Are you all right?"

His only answer was the continued running of the water.

You go charging in there like some sort of knight in search of the Holy Grail and you're going to scare her to death, a caustic voice warned in his ear. *Especially since you've already grabbed her and kissed her once tonight. Hold your horses and let her have her privacy. She'll be out when she's done.*

But another ten minutes passed and Annie showed no sign of cutting off the water. Struggling for patience, Joe paced and cursed and tried to ignore the worry squeezing his heart. But he was fighting a losing battle, and with a muttered curse, he knocked on the bathroom door, then pushed it open before she could say yea or nay. Like it or not, he was going in.

He half expected her to scream, but with the shower door closed, she didn't even see him. "Annie? Are you all right?" he called over the steady drone of the shower. "You've been in there an awful long time."

She'd heard him—she had to. But silence was his only answer. Truly worried now, he strode over to the shower stall. Later, he couldn't have said what he expected to see when he jerked open the door, but it wasn't the sight of Annie standing under a cold spray of water, her face as pale as death, her arms heavy with exhaustion as she dragged a washcloth over herself again and again. In some spots on her breasts and thighs, her skin was red and nearly rubbed raw.

Alarmed, he didn't even stop to think, but stepped into the shower fully clothed. "Annie? Honey? What is it? What's wrong?"

She glanced up at the first sound of her name, her hands stilling, and it was then that Joe's heart stopped in his chest. He'd never seen such stark terror in anyone's eyes before and it scared the hell out of him. He wanted to reach for her, to wrap her close and demand to know what had happened, but he was afraid to touch her.

She blinked, her gaze locked and focused on his, and suddenly her blue eyes were swimming in tears. "J-Joe...help m-me. I—I c-can't g-get clean."

He'd sworn when she left him that he'd never let her break his heart again, but he felt it crack then, and it didn't matter. Nothing mattered but Annie. "Oh, baby," he rasped, his own eyes stinging as he reached to take the washcloth from her, "you're so clean, you're squeaky. Here, let's turn the water off and get you out of here."

With a savage twist of his hands, he shut off the cold spray, plunging the bathroom into a thick, heavy silence. Her arms climbing up her body to hug herself, Annie tried to say something, but suddenly her teeth were chattering and she was shaking with cold and shock. Joe ached to hold her, but he wasn't sure how she'd react and he didn't want to upset her any more than she already was.

"Don't try to talk," he murmured soothingly as he pulled towels from the linen closet and wrapped them around her as tenderly as if she were a child. "Whatever the problem is, I'll handle it. Just stand there and let me take care of you, honey. Everything's going to be okay."

Biting her bottom lip to still its trembling, she nodded and docilely did as he said, not uttering so much as a whimper as Joe gently patted the water from her breasts and hips and legs. His emotions fiercely held in check, he told himself to get a grip.

But a muscle jumped in his jaw every time he touched her poor chafed skin. Lord, she had to be hurting—it hurt him just to look at her.

What happened while he was gone? he wondered furiously. Why had she done this to herself? Questions tore at him, but she was in no shape to give him any answers. Not now. She could barely stand and words were beyond her as goose bumps rippled across her skin. Wrapping a towel around her dripping hair and another around her shivering body, he urged her into the bedroom. "C'mon, sweetheart. Let me find you a nightgown and then I'll put you to bed. Once you warm up, you'll feel better. Okay?"

Only able to manage a jerky nod, she stumbled over to the bed and perched hesitantly on the side of the mattress. By the time Joe finally found her a gown and robe, some color had seeped back into her face, but her knuckles were white with strain as she clutched at the towel that covered her. And when her gaze lifted to his, awareness of her own nakedness was there in her eyes.

Hesitating, Joe unconsciously curled his fingers into the softness of her nightclothes. "Can you dress yourself?" he asked huskily.

Heat climbing in her cheeks, she swallowed thickly. "Y-yes. I—I think s-so."

He didn't want to leave her by herself, but she couldn't have made it plainer that she needed a few minutes to herself. Crossing to her, he laid her clothes next to her on the bed. "I'll just be in the living room," he told her quietly. "If you need some help, just holler."

Walking away from her when he knew she still needed him was one of the hardest things he'd ever done, but he didn't intend to be gone for long. Grabbing some dry clothes for himself from their closet, he hurried into the guest bathroom to dry off and change, then headed for the kitchen to make her a cup of hot cocoa. Within minutes, he was back, knocking at the bedroom door.

"You okay, honey? I brought you some cocoa. I thought it might steady your nerves. Are you decent?"

Cold all the way to her soul in spite of the gown and robe that now covered her from her ankles to her throat, Annie hugged herself and had to swallow twice before she could answer. "Yes. You can c-come in."

The words were hardly out of her mouth, and he was there in front of her, studying her with eyes that were dark with worry. And, just as quickly, the tears that she'd thought she'd cried out in the shower were back, spilling over her lashes. He was being so sweet to her, and she was acting like a basket case. God, what must he think of her?

"I'm sorry," she sniffed.

"Don't be ridiculous," he chided. "After everything you've been through, I imagine you're entitled to a few tears." He held the steaming mug out to her and smiled coaxingly. "I made it just the way you like it—with an obscene amount of whipped cream."

Sure her stomach would revolt if she dared to put so much as a swallow in it, she took the cup to warm her hands. The scent of chocolate, dark and sinful, drifted to her nose, tempting her. Staring down at the mound of whipped cream floating in the chocolate, she hesitated.

"Go ahead," Joe urged softly. "It'll make you feel better."

She didn't think she would ever feel better again, but she took a sip, then another, and felt heat spread through her like liquid sunshine. She sighed and held the mug to her chest. For the first time in what seemed like hours, she had some body heat to fight the cold that invaded her very soul.

When she glanced up, Joe was watching her with eyes that were as fierce as a hawk's. "What happened while I was gone?"

She didn't want to tell him, but one look at his set face and she knew he would never be satisfied with anything less than the truth. But God, how did she tell him without sounding like a baby who was afraid of her own shadow? "This is so stupid," she blurted out, dashing impatiently at the tears that slid down her cheeks as she stepped past him to pace the length of the bedroom. "I don't know what's the matter with me. Nothing really happened. It was just a phone call—"

"Someone called? Who? When?"

She nodded. "About five minutes after you went back to the restaurant. Actually, it was two phone calls. I thought the first one was a wrong number because no one said anything, so I hung up. Then a few minutes later, the phone rang again. I almost didn't answer it, but I knew you'd be worried if it was you...."

"And?"

"A man said my name—"

"And?"

"And that was it." A strangled laugh, verging on hysteria, forced its way through her tight throat. "I know—it sounds ridiculous. There was nothing to be afraid of, but the second he said my name, I was terrified. And I don't even know why! He didn't threaten me or anything. For all

I know, he could have been an old friend of yours who's wondering right now why I hung up on him. God, I feel like such an idiot!''

"Why? Because you're afraid? Honey, if we could explain away fear, nobody would be scared of anything." Moving to her side, he slung a brotherly arm around her shoulders. "You don't have to apologize for being scared. You were, and now we have to figure out why. Did you recognize the caller's voice? Did it sound familiar at all? Maybe you knew him."

For a second, just a second, the weight of his arm across her shoulders felt like heaven, and she allowed herself the luxury of melting against him. But then she could hear the caller's voice in her ear, saying her name, and suddenly she couldn't bear to be touched.

Shrugging out from under his arm, she was halfway across the room before he even realized there was a problem. She saw his surprise, the slight tightening of his jaw, but there was nothing she could say, no explanation she could give, that would make sense. He would think it was because of the kiss—that she didn't trust him—but the wariness he'd stirred in her then was nothing compared to this.

Regret darkening her eyes, she turned away. "No. At least I don't think so," she amended. "I don't remember ever having heard it before, but I guess that doesn't mean much, does it?"

She couldn't have made it clearer that she didn't want his touch if she'd screamed and fought her way free of him. His expression carefully shuttered, Joe didn't so much as flinch. "Okay, so you don't remember his voice, but he had to know you since he called you by name. What did he do after that?"

"I—I don't know. I hung up." Emotions skittered across her face, as easy to read as a Dr. Seuss book. Fear, trepidation, revulsion. Her gaze unfocused, directed toward something Joe couldn't see, she swallowed and dazedly rubbed her hands up and down her arms just as she'd done when he'd found her in the shower. "I felt so dirty, I couldn't stand it," she whispered half to herself. She blinked then, her eyes lifting to his with painful, helpless bewilderment. "I couldn't get clean, Joe. I tried, but it didn't matter how much soap I used, I still felt dirty. And I don't know why."

He went to her then because he couldn't help himself, because she needed him, whether she knew it or not. And he, God help him, needed her. "You're not dirty, honey." Taking a chance, he lifted his hand and lightly ran a finger down her smooth cheek. "You're clean and beautiful, and if someone made you feel otherwise, they're the one with the problem, not you."

He was so close he could see the doubts in her eyes. He knew he was crowding her, but God, he ached to just hold her, dammit! To feel her against him and forget for a moment they'd ever been apart. But he hadn't forgotten the shock in her eyes when he'd kissed her. And a man could only watch his wife cringe from his touch so much before he learned to keep his hands to himself.

Stepping back, he gave her the room she needed. "Now that we've got that straightened out," he began, "why don't I—"

The sudden knock on the front door was sharp and demanding. Startled, Annie stiffened, every line of her body tight with apprehension as her eyes flew to Joe's. Swearing, he growled, "Who the hell is that at this time of night? Stay here, honey, while I check it out."

The last person he expected to find knocking on his front door at ten o'clock at night was Sam Kelly. Jerking the door wide, he motioned him inside. "You don't usually come calling this time of night. What's up?"

"I probably should have waited until tomorrow for this, but I've got some news and I thought you'd want to hear it as soon as possible." Stepping into the living room, he glanced around. "Where's Annie?"

"Here," she said from the short hallway that led to the bedrooms. "What's wrong? Did you find out what happened to me?"

"Not to you, no," he said regretfully. "But I did find out what happened to Sal Larkin." At her blank look, he said, "You know, the renter you were supposed to meet with at the Transit Tower the other night. He never showed because he was in a car accident on the way in from Houston. He's been in the hospital ever since."

"Oh, no!"

"I know it's not much consolation, but at least we know he wasn't involved in what happened to you," he said. "He was in emergency surgery at the time and couldn't have possibly had anything to do with whatever went down in the Transit Tower parking garage. That means someone else is involved. All we've got to do is figure out who."

"That may be simpler than you think," Joe told him gravely. "Annie got a couple of strange phone calls tonight when I was at the restaurant."

"What kind of phone calls?"

Pale, she grimaced. "One was a hang-up. The next one was a man. He called me by n-name—"

"And scared her out of her mind," Joe finished for her angrily.

He told him then about Annie's reaction to the call. "Whoever he was, he had to have something to do with her amnesia," he said grimly. "She was terrified of him. And I'm telling you right now, Sam, if I ever get my hands on him, the miserable piece of scum is going to wish he'd never been born.''

Sam understood exactly how he felt—in his shoes, he'd have been as outraged as Joe, but the last thing this case needed right now was an outraged husband muddying the water. ''Hold your horses, Kemosabe,'' he warned, shooting him a hard look. ''For all we know, this could be just a case of a simple wrong number—''

''The hell it is! He called her by name!''

''Her name's in the phone book, isn't it? She's a licensed Realtor, Joe. Doesn't she have both her home and business numbers listed? It could have been a business call that scared her for some reason.''

It could have, but Joe wasn't buying that for a second. ''You didn't see her in that shower, Sam. She was freaked, and you know Annie's not the type to freak easily.''

''Which is all the more reason for you to take care of her and let us handle whoever made that call,'' he replied. ''Annie's shaky enough over this without you trying to take the law into your own hands.'' Turning back to Annie, he motioned for her to join him on the couch. ''Why don't you come over here and tell me about this call, Annie—''

''All he said was my name.''

''I know,'' he said patiently, as she reluctantly crossed to the couch, ''but what did he sound like? Did he have an accent? Were there any noises that you could pick up in the background? Any strange sounds that might tell us where he was calling from? Close your eyes and just think a minute. Maybe there was a train whistle or some music...''

Obediently, Annie did as he asked, praying that in her terror, she might have missed something, anything. But all she could hear when she replayed the call in her head was that voice...flat, totally without emotion, yet somehow horribly frightening at the same time. Who was this man who could terrify her with just the sound of his voice? What did he want with her? And when would he call again?

Her eyes flew open, the new fear draining the last of the color from cheeks that were already lily-white. "There was nothing," she rasped hoarsely. "Nothing. He called me by name, and then there was this long silence. Do you think he'll call back? I can't talk to him again. I won't!"

"You're damn right you won't," Joe growled. There was no way he was standing back and letting some sick joker terrorize her this way. "From now on, I'll answer the damn phone, or we'll let the machine get it." And she wasn't going to be left alone again either. When he couldn't be with her, he'd make sure someone else was.

Turning to Sam, he arched a dark brow. "Well?" he demanded. "You still think this was a simple wrong number?"

He didn't, but it didn't matter what he thought. He had to go by the law. "At this point, it doesn't matter, Joe. It's not against the law to call someone by their name over the phone. If we could prove he knew what he was doing to her when he did it, we might have a slim case of harassment, but he'd have to call a heck of a lot more than twice. If I were you, I'd get caller ID on your phone just in case this joker calls back. At least then we'd know where he was calling from and we might be able to find out who the devil he is."

It was a long shot, but the only one they had. Joe nodded. "I'll make the arrangements the first thing Monday morning."

By ten o'clock Monday morning, Joe had someone from the telephone company installing caller ID at the apartment and, to the amusement of the telephone repairman, a new phone in both bathrooms. Over the next few days, however, the new service turned out to be unnecessary. Whoever had called Saturday night and scared the living daylights out of Annie hadn't called back. Not taking any chances, though, Joe made sure she wasn't left alone again. If she wasn't with him at the restaurant, she was with Phoebe, or he brought work home with him.

As promised, Sam got back to them with the results of the lab tests on Annie's clothes and the stain in the parking garage, and the news wasn't anything they hadn't expected. The bloodstains matched each other, but not Annie. As for the fingerprints on her car, they all turned out to be hers.

With the case at a standstill, they seldom discussed it, but settled into a routine that seemed to take the anxiety from Annie's eyes. Her memory still persisted in eluding her, but she was more relaxed...as long as they remained in the apartment. The second they stepped outside, however, the fear was back, the tension gripping her visibly—a thing that was difficult to watch. Realizing that she didn't know friend from foe, Joe took immediate steps to remedy the situation.

"C'mon," he told her after breakfast one morning. "I'm going to introduce you around so if someone speaks to you in the hall, you'll know if it's someone you can trust."

He didn't have to think twice about who to introduce her to first—he took her straight downstairs to Alice Truelove, who lived in the smaller of the two apartments at the back of the mansion. And as he'd hoped, Alice beamed in delight at the sight of Annie by his side and snatched her into her arms for a fierce hug. "I wondered when you were going to get down here and tell me you were back! I saw you and Joe go out to dinner the other night, but I didn't want to intrude. Lordy, lordy, look at you! I knew this old house would work its magic if you two would just give it enough time. Joe, isn't she a sight for sore eyes?"

"Yes, ma'am, she is," he replied, grinning when Annie couldn't help returning the small, spry woman's enthusiastic hug. "I thought it was time I got her down here—she needs a friend she can trust."

Quickly and efficiently, he told her the whole story and wasn't the least surprised when Alice's faded blue eyes took on a hard gleam. With her plump figure, beautifully lined face, and cloud of stark white hair that she invariably wore twisted up in a bun, she might look a soft pushover of a granny, but she could be tough as nails when she wanted to be.

"You visit me whenever you want, sweetie," she told Annie. "I just dare anyone to try and bother you. I've got my Colt .45 that my daddy gave me in my bedroom, and you can bet the bank that I know how to use it."

"I don't think you'll need the peashooter," Joe drawled, grinning, "but Annie might drop by sometime when I have to take care of some things at the restaurant. Thanks, Alice."

"For what?" she sniffed. "You two are like family. You call on me whenever you need me. Since Annie doesn't remember the stories about the mansion, I can tell them to her all over again."

"Later," Joe laughed, tugging Annie down the hall to the next apartment. "She'll get back to you later."

Over the course of the next few days, he took her around to all their neighbors in the mansion and reintroduced her to them.

Not surprisingly, it was the women she was most at ease with. She chatted every morning with Mrs. Sanchez across the hall and asked Susan Lucas, a renter who lived downstairs and had just had her second baby two months ago, everything she could think of about pregnancy and babies and parenting. But it was Alice she kept going back to. And true to her word, the old lady spent hours entertaining her with stories about the Lone Star Social Club.

After one particularly entertaining afternoon, Annie's eyes were sparkling when she and Joe went to the restaurant for dinner. "How old do you think Alice is?" she asked him after they'd given their orders to the waiter. "I know you said she's supposed to be the original owner's granddaughter, but if I didn't know better, I'd swear she was the original owner herself. She knows the names of everyone who ever met and fell in love there all the way back to the turn of the century. But she couldn't be that old, could she?"

Joe grinned. "God only knows. From what I hear, she was here long before the Riverwalk was ever thought of."

"Do you think that old legend about unmarried renters falling in love is for real? How could it be? It's just a house."

"With a heck of a wallop," he replied, chuckling. "I can't explain how it works, but I've lived there for nearly six years, and nobody remains single for long. Even Bob Jackson bit the dust, and he was the most hardened bachelor I ever met. He swore when he moved in that the *curse* wasn't going to get him, but I'll be damned if he didn't elope with his new secretary five months later. Talk about shaking up a few people. One of Jackson's best friends lived on the first floor and moved out immediately."

"So he's still a bachelor?"

"Are you kidding? His sister introduced him to her roommate and he found himself walking down the aisle three months later. Last I heard, they had three kids and were expecting another one on Valentine's Day. And then there was you, of course," he added. "I took one look at you and knew my days as a bachelor were numbered."

He said it teasingly, with a twinkle in his eye, but there was nothing funny about what she'd done to him. She'd turned his life upside down and filled a void that he hadn't even known was there, and he'd loved her for it. He hadn't realized how much until she walked out and he'd found himself faced with the emptiness of his own lonely existence.

He wanted her back, dammit. Wanted back what they'd once had together. Needed back what he'd carelessly let slip through his fingers. But she wasn't the same woman who married him or even the same one who'd walked out on him. Staring soul deep into her sapphire eyes, he didn't see how they could ever find their way back to what they had once had. Not if she'd betrayed him with another man.

"Joe? Are you okay?"

Lost in his thoughts, he blinked and brought her back into focus to find her frowning at him in concern. "Yeah, I'm fine," he said in a gravelly voice, then deliberately changed the subject. "So what are you and Phoebe doing tomorrow?"

"Showing a ranch up by Kerrville," she said promptly. "A couple from Corpus is driving up to look at it and another one west of Bandera, so we should be gone most of the day. What about you? You going to be at the new place all day?"

"Probably," he said, fighting a smile as their food was set before them and the waiter automatically set a bottle of ketchup on the table. Over the last few days, she had developed a fondness for the red stuff that bordered on a craving. Most of the restaurant staff had learned that it didn't matter what she ordered to eat, she was going to ask for ketchup before the meal was over. "The opening's just around the corner and there's still a lot to do. The painters are finishing up in the morning in the dining area, and the kitchen appliances are supposed to be delivered Thursday. The printer's also delivering the invitations sometime tomorrow, but they still have to be addressed."

"I'll help you if you'll bring the guest list home," she promised, digging into her food with gusto. "Why don't we eat at home tomorrow night and order in a pizza?"

That was an offer she wouldn't have made three months ago, not when she was so dead set against him opening another restaurant. Remembering the times she'd accused him of being more concerned with the shape of his business than the condition of their marriage, Joe knew he should tell her about the day she'd left him. If he didn't, he would be giving her just one more reason to resent him when she got her memory back.

But he was damned either way, and he hated to ruin the mood when there hadn't been a tense moment between them in days. The decision made, he said, "Good idea," and damned the consequences. "Have Phoebe drop you by here when you get back tomorrow and we'll walk home together."

The florist's box was propped against their front door, but Annie never noticed it. She and Phoebe had driven away from the ranch in Kerrville with a huge contract in hand and should have celebrated, but all Annie had wanted to do was get back to Joe and tell him about her day. She'd missed him. She hadn't expected that, and she had to admit that the idea shook her. After all, it wasn't as if she spent every waking moment with him. He had a business to run, not to mention a second restaurant to open, and over the course of the last few days, she'd spent hours at a time with Phoebe and other friends and neighbors while he worked.

He couldn't devote all his time to her, and she didn't expect him to.

But today had been different. She'd been gone since morning, and in spite of the fun she'd had with Phoebe, she'd found herself wondering what he was doing, where he was, if he'd given her so much as a second thought since she'd left. Then, when Phoebe had dropped her off at the restaurant and she walked in to discover him in conversation with Drake near the riverfront entrance, her eyes met his and her heart just seemed to stumble.

A fanciful woman might have thought he was waiting for her, especially when a slow smile quirked up one corner of his mouth the second he saw her. Trapped in the heat of his gaze, she didn't have a clue if she was fanciful or not. She just knew that for the first time that she remembered, she was having dinner with her husband alone. There would be no waiters to interrupt them, no old friends to wander in and greet them. It would just be the two of them, like any other married couple, spending a night in at home. Her mouth went dry just at the thought of it.

He greeted her with a kiss on the cheek that set her skin tingling and her mind jumping forward to the moment when he shut their front door and they were alone. She hardly heard Drake greet her or wish her good-night after Joe collected the invitations for the grand opening to the new restaurant from his office. They started home, and before she was ready for it, they were walking down the second-floor hall to their apartment.

Struggling to get control of the smile that kept breaking out on her face, she told herself that the only reason she was looking forward to spending time alone with him was that this man who called himself her husband was still such a mystery to her. But her wildly thumping heart wasn't buying that, and she didn't care. They were only going home, but it felt like a date, and she intended to enjoy herself.

Turning to face him as they reached their front door, she grinned. "So what do you want on your pizza? Or maybe I should ask what do *I* want? I do like pizza, don't I?"

"Are you kidding?" he chuckled. "You can eat your weight in the stuff. And just for the record, you like sausage and pepperoni…just like I do." He started to insert the key in the dead bolt, only to stop in surprise as his gaze dropped to the florist's box propped against the door. "Hey, what's this?"

"I don't know," she said, eyeing the white box curiously as he bent down to pick it up. "I didn't order anything. Did you?"

"No, but it's got your name on it. Have you got a secret admirer you haven't told me about?"

It was, to say the least, an unfortunate choice of words. Suddenly realizing what he'd said, he unconsciously dropped his gaze to her slightly rounded stomach, which was barely concealed by her long, thigh-length sweater. In the damning silence that fell between them, they both knew there was a good possibility that over the last few months she'd had not only an admirer, but a lover as well.

"If I do, I seriously doubt he would be sending me presents here," she replied quietly. "There must be some mistake."

"Maybe," he agreed, frowning. "Let's go inside and see what's in it."

He set the invitations on the entrance-hall table as soon as they were inside, then carried the box into the living room and set it on the coffee table. It was harmless-looking cardboard, the kind of box roses came in, but tied with twine. And the card with Annie's name on it was unsigned.

With no florist's stamp on it there was no way to tell where it had come from.

"Maybe we should call Sam," Annie suggested worriedly, chewing on her bottom lip as she sank down onto the couch next to him. "He'd probably want to know about this."

"Let's see what's in it first," Joe said, and cut the twine with his pocketknife. "For all we know, it could be a welcome-home present from one of the neighbors who didn't want you to make a fuss."

Knowing what a matchmaker Alice Truelove was, Annie had to admit that it would be just like the old lady to send flowers without signing the card in the hopes that she would mistakenly think they were from her husband. Her mouth softened into a smile. "You're talking about Alice, aren't you?"

He nodded, but it wasn't flowers in the box. Instead, it was a single piece of cedar, and a dead one at that. The needles on it had long since turned brown. Confused, Joe frowned. "What the hell!"

Her blood roaring in her ears, Annie stared at the small branch in puzzlement. It was harmless; it couldn't hurt her. But then Joe picked it up and the scent drifted under her nose, and suddenly her stomach turned over. "Oh, God!"

"Annie? Honey? What's wrong?"

Her eyes wide, her hand pressed to her mouth, she couldn't answer him. With a muffled moan, she ran for the bathroom. Swearing, Joe threw down the cedar branch and rushed after her.

She'd been sick every morning, losing the contents of her stomach almost as soon as she crawled out of bed, but even when the nausea was at its worst, it had never been like this. She was violently ill and there wasn't a damn thing Joe could do but hold her head and curse with worry.

Murmuring to her when she was finally spent, he jerked down the toilet lid, helped her sit down, and quickly wet a washcloth. "Just close your eyes and ride it out, sweetheart," he murmured as he gently wiped her face with the cool cloth. "You're going to be fine."

She should have been—she always had been before. But as a faint bit of color came back into her cheeks, the fine trembling that hit her told her this wasn't going to be like the other times. "I'm s-sorry," she stuttered, winding her arms around herself. "I—I don't know what's the m-matter with m-me. The s-second I smelled the c-cedar, I j-just got s-so scared I felt l-like someone had p-punched me in the stomach."

Swearing, Joe didn't stop to think, he just scooped her up in his arms and sat back down with her on his lap. When she automatically froze, he knew she was going to fight her way out of his hold any second, but then something in her just seemed to give. With a sob, she collapsed against him and let him hold her, really hold her, for the first time since she'd come home. And in her misery, she had no idea how close she came to destroying him.

Softly cooing to her, he soothed her with endearments and caresses, and all the while the voice of reason cautioned him to be careful. She was scared and vulnerable, and he was setting himself up for a fall, big-time. Any warm body would do when you were scared, but once she calmed down, she'd shy away from his touch just as she always did.

But he ached for her, dammit! He didn't want to. He didn't like it, but there it was, like it or not. And there was no way he was letting her go as long as she needed him. For now, he found to his surprise, that was enough.

Chapter 6

The dream crept out of the darkness like something wicked that only dared to expose itself in the blackest hours of the night. Sweeping over Annie's defenseless, sleeping body, it swallowed her whole with no warning whatsoever. One second her breathing was slow and steady, her sleep deep and restful, and the next she was being hurtled into the middle of a horrifying nightmare. Her throat clenched tight, she tried to scream, to move, to escape, but fear paralyzed her. Helpless, all she could do was shrink into herself and ride out a terror that had no beginning or end.

It was dark. God, it was so dark! There were no city lights, no moon, no houses close by, no one to see her. And no one to help her. She wanted to run, to hide, but it was too late for that. Staring down at the shovel in her hands, she started to tremble. How could she do this? How could she not? Swallowing a sob, she drew in a deep breath and deliberately made her mind go blank. Then she began to dig.

The ground was soft from the rain that had fallen earlier in the evening, the air tangy-sweet with the scent of cedars that surrounded her like a forest. Another time, she might have enjoyed toiling in the earth after an autumn rain. But not now. Not here. This was no garden that she dug; and the deeper and longer the hole got, the sicker she felt. Her fingers wouldn't stop shaking, and the handle of the shovel kept slipping from her grip, scraping the soft skin of her palm. Once, she almost pitched headlong into the pit and felt her stomach roil. Sweat broke out on her brow, and she wiped it away with a hand that felt as if it would never be steady again.

Time slowed, then stopped altogether, and torture took on a whole new meaning. With the coppery taste of fear on her tongue, she didn't allow her attention to wander from the shovel and the dirt. And an ever-deepening hole that yawned like the entrance of Hell at her feet. Then, before she was ready, it was long enough, wide enough, deep enough.

She stared at it and almost gagged. Merciful God, she couldn't do this! But she wasn't given a choice. The cold form lying on the ground next to her rolled into the shallow grave with a soft, sickening thud and landed face up. Glazed, sightless eyes stared unblinkingly up at the night sky.

A sob lodged in her throat. Her eyes shied violently away, but not before her gaze locked in fascinated horror on the small, fatal bullet hole in the middle of the dead man's forehead. Inanely, she wondered where all the blood was. There should have been blood.

Images stirred in her head. Terrible, tormenting images that made her heart stumble in her breast and her throat constrict on a frozen scream. She slammed her eyes shut, but still she could see him, this same man, standing before her, his startled gaze locked on the gun, the sure knowledge in his pale blue eyes that he was looking at his executioner. The gun exploded, and in the next instant, he was flat on his back, much as he was now, his life force draining out of him onto the pavement before he could even ask God to have mercy on his soul.

And now she had to bury him.

Oh, God, oh, God. The shovel fell numbly from her fingers, and she couldn't make herself move to catch it. Her tongue thickened; bile pooled in her mouth. Her flesh crawling, she sank to her knees and cupped her trembling hands in the loose dirt piled next to the grave.

Don't look at its face! It's not real. It's not a man if you don't look at his eyes. Think about the dirt, the grittiness of it under your nails and covering your skin. When this is all over, you're going to go home and scrub it off. Then you'll be clean and all of this will go away like a bad dream.

Her movements stiff and jerky, she scooped up dirt and tossed it, scooped it and tossed it, and never once looked to see where it landed. Instead, her gaze was fixed, and in her mind, she was already in that shower. She could feel the soap against her bare skin, the water beating down on her, pounding the tension out of her tight shoulders, relaxing her, cleansing her. Just the thought of it brought tears to her eyes.

But the face. She had to cover the face.

There was a roaring in her ears. Her fingers curled into the dirt, and the scent of cedar needles and fresh dirt rose to her nose.

No! a frantic voice in her head cried out in protest. *Don't do this! Please don't do this.*

But her hands took on a life of their own. In slow motion, they lifted the dirt and carried it up the long length of the still, half-buried form before her. And then, before she was ready for it, her hands were hovering right over the dead man's face.

She tried not to look, but she couldn't stop herself. His skin was pasty white, the mouth frozen in a silent scream. With his square-cut jaw, chiseled bone structure and thick cloud of black hair, he might once have been a handsome man in spite of the small scar that marred one corner of his mouth. But not now. Not in death. Death had robbed him of life, of spark, and left behind a bloodless, macabre monster that she knew would haunt her nightmares the rest of her life.

Frozen, so close she could smell the death that rose from him, she felt the trembling of her fingers worsen and could do nothing to stop it. In what seemed like slow motion, the dirt cupped in her hands trickled into his eyes and mouth and nose.

"No!"

Her unholy scream echoed through the apartment like the screech of a banshee. Slumped against the headboard of their bed, where they'd both fallen asleep while he'd held her after she was sick, Joe bolted up, his heart in his throat and his eyes wild and confused. "What the hell! Annie? My God, what's wrong?"

She didn't hear him. Devastated, tears streaming down her bloodless face, she bent over, her arms wrapped around her middle, and rocked in misery. "What have I done? Oh, God, what have I done?"

She sounded so horrified, so revolted with herself, he reached for her without thinking. "Honey, you haven't done anything. What makes you think you have? You were just dreaming—"

"No!" Already shaking her head, she didn't let him finish...or touch her. Scrambling out of bed, she backed out of reach until she stood all alone, her face etched in despair. "You don't understand!" she cried. "It wasn't a dream. It was a memory. I think I killed a man."

Joe paced the confines of the kitchen like an innocent man who had just been convicted of a felony, more frustrated than he'd ever been in his life. *I think I killed a man.* Dear God, she'd meant it! She actually thought she'd killed a man. And no amount of talking on his part had changed her mind. She didn't know how or why or even who the man was, but there was no other explanation for her burying a dead man in a stand of cedars. It all fit, she'd claimed. The blood on her clothes and on the pavement in the parking garage, her desperate need to get clean, the sick despair that had spilled into her stomach at the sight of that cedar branch. She'd killed a man—and someone out there knew it.

She'd been so serious, so *sure,* that she'd scared the hell out of him. Shaken, he'd immediately hustled her into the kitchen, warmed her some cocoa, then spent the next fifteen minutes trying to convince her that she'd just had a night terror. Granted, it had been a particularly nasty one and horrifyingly real, but it was still a far cry from a memory.

He might as well have saved his breath. Her chin took on that stubborn set he'd come to know too well over the course of their marriage, and nothing he'd said so far had persuaded her that there was no need to call Sam.

"Dammit, this is ridiculous!" Quelling the small niggling doubt that whispered in his ear—dear God, was it possible that she'd done such a thing?—he pushed back from the kitchen table and rose to glower down at her. "I know you—better than you know yourself right now, I might add—and you just haven't got what it takes to kill anyone. You're a soft touch, Annie Taylor. If I'd let you, you'd pull every bum off the street into the restaurant kitchen and feed them. You could no more shoot someone between the eyes than you could fly.''

Even to his own ears, his tone was desperate and edged on panic. He couldn't tell who he was trying to convince— her or himself—and she knew it.

''No one wants to believe that more than I do,'' she said hollowly, ''but I can't. The evidence is too damning.''

''A dream isn't evidence!'' he snapped. ''Your mind's just playing tricks on you. You got that damn package with the cedar in it this afternoon and it scared you. So tonight your subconscious came up with a way to explain your fear. That's all it was.''

It was a logical explanation, and more than anything else in the world, Annie wanted to believe it. But she couldn't. Not when she could still feel the grit of the dirt on her skin and smell that damn cedar. Just thinking about it made her want to gag. She'd buried a dead man—she knew it.

Her cocoa turning cold in her hands, she pushed it away. ''We have to call Sam, Joe. He needs to know about this.''

''No.''

''If you won't call him, I'll do it myself.''

''The hell you will!''

She flinched at his roar but her stubborn jaw only lifted a notch higher. ''Raising your voice isn't going to change my mind. Sam said to call him if I remembered anything, and that's what I'm going to do.''

He wanted to shake her. He wanted to lock her up in their bedroom and not let her go anywhere near Sam or any other cop who might take her ridiculous story seriously. But she'd fight him on that, so all he could do was pretend to go along with her, and in the process, appeal to her maternal instincts.

"All right," he said flatly. "If you really want to call him, I can't stop you. But in case you hadn't noticed, it's three o'clock in the morning. If you call him tonight, you probably won't get any sleep the rest of the night. Do you think that's good for the baby?"

He saw the answer in her eyes and pressed the advantage. "If you really shot someone and buried him, which I strongly doubt, he's not going anywhere tonight. Waiting another few hours to notify the authorities isn't going to hurt anything."

He was right, but she was afraid to close her eyes again, afraid that she'd get caught up in that nightmare again and never find her way home. Swallowing a sob, she shivered and wished Joe would hold her. But she couldn't ask, and he didn't take the initiative. Considering the circumstances, she really couldn't say she blamed him. She'd killed a man. When Joe had vowed to love and cherish her for better or for worse, she doubted that he'd expected *worse* to include murder.

Jerking to her feet abruptly, she needed to walk, to pace, to work this out in her head, but there was no place to go. No place but back to bed, and she couldn't do that. Turning away, she stared blindly out onto the balcony. "All right, I'll wait until the morning to call him, but I can't go back to bed. I just can't."

"You're not going to dream, honey," he said softly from behind her.

"You can't be sure of that."

"Yes, I can. I'll sit by the bed and wake you the second I think you're dreaming."

Surprised, touched that he would even suggest such a thing, she whirled to face him. "I can't ask you to sit up the rest of the night. You've got to work tomorrow."

"I don't need much sleep," he fibbed easily. "Don't you

remember? Give me a two- or three-hour catnap and I can go for another twenty hours easy. I'm wide-awake, so while you're sleeping, I'll just sit by the bed and address the invitations. We never got around to that, remember?''

She should have said no—she couldn't take advantage of him that way. But she was punch-drunk, she was so tired. She desperately needed to get horizontal, but if she closed her eyes even for a second, the dream would be on her, and she might not be able to fight it off a second time.

"All right," she agreed. "But only if you promise to go to bed if you get tired. I'd feel terribly guilty if you stayed awake just because of me."

His fingers crossed behind his back, he nodded solemnly. "On my honor as a Boy Scout. Now will you go to bed before you fall on your face? You can barely keep your eyes open as it is."

Another time, Annie would have quizzed him about being a Boy Scout, but the last of her energy was spent and she couldn't manage any more protests. Sighing as he slipped a supporting arm around her waist, she let him lead her to the bedroom.

She didn't dream, but she didn't sleep very well, either, and she woke the next morning with sandy eyes and a headache. For once her stomach wasn't acting up, but she found little comfort in that. Before she even opened her eyes, the events of the previous evening came flooding back. The cedar branch left on their doorstep, the dream, the face of a dead man that was indelibly sketched in her memory. "Oh, God!"

She would have bolted right out of bed, but before she could even think about throwing back the covers, her gaze landed on Joe. He was seated in the chair next to the bed, just as he had been last night when she'd closed her eyes for the last time and drifted back to sleep, only he wasn't working on the invitations for the restaurant opening as he had been then. Instead, he was slumped in the chair, asleep, his chin resting on his chest and his pen still clutched in his hand, the invitations spread out around his feet on the floor.

Something shifted in her heart, a barrier that she hadn't even known was there, giving way to a rush of emotions that pulled at her heartstrings and made it impossible for her to drag her gaze away from him. Settling back against her pillow, she studied him quietly, noting the night's growth of beard that darkened his shadowed jaw, the enticing curve of his sensuous mouth, the sweep of dark lashes that any woman would have killed for. He was, she couldn't help noticing, an incredibly sexy man. And he was her husband.

That knowledge no longer shook her as it had at first. She'd come to accept the fact that he was a part of her life. She didn't remember loving him, but at one time, he must have loved her fiercely. She could still see the lingering traces of it in the dark secret depths of his eyes, still feel it in the gentleness of his touch and the way her own heart leapt at the sight of him.

What kind of lover was this man who was her husband? she wondered, her eyes searching as they traveled the lines of his sleeping face. Was he generous and caring and as interested in pleasuring her as he was himself, or were his own needs his only concern? Did he hold her afterward or just roll away and go to sleep? He seemed to be a toucher, but that could be wishful thinking on her part. She couldn't remember, but she thought she must be the kind of woman who needed the man she loved to keep her close after the loving. Would Joe know that without having to be told?

Was he that sensitive to his lover's needs? Would the time ever come when she would find that out for herself?

Images stole into her mind, hot, intimate imaginings that fired her cheeks and stole her breath. With an ease that shocked her, she could picture herself stroking him, loving him, giving herself totally and completely to him. Just him. Until they were both spent, replete, sated. Just thinking about it left her weak. And hot on a chilly autumn morning.

He shifted slightly, and her heart jerked in alarm. *What are you doing, Annie?* a voice cried in her head. *Get out of that bed before he wakes up and finds you staring at him like a sex-starved spinster just waiting for the chance to jump his bones!*

But even as she moved to throw off the covers, it was too late. The pen slipped from his fingers and fell to the floor, barely making a sound. But it was enough to wake him. Wincing, he stirred, rubbing at the back of his neck, and she watched in fascination as he slowly came awake. As rested as if he'd lain on the bed beside her all night, he stretched and yawned with an animal grace that did funny things to her stomach. Then his eyes opened and settled on her as if he'd known all along that she was watching him, and she could do nothing to stop the damning blush that slowly stole into her cheeks.

A sleepy smile tugged up the corners of his mouth, then, before she could even begin to guess his intentions, he leaned over and kissed her. Startled, her heart missed a beat, and she couldn't for the life of her raise her hands to push him away. He was still half-asleep, she told herself weakly. He'd forgotten that he'd promised not to kiss her again. He didn't know what he was doing. He couldn't. But the second his lips settled gently on hers, he showed her in two seconds flat that he was a man who knew exactly what he was doing.

His mouth moved on hers, as soft as a summer breeze, gently wooing, seducing, so different from the heat and flash and hunger of that other time, when he'd caught her so completely off guard. Captivated, she trembled, her eyes closing on a sigh. Her heart murmuring a languid rhythm that seemed to echo in her blood, she wanted to reach for him, to wrap her arms around him and never let go. But she was afraid that if she did, this would all turn into a dream. So she curled her fingers into the covers and focused all her attention on just his mouth. The taste, the feel, the heat of it. How could she have forgotten him? she wondered dizzily. Forgotten *this?*

Need crawling through him, raking him with silken claws, Joe fought to keep the kiss light and easy. But damn, it was hard! He'd been dreaming about making love with her when he woke up to find her staring up at him from their bed, and it had seemed the most natural thing in the world to lean over and kiss her. Just a simple good-morning kiss—that was all it had started out to be. But he'd still been caught up in that damn dream and his defenses had been down, his body hot for her. The second his mouth had touched hers, he was lost.

Dear God, he ached for her! It had been too long since he'd kissed her, too long since he held her close and loved her until they were both so weak they could hardly move. She was his wife, dammit, and he wanted her! She might not remember anything about their life together, but she wasn't indifferent to him—not if those soft little whimpers she made at the back of her throat were anything to go by. He could crawl into bed with her and love her like there was no tomorrow, and she'd never utter a word of protest.

But there was a tomorrow. And a yesterday, one where she might have gotten pregnant by another man. And as much as he wanted to forget that, he couldn't.

Cursing his raging hormones, calling himself seven kinds of a fool, he reluctantly lifted his head. And nearly kissed her again when he saw the glazed desire in her eyes. Swallowing a silent groan, he forced a crooked smile and told himself to keep it light. "Good morning, sleepyhead. I guess I don't have to ask you if you slept all right. You were rattling the windows."

Surprised, her pulse still skipping madly, she gasped, "I was not!"

"You were snoring a beat you could dance to halfway down the Riverwalk," he claimed outrageously. "I spent most of the night waiting for Alice to break into song downstairs."

He was so solemn, she might have believed him if it hadn't been for the twinkle dancing in his eyes. The need humming in her veins giving way to amusement, she laughed. "You're making that up! Anyway, you're a fine one to be talking. *I don't need much sleep,*" she mimicked. *"Give me a two- or three-hour catnap and I can go for another twenty hours easy."*

His grin unrepentant, he shrugged lazily. "So I exaggerated a little." When she lifted an eyebrow at that, he laughed. "Okay, so make that a lot. My intentions were good. You needed to sleep and you did. Mission accomplished. Now, how about breakfast?" he asked, deliberately changing the subject. "Is the baby up to ham and eggs this morning, or are we sticking with dry toast?"

She knew what he was doing—deliberately mentioning the baby in order to distract her about last night—and for that, she wanted to kiss him. But she'd already done that, and he'd been the one to pull back.

Her pride battered slightly, she forced a smile, determined to keep things as light as he. "I don't know about the baby," she said easily, "but if you're talking scrambled, with hash browns and plenty of ketchup, you've got a deal.''

"Somehow I had a feeling you'd say that," he said dryly. "So I had a whole case of the stuff delivered yesterday. You want ketchup, sweetheart, you've got ketchup." Playfully swatting her on the thigh, he grinned. "So up and at 'em, lazybones. It's your turn to cook."

She wasn't, by any stretch of the imagination, a gourmet cook, but she had discovered over the last few mornings that she could handle breakfast quite well, thank you very much. So as soon as she was dressed, she set to work at the stove while Joe made the toast and orange juice. The kitchen was large enough to hold a small army, but every time she turned around, she seemed to find Joe in her path. He teasingly accused her of throwing herself at him, but he was the one who was always brushing up against her, making her laugh and her heart skip. By the time they finally sat down to eat, the last thing she was interested in was food. Breathless and flushed, she was hungry for something a lot hotter than ham and eggs.

But she'd been so upset last night over the package left on their doorstep that they'd never gotten around to ordering pizza. She took one bite of the eggs she'd scrambled, and her stomach reminded her that it had been nearly twenty hours since she'd eaten. With a murmur of pleasure, she dug in.

Given a choice, she would have lingered over the meal for most of the morning, enjoying the food and coffee and Joe's company. But she couldn't. Not when last night's nightmare was still so fresh in her mind. As soon as they were both finished eating, she rose to carry their dishes to the sink. When she turned back to face Joe, her jaw was set. "I want to go to the police station and talk to Sam this morning. He needs to know what I've remembered."

"Honey, that was just a dream—"

"No, it wasn't," she insisted stubbornly. "It happened, Joe. I remember."

Startled, he followed her to the sink, his dark eyebrows snapping together into a straight line over his narrowed brown eyes. "What do you mean, you remember? Are you saying you've got your memory back?"

"No. Not much of it, anyway. But I remember kneeling on the ground covering a dead man with dirt." Haunting bits and pieces of too real images rose before her eyes, sickening her. "I can still see his face," she said faintly, shuddering. "I didn't imagine it."

"You didn't kill him," he said flatly. "I don't care what you dreamed, you didn't kill anyone."

His belief in her warmed her heart, but nothing he could say could erase the doubts that were lodged like a fist in her throat. "I need to find that out for myself. Please, Joe."

He wanted to argue. Dammit, he wanted to grab her and shake some sense into her! But there was a pain in her eyes that stabbed him right in the heart and as much as he wanted to believe she was being paranoid, he couldn't dismiss her fears nearly as easily as he would have liked. "All right," he sighed. "We'll go talk to Sam. But I still don't think it's necessary."

Thirty minutes later when Sam escorted them into a small interview room at the police station where they could talk in private, Joe hadn't changed his mind. "I told her she just had a vivid dream," he told his friend as they each took a chair at the table in the middle of the room, "but she insists it was real."

"It was real," Annie retorted. "I think I killed someone, Sam."

Unlike Joe, Sam didn't automatically dismiss her claim as just a trick of her overactive imagination. Instead, he sat back in his chair and regarded her steadily, his thoughts well hidden behind his steady gaze. "Tell me about it," he suggested.

She started at the beginning, with the delivery of the cedar branch to the apartment, and told him how the sight and smell of it sickened her. Just thinking about it made her fingers tremble and she quickly locked them together in her lap, then began to recount the memories that had assaulted her in the middle of the night. "It wasn't just a dream," she said finally. "The details were too exact. I could feel the dirt, smell the cedar, everything."

"But you don't remember shooting him? Or even holding a gun?"

"Well, no, but—"

"Then how do you know you killed him? Just because you buried the man doesn't mean you're the one who murdered him," he pointed out logically.

"But there was no one else there," she argued.

"Maybe not in your dream, no. But dreams aren't always reliable. How big was the dead man?"

Caught off guard, she blinked. "I don't know. Six-one or so, maybe a hundred and ninety pounds."

"And you think you not only killed him in that parking garage, but somehow managed to get him in your car, then drive him out in the sticks somewhere and bury him? All by yourself? C'mon, Annie, I know you're tough, but there's just no way you could have done that. There had to be somebody else."

"Which would explain a hell of a lot," Joe said promptly. "Like why someone keeps trying to terrorize her with phone calls and this damn thing..." he motioned to the cedar branch, which lay brown and stiff in the box it had been delivered in. "If she really did bury a corpse in a bunch of cedars, that damn branch wouldn't mean anything to anyone but Annie and whoever was with her."

"But why would this person want to terrorize me?" she cried. "I don't even remember him."

"Exactly," Sam replied. "As long as you have amnesia, he's safe. You can't identify him."

His brown eyes black with rage, Joe swore. "He scared her out of remembering her own name once. Now he's trying to do it again, only this time he wants to make sure she doesn't remember him."

"Because as long as she hasn't got a clue who he is, all we have to work with is a body that could be buried anywhere in the state of Texas," Sam concluded. "So that's where we'll start." Turning back to Annie, he said, "I know this isn't pleasant for you, but can you describe the dead man for me? I'm going to check missing persons and anything you remember might help identify him."

Her mouth cotton-dry, she could see the corpse as clearly as if it lay stretched out before her on the table. "He was a white man, with thick black hair, a square jaw and chiseled face. I—I don't know how o-old he w-was. It was kinda hard to tell."

"You're doing fine," he assured her. "Just take your time and try to remember everything you can. Was there anything odd about him? Any identifying marks like a mole or something that would make him stand out in a crowd?"

"A scar!" she blurted out, suddenly remembering. "Right by the left side of his mouth. I remember thinking that he must have been handsome even with the scar."

Frowning at the description, Sam rose abruptly to his

feet. "That sounds familiar. Hold it a second and let me check something. I'll be right back."

He was back almost immediately with an eight-by-ten photo he held out to Annie. "Have you ever seen this guy before?"

It was the picture of a man in a business suit. Lean and rugged, his black hair conservatively cut and styled, he had the kind of good looks that would inevitably draw women's eyes wherever he went...in spite of the small scar that marred the left side of his mouth.

Annie took one look and blanched. "Oh, God, that's him!"

"Easy, honey," Joe said soothingly. "Whoever the hell he is, he can't hurt you."

"He's Robert Freeman," Sam informed them, tossing the picture onto the table. "The president of Brackenridge State Bank. He's been missing for over a week. And so has a hell of a lot of money from the bank. Up until now, we had reason to believe that Mr. Freeman had embezzled the money, then skipped the country. Apparently, we were wrong...at least about him skipping the country."

"You think Annie stumbled across someone killing him in the Transit Tower parking garage?" Joe asked shrewdly.

Sam nodded grimly. "That makes more sense than her shooting Freeman between the eyes. She was probably just in the wrong place at the wrong time and got dragged into a murder. In all likelihood, the murderer planned to kill her, too, but somehow she managed to get away."

His jaw rigid, Joe would have given anything to have five minutes alone with the bastard who had terrorized her. No wonder she'd blocked it from her memory! Frowning at her pale face, he reached over to cover her clenched fingers with his. "Does any of this sound familiar, sweetheart?"

"Not really," she said with a regretful shake of her head. "I know I buried him. That's all. Whenever I try to remember anything else, I just run into this black wall."

And it was that black wall of forgetfulness that could get her killed. Somehow the killer had found out who she was and where she lived and was doing a good job of scaring her. But as long as she lived, there was a possibility that she could remember him at any time. Eventually, he would have to come after her. And when he did, he would have a distinct advantage. Because he could pass her on the street and look her right in the eye, and she probably wouldn't know him.

Joe glanced at Sam and saw the same knowledge in his friend's eyes. "I think this would be a good time to get Annie out of town for a while," he told Sam. "We've got a cabin in the Davis Mountains that we used to get away to when we were first married, but we haven't been there in a few years. She'll be safe there. It's forty miles from town and out of sight of the road. No one will even know we're there."

"But what about the restaurant?" Annie protested. "And the opening for the new place? It's just a couple of weeks away, isn't it? I can't ask you to drop all that and run away to the mountains with me. You need to be here to handle things."

If he hadn't been so worried about her safety, Joe would have laughed at the irony of the situation. In the months before she'd left him, she'd done nothing but complain about how little time they spent together because he was always working. And now she was finding excuses for him to stay in town and work.

"Your safety is more important than the damn restaurant," he said. "Anyway, Drake can handle a lot of things for me. And it's not like I'll be completely out of touch. If something crops up that I need to handle personally, he can call me on my cellular. Anything else will just have to wait until we get back."

"But when will that be?"

"When you get your memory back or Sam catches the bastard who did this to you—whichever happens first."

"But that could be months!"

"You're already starting to remember things," Sam pointed out. "Granted, there are still a lot of pieces missing, but knowing that you're safe at the cabin may be just what you need to let your guard down and remember the rest. And while you're gone, we've got some new leads to follow," he added. "Knowing Freeman is dead changes things. We've been looking for him in Canada and Mexico, not in a grave in the country. We'll find him, Annie. Then we'll find his killer."

"But he could be buried anywhere. There's cedar all over Texas. You could look for years and never find his body."

"True, but you've given us more information about that night than you realize. We know that you had an eight-o'clock meeting at the Transit Tower and that you showed up at your and Joe's apartment sometime around two or three in the morning. You didn't have a car or any money to catch a cab or bus, so you must have walked all the way home once you got away from the killer. That means he couldn't have taken you too far out in the country to bury Freeman. That narrows our search considerably."

"So you see? It won't be that long," Joe said. "Just a couple of weeks. And getting away will be good for you and the baby. You need the rest."

And they needed this time together. *He* needed it. He didn't know if he'd ever be able to trust her again, and when she got her memory back, she could hurt him all over again, but that was just a chance he would have to take. There were still feelings between them, and he had to see if there was any chance of a future between them.

Her eyes searching his, she hesitated, but he saw in a glance that he'd already won. Giving in, she grumbled, "I still feel guilty about taking you away from your work, but if the two of you think this is for the best, who am I to argue?"

Elated, he only nodded. "Good. We'll leave at dawn."

Chapter 7

When Joe had first started looking for property to buy, six years ago, he'd wanted someplace completely isolated from the rest of the world, a retreat from phones and faxes and temperamental chefs, not to mention a never-ending stream of customers it was his responsibility to please. He worked long, hard hours and seldom took any time off for himself, and when he did, he wanted to look out his front door and see nothing but a wide expanse of uninhabited land that stretched all the way to the horizon. He'd had to go all the way to West Texas, but he'd finally found what he was looking for in the Davis Mountains.

There, the air was clean and dry, the population minimal. His neighbors were hard-working ranchers who minded their own business and didn't have time to come calling, which was just fine with him. He didn't want to be rude, but he didn't want to be bothered, either. Not here. And he wasn't. With his cabin located at the end of a private road halfway up the side of a mountain, his only visitors were mule deer and skunks and an occasional mountain lion.

He'd brought Annie there for the first time on their honeymoon, and now, as they drove up the drive to the cabin, memories came sweeping back. God, it seemed like yesterday! The night had been clear, the stars brighter than anywhere else in the country, but not nearly as bright as the love shining in Annie's eyes. She'd spied a falling star and tried to get him to wish on it, but he hadn't been able to look away from her. She was everything he'd ever wanted, and that week they'd spent there—and the getaways they'd managed over the next few years after that—had been the happiest of his life.

Wondering if the simple frame structure would strike a spark in her memory, he braked to a stop next to the front porch and cut the engine. Silence, soul deep, immediately engulfed them. Watching her in the starlight, he waited for recognition to flare in her eyes, but there was nothing there but natural curiosity. She didn't remember.

Not sure if he was disappointed or relieved, he reminded himself he was going to have to be careful not to rush her into something that either one of them might not be ready for. He shouldn't have needed the reminder—he hadn't forgotten that she could be carrying someone else's baby—but lately, he found it harder and harder to believe that she'd walked into another man's arms and bed so quickly after leaving him. For the sake of his own bruised heart, he needed to keep his distance until he knew if he could live with that or not if she had, but with every passing day, that became more and more difficult. He wanted her close, skin to skin, without the past between them. He dreamed of her, ached for her, longed for what they had once had, even though he knew what they'd once had could be gone forever.

Another man might have hated her for that, for the doubts that he was now forced to live with because of her, for the limbo that there was no way out of until she got her memory back, but he couldn't. He still loved her. He'd suspected it the first time she'd had morning sickness, and he'd known it for sure when she'd opened that damn florist's box and seen that cedar branch. The terror in her eyes was something he never hoped to see again, and given the chance, he would have gladly turned back the clock and been the one in the parking garage that Thursday night when she stumbled across a murder and changed their lives forever.

He was a one-woman man—he knew that now and accepted it. And she'd been his woman from the first time he laid eyes on her. They didn't, however, live in a fairy tale, and he had some serious thinking to do. If the baby turned out not to be his, could he raise another man's child without seeing Annie's betrayal every time he looked at it? Because it was a part of her, he wouldn't be able to stop himself from loving it if he tried. But a dagger of jealousy twisted in his heart at the thought of her loving another man. Until he could get past that, he had no business touching her.

It was, he thought, clenching his jaw, going to be a long couple of weeks.

"Well, this is it," he said, shattering the silence. "Does anything look familiar?"

Annie stared at the rustic cabin that sat like a hulking shadow in the darkness and shook her head. She was sure that it was probably charming by the light of day, but right now, it was hard to tell. During the long drive from San Antonio, Joe had told her that the place had all the comforts of home, including hot and cold running water and electricity, not to mention a view that was out of this world. And gazing at the stars that twinkled overhead like a brilliant, glittering canopy, she had to admit that the promised view, at least, was spectacular. But the cabin looked awfully small.

"No," she said regretfully, "but things might look different in the morning. Did we spend a lot of time here?"

"As much as we could when we were first married. Not so much over the last couple of years." Pulling the keys from the ignition, he pushed open his door. "Why don't you stay here while I open up and check for uninvited visitors?"

Surprised, she lifted an eyebrow at him. "I beg your pardon?"

"Snakes," he said succinctly. "They have a way of finding a way inside since the place sits empty for so long."

"Oh, God," she whispered faintly. "And this is where you come to *relax?*"

"Yeah," he laughed. "I guess I'm a glutton for punishment. Hold on, and I'll be right back."

He was out of the car and striding up the porch steps before she could warn him to be careful, and a split second later, a light flared on as he unlocked the cabin door and stepped inside. He disappeared from view. Suddenly cold, she shivered. She didn't have to search her nonexistent memory to know that she didn't like snakes.

He was back almost immediately and pulling open her door for her. "All clear," he announced. "Let's get this stuff inside and then we'll see about supper. You're probably starving."

She'd passed that state about fifty miles back, but she hadn't wanted to suggest that they stop because it was getting so late and he'd seemed in a hurry to reach the cabin. Now, at the mere mention of food, her stomach growled with embarrassing enthusiasm. Laughing, she admitted, "I guess it wouldn't do any good to deny it, would it? What can I carry?"

Chuckling, he handed her a grocery bag of fruit. "Maybe you'd better start with something edible. I know how you are when you haven't eaten in a while. Even the furniture starts to look good."

"I'm not that bad." She gave him a withering look, only to ruin the effect by reaching into the bag for an apple.

Grinning, he said, "I rest my case. Get the screen door, will you?"

He hefted a large ice chest filled with perishable items and started up the porch steps. Hurrying around him, Annie quickly pulled open the screen door for him to pass through, then followed him inside. Two steps past the threshold, she stopped abruptly and swallowed, her heart knocking against her ribs as she got her first good look at where they would be spending the next few weeks, possibly the next few months.

Except for the small partitioned area that jutted out of a corner, which she presumed was a bathroom, the cabin consisted of one room. One very *small* room when compared to the apartment they'd left behind in San Antonio. There were no other walls or partitions, nothing but pockets of living space and no privacy whatsoever. The kitchen, with its apartment-size stove, refrigerator, and tiny table took up one corner, while an overstuffed couch sat before a corner fireplace in what served as the living room. It was the last remaining corner, however, that drew her gaze and made her heart stumble in her chest.

A bed. There was one bed, a double, that looked like it had come right out of a bordello in an old western movie. Made of iron and painted white, the headboard and footboard were shaped like hearts and delicately decorated with iron roses. Annie took one look at it and knew somehow that this was where she and Joe had spent their honeymoon.

Her knees weak and her pulse wild, she stared at it, trans-fixed, and wondered why he'd brought her there. Was this his way of telling her that he didn't care whose baby she was carrying—he was ready to resume their marriage? Or was he so completely over her that it truly didn't bother him to bring her there because the place had no meaning for him?

No! What about the kisses they'd shared? she wanted to cry, and knew she was in trouble. She had no right to ask him to explain himself, no right to expect him to feel any-thing for her but possibly lust and a whole lot of distrust. She was the one who had left him. She was the one who'd returned pregnant, with no idea of who the father of her baby was. And she was the one who'd buried a dead man, a man she still wasn't convinced she hadn't killed. Consid-ering all that, she was lucky that he even spoke to her, let alone went out of his way to see to her welfare.

But, God, she hated this! She hated not knowing who she was, what she was capable of. Thinking that she might have killed a man was bad enough, but not being able to recall the circumstances of her baby's conception tore her up. What kind of woman was she? Why couldn't she re-member? She wanted to believe that it was because her mind had chosen to forget everything rather than remember whatever violence she'd faced in the Transit Tower parking garage. But what if that was just wishful thinking on her part? What if it was the truth about herself and the choices she'd made in her life that she really couldn't face?

"Well, that's it," Joe said as he unloaded the contents of the ice chest into the refrigerator. "I'll get the luggage after we eat. Since it's so late, how about soup and sand-wiches for supper?"

Thankful for the distraction, Annie pushed back her troubled thoughts and forced a smile. "That sounds great. I'll set the table."

By nine-thirty, they had finished eating, done the dishes, and brought in their luggage from the car. There was no television, no paperwork to catch up on, nothing to do but go to bed. And though they'd both managed to look anywhere but at the sleeping alcove while they were eating, there was no avoiding it now.

Annie told herself there was nothing to be concerned about. It was a bed just like any other bed—nothing was going to happen in it that she didn't want to. And it wasn't as if this was the first time they'd slept together. Whenever she'd cried out in the night, he'd been there to hold her until she fell back asleep, and most mornings, he was still there when she woke up. Another man might have already pushed for his husbandly rights by now, but if she'd learned anything about Joe in the last week, it was that he would never insist on any kind of intimacy between them that she wasn't ready for. Even if they shared a bed, he wouldn't lay a finger on her if she didn't want him to.

She knew that, accepted that, was thankful that he was such a patient, caring man. So why was her heart pounding like a hammer? They'd chatted like old friends all through supper, but suddenly the cabin was filled with a silence that seemed to throb with expectation. Her gaze clashed with his, then quickly skittered away. Swallowing, she snatched up her overnight bag and hugged it to her breast like a shield. She knew she was acting like a nervous virgin, but she couldn't seem to help herself.

"I'll take the bathroom first, if you don't mind," she said huskily, and swept past him with a speed that was embarrassingly close to a run.

"Smooth, Annie," she muttered under her breath as she shut the bathroom door and leaned back against it. "Real smooth. What do you think you accomplished by running in here? Unless you plan on sleeping in the tub, you're going to have to face him eventually. Why don't you just do it now and get it over with?"

She should have, but she couldn't. So she hastily pulled off her clothes and eased down into a tub of warm water. Twenty minutes later, her skin pink and clean, her hair a riot of dark curls, she pulled on her flannel gown and robe and knee socks. The coward in her hoped that Joe had already gone to bed, but the chances of that were slim. Left with no choice but to deal with the situation, she drew in a fortifying breath and pulled open the bathroom door.

The first thing she saw was the bed. Joe had pulled back the patchwork quilt that covered it and turned on the bedside lamp, leaving the rest of the cabin bathed in shadows. The pillows were plumped, and even from halfway across the room, she could see that the sheets were fresh and clean. In spite of the ruggedness of its surroundings, with nothing more than the addition of a rose on the pillow and a bottle of champagne on the nightstand, it could have been as elegant as the honeymoon suite at the Hilton.

All it needed to be complete was the bridegroom.

Automatically, her eyes went looking for him. She found him on the couch. He sat slouched low on his spine, his legs stretched out before him and crossed at the ankles, watching her with dark, enigmatic eyes. A pillow and a neatly folded blanket sat on the cushions next to him.

When her eyes widened at the sight of the bedding, he pushed to his feet and started toward her like a lion on the prowl. Caught in the trap of his heated gaze, she stood rooted to the spot, horribly afraid that the granny gown she'd been so sure only moments before was hardly appealing was now far too revealing.

She expected him to walk past her to the bathroom, but he stopped right in front of her instead, so close that when she drew in a sharp breath, the tips of her breasts brushed his chest. "I'm going to sleep on the couch," he said in a low growl that stroked over her like a caress. "Because if I don't, I won't be able to keep my hands to myself. Unless, of course, you don't want to sleep alone."

He arched an eyebrow at her, time rolling to a stop while he waited for her answer. When she mutely shook her head, a wry smile twisted his mouth. "I had a feeling you'd say that. And you're probably right. If you weren't, I just might try to change your mind. But not tonight. You look tired, sweetheart. Go to bed. It's been a long day."

Leaning down, he pressed a fleeting kiss to her mouth, then stepped around her into the bathroom and quietly shut the door behind him. Dazed, her blood humming in her veins, it was a full two minutes before Annie moved to the bed.

When she slipped between the sheets and snapped off the bedside light, she was sure she'd never be able to sleep. But she'd been up before dawn, and the sound of the shower running in the bathroom was a steady, hypnotic lull. Settling against the pillows, she closed her eyes and sighed. Long before Joe stepped out of the bathroom, she was asleep.

Lost in her dreams, she never saw him move to the side of the bed and stand there in the dark, staring down at her. Her breathing slow and easy in sleep, she never saw his expression soften, never saw him lift his hand to her hair and caress a wayward curl. If she'd opened her eyes, just for a second, she would have seen him hesitate, would have seen the pain and regret that registered in every line of his body. But she didn't, and when he turned away, she was none the wiser.

It was the steady thud of an ax hitting wood that woke her late the next morning. Stirring, she frowned, then jolted awake, startled, when something hit the side of the cabin, hard. Blinking the sleep from her eyes, she was still trying to figure out what woke her when another loud thunk reverberated through the cabin. Frowning, she pushed her tangled hair from her eyes. "What the devil's going on?"

She spoke to an empty cabin. In a single, all-encompassing glance, she saw that the couch where Joe had slept was just as it had been when she'd gone to bed last night. The blanket and sheets were neatly folded and piled in a stack, with the pillow on top. She might have thought he hadn't slept there at all if she hadn't gotten up during the night to go to the bathroom a zillion times. Every time she'd passed the couch, he'd been lying in exactly the same position, dead to the world.

So where was he? Throwing back the antique quilt that had kept her as warm as toast all night in the cool mountain air, she rushed over to the window and pulled back the curtain to find Joe chopping firewood right by the cabin's back porch. He'd already worked up a sweat and pulled off his shirt, and in the morning light, his skin gleamed like bronze as he brought the well-sharpened ax down with gratifying force on the wood. Without breaking rhythm, he lifted the ax again and swung with all his might.

The wood split without so much as a groan, but Annie couldn't take her eyes from Joe. Lord, the man was put together well! He wasn't one of those muscle-bound jocks who liked to work out and lift weights, but he managed to keep fit nevertheless. He had a lean, rangy body, with strength evident in every clean line of his broad shoulders and slim hips. With no effort whatsoever, he split the length of wood into kindling, then tossed the pieces into a pile at one end of the porch. One of them missed and hit the wall of the cabin instead, causing a thump like the one that woke her.

Leaning against the window frame, Annie felt something warm spill into her stomach. She could have stood there for hours, but then he turned unexpectedly toward the window where she stood, and her heart jumped in her throat. Hastily stepping back out of sight, she grinned at her own foolishness. He was her husband; they'd been married for over five years—she should be able to look at him without self-consciousness, she chided herself.

But she had no memory of the past, only of the last week and a half. She knew she could trust him with her life, but her heart was another matter. He made her weak at the knees with a touch, breathless with a fleeting kiss. She didn't know what had driven her to leave him, but there was no doubt that there was still something between them. Something strong and exhilarating and scary in the kind of way that had her constantly fighting the need to smile.

They both knew that it was just a matter of time before they did something about it. But not yet, she thought as she grabbed jeans and a blouse from her suitcase and stepped into the bathroom. She wanted time. Time to get to know him better. Time to remember not what had driven them apart two months ago, but what had brought them together five years ago. Because she had a feeling that when she did remember why she'd left him, she was going to need the memory of her love for him to hold on to and ease the hurt she wasn't ready to remember.

Lost in her thoughts, she washed her face and brushed her teeth, then automatically tugged on her clothes, hardly paying any attention to what she was doing. Until she tried to snap her jeans and couldn't. Surprised, she adjusted the fit and tried again, with the same results. Frowning, she glanced down to see what the problem was and found her stomach in the way.

Only then did it hit her. The baby. She was really starting to show and her jeans no longer fit.

Stunned, she felt a silly grin curl around her mouth and almost laughed out loud. Every time she'd had to deal with morning sickness, she was reminded of the changes taking place in her body, but up until then, she'd only associated her pregnancy with discomforts she had no control over. Nausea, backaches, tiredness that seemed to zap all her energy. But now she only had to look at her rounded stomach to see the baby safely cradled inside her.

A baby, she thought, smiling tenderly. She really was going to have a baby. A sweet tide of love flooded her, a rush of warmth that melted her bones and brought the sting of tears to her eyes. Turning, she pulled open the bathroom door. She had to tell Joe!

He was in the process of straightening the woodpile on the porch when Annie rushed outside with a funny look on her face and tears streaming down her cheeks. Her hair was wild, the smile that flirted with her mouth tremulous. Stopping short at the sight of him, she hesitated, a wealth of emotions he couldn't begin to identify flickering in her eyes.

Straightening, he frowned. "You okay? What's going on?"

She laughed, a shaky sound that he'd never heard from her before. "Nothing. I'm fine. I was just getting dressed…"

When she stopped and pressed a hand to the smile that

kept turning up the corners of her mouth, he arched a brow. "And?"

"And I can't snap my jeans," she admitted, grinning.

Joe's gaze automatically dropped to her belly, which was concealed by the loose-fitting gingham blouse she wore. From her happy expression, he was obviously missing something, but he couldn't for the life of him say what it was. "So?"

"So they don't fit," she laughed. "Look."

She held up her blouse, revealing her slim hips and barely zipped, unsnapped jeans. His gaze drawn like a magnet, Joe could no more have dragged his eyes away than he could have chopped wood with an ice pick. He told himself there was nothing the least bit seductive about the way she lifted her shirt. In fact, she was so damn pleased with her condition that it obviously hadn't occurred to her that he might be affected by her pose one way or the other.

But he was. God, was he! He took one look and felt like all the air had been sucked from his lungs.

Her jeans didn't gap open much, but through the narrow V, Joe could see pink panties trimmed in lace and the soft white skin of her rounding belly. Her still small, but blatantly pregnant, belly. Fascinated, he stared at her long and hard, his fingers itching to touch her, to skim across her bare skin and chart the changes occurring almost before his eyes in her body.

That was his baby she could be carrying, his child. He'd always known one day that they would have children, but he'd never given much thought to what pregnancy would do to Annie. Oh, he'd known she'd gain a hefty amount of weight and, like all expectant mothers, she'd walk around with her stomach leading the way. What he hadn't expected was the beautiful glow of her skin or the way she seemed to grow softer, more vulnerable, with every passing day.

And then there were the changes in himself. She'd always been a woman who could take care of herself, and he'd loved that about her. But now, seeing the remains of her tears clinging to her cheeks, protectiveness raged like a storm inside him. All he could think of was wrapping her close in his arms so that nothing and no one could ever hurt her or the baby again. She was his. *They* were his....

Even as he tried to convince himself, his mind taunted him with images of Annie in the arms of another man. No! he wanted to roar. She wouldn't have done that to him, to *them*. She couldn't have.

But then again, he'd never thought she'd leave him, either.

His blood running cold at the thought, he jerked his eyes back up to hers. "We'll have to get you some maternity clothes the next time we go into town," he said woodenly. "Until then, just leave your jeans unsnapped. There's no one out here to see anything."

That wasn't the response she'd expected—he knew that the minute the words left his mouth. The light died in her eyes; her happy smile dropped from her mouth. Not a word of reproach passed her lips, but guilt still stabbed him in the heart. He felt like the lowest form of heel, but he couldn't give her the enthusiasm she seemed to need from him. Not yet. Turning away before he said something he would regret, he picked up the ax and returned to the woodpile.

Letting him go, Annie stared after him, more encouraged than her common sense told her she had any right to be. Another woman might have been hurt by what appeared to be his total lack of interest in her pregnancy, but he hadn't fooled her for a second. He wasn't a cold or indifferent man, and she'd seen the flash of heated emotion that had flared in his eyes when she'd lifted her shirt and shown him her belly. He'd wanted to touch her as badly as she'd needed him to, and for a moment there, she'd half expected him to sweep her up into his arms and carry her to bed. When he hadn't, she'd known to the second when he'd remembered the baby might not be his.

Oh, he'd hidden it well, but she hadn't missed the clenching of his jaw or the green-eyed monster that had glared at her through his eyes when he thought that she might have betrayed him. He was jealous, and she was thrilled. Because a man who didn't care wouldn't have blinked an eye at the thought of her leaving him for another man.

After sitting empty for over a year, the cabin and yard were in desperate need of maintenance. The gutters were in terrible shape, sunlight peeked through some of the roof tiles on the porch, and the inside of the structure needed a thorough scrubbing and dusting. So, after breakfast, Joe attacked the porch roof and Annie went to work inside.

It was hot, dirty work. Annie couldn't remember the last time she'd done any physical work around a house, and she thoroughly enjoyed herself in spite of the fact that there was no dishwasher or vacuum cleaner or even a radio to break the silence while she worked. Humming to herself, she washed not only the breakfast dishes by hand, but every dish and skillet in the cabinets.

While they were draining, she pulled the dusty curtains from the windows and tossed them in the washing machine, then made up a solution of water and vinegar to clean the windows. Outside, she could hear Joe hammering on the roof, then his muttered curse when he accidentally hit a finger. When the curtains finished washing and she stepped outside to hang them on the clothesline strung between two cedar posts just yards from the back porch, she couldn't stop her eyes from lifting to the roof. There in the bright sun, Joe was down on his knees and bent over the leaky tiles of the roof, frowning with concentration as he hammered a crooked cedar tile back into place.

It was a sight that was to become very familiar to her over the course of the day. When he finished the roof, he turned his attention to the gutters, then the porch railing. He never seemed to run out of things to do, and every time Annie stepped outside, she found herself looking for him. A couple of times, he caught her watching, and the looks that passed between them all but sizzled. Then he turned his attention back to his work, and her breathing slowly returned to normal. Until she stepped outside again. And she found a lot of reasons to step outside.

Just a week ago, she hadn't wanted him to come anywhere near her, but there was something about him that she couldn't resist. And their situation didn't help matters any. Only Drake, Phoebe, and Sam knew where they were, and for all practical purposes, they were completely alone in the world. He couldn't make a move, a sound, without her being aware of it. And when they sat down at the table for lunch and supper, it was his dark, watchful eyes she found herself looking into, his deep, sexy voice that she silently sighed over.

But it was the nights, she was to discover, that were the worst. Her body was exhausted, but when she crawled into bed later that evening and he stretched out on the couch in the dark, sleep was a thousand miles away. Restless, she shifted, trying to get more comfortable, only to freeze as the darkness seemed to amplify every single sound. Could he hear the thunder of her heart? The way her breath hitched in her throat?

A nervous giggle bubbled in her throat at the thought and was hastily swallowed. She had to stop this! After five years of marriage, she was supposed to be well past the stage of mooning over her husband. But he made her want things she couldn't remember and yearn for a closeness that they'd lost somewhere along the way. Why? What had happened to them? How could they have let what they'd once had slip through their fingers without a fight?

She fell asleep, wondering and worrying in her dreams, knowing that if she didn't remember soon, it was going to be too late. She cared for him so much more than she should, and they could be here, alone together, for who knew how long. How was she supposed to protect her heart, when the pull he had on her grew stronger with every passing hour?

The next day, she was still asking herself the same questions, and the answers were as elusive as ever. And that was when the panic started. She was falling in love with him for the second time in her life, but the knowledge brought her little peace. They were on a collision course with heartache and quickly running out of time. There was no way to avoid the inevitable disaster unless she somehow got her memory back.

So while he spent the day recaulking the cabin windows and trimming the trees that brushed against the eaves, she tried her damnedest to remember not only the day she'd first fallen in love with him, but the exact moment she'd turned her back on him and walked away. In doing so, she knew she might get more than she bargained for. Not only could she turn out to be a woman she didn't like at all, but by trying to force one memory, she could be opening herself up to a whole flood of bad ones. Either way, she was probably going to get hurt, but at least she'd have some answers.

All she got for her efforts, however, was a low-grade headache that stayed with her all day. By the time they'd finished supper and retired to opposite ends of the couch to relax in front of the fire before going to bed, it had progressed to a constant pain that pounded at her temples. Unable to concentrate on one of the paperback novels they'd brought along to pass the time, she let it fall to her lap and squeezed her eyes shut. It didn't help.

"Problems?"

Her eyes still closed against the light that only seemed to intensify the pain, she nodded and rubbed tiredly at her temples. "It's just a stupid headache."

"Have you taken anything?"

"No. The baby…"

She didn't have to say anything more—he knew she would never chance doing anything that might hurt the baby. Silence stretched between them, but she couldn't bring herself to find some tidbit of conversation to break it. Then she heard him move, and before she could begin to guess his intentions, he slid across the couch, not stopping until he was sitting right next to her, his thigh firm against hers. Startled, she tensed and her eyes flew open. "What—"

"Shhh," he murmured, resting his hands on her shoulders. "Don't go getting all skittish on me. I'm just trying to make you feel better."

"Said the spider to the fly," she drawled. Drawing back slightly, she eyed him warily. "What *are* you doing?"

"Just giving you a massage," he retorted, grinning. "Why? What'd you think I was doing?"

Her mind drifted to hot, slow-moving images of the two of them touching, kissing, loving. And an ache that had nothing to do with the one in her head settled low in her abdomen.

"Annie? Are you in there? Where'd you go?"

She blinked and looked up to find him staring into her

eyes, trying to follow her into her thoughts. Mortified, she felt a hot blush steal into her cheeks, and wanted to die right there on the spot. "Sorry," she said in a rough voice she hardly recognized as her own. "I guess my mind just wandered for a second. Maybe I should go to bed."

"Not yet. Turn around and let me give you a back rub. It'll make you feel better."

She shouldn't have, but when his hands urged her to scoot around and present her back to him, she couldn't summon the will to resist. Without a word of protest, she settled sideways on the couch with him right behind her. Then his hands worked their way down her spine and back up to her neck, massaging the tension out of her tight muscles, and she melted like a candle in the sun. By the time his fingers slid into her hair and found the throbbing in her temples, she was boneless. Groaning, her eyes still closed and a soft smile curving her mouth, she leaned back into his touch.

She was falling asleep in his hands and seemed to have no idea what she was doing to him. *Don't!* he wanted to warn her. *Don't trust me that much. I want you too badly.*

But he couldn't say the words any more than he could push her from him. Unable to resist temptation, he leaned down and kissed the side of her neck. Under his mouth, her skin was soft and warm and far too tempting. His teeth hurt, he wanted her so badly. And there wasn't a damn thing he could do about it. Not when her head was hurting and she was so tired she could barely string two words together.

"That's it, sweetheart," he whispered. "Just relax. You were probably out in the sun too much today. Tomorrow I'm going to make sure you stay inside with your feet up."

"No," she muttered, leaning more heavily against him. "It wasn't that. I was trying to remember."

His fingers stilled at her temples. "Grant said you were supposed to just take it easy and let everything come back at its own pace."

"I tried that. It isn't working."

"What about your dream?" he reminded her. "You described that dead banker to a T, so he must have had something to do with whatever happened in the garage. Give yourself time. The rest will come when you're ready to deal with it."

"But what if it doesn't?" Voicing her worst fear, she turned to face him, her eyes troubled and dark with worry. "What if I never remember anything?"

His gaze locked with hers, Joe didn't pretend to misunderstand. She wanted to know about them. What was going to happen to them if she couldn't tell him where she'd been for the last two months? Who she'd been seeing? Who she might have been sleeping with when she still had a husband at home? Did they even have a prayer of a chance with so many unanswered questions between them?

She needed reassurance—he could see it in her eyes, hear it in her voice—but he couldn't give it to her. "I don't know," he said, letting her go. "I guess we'll have to wait and cross that bridge when we come to it, won't we?"

Chapter 8

By unspoken agreement, they strictly avoided discussing the future after that. And all physical contact, including massages. Knowing it was for the best didn't make it easy on either one of them, but somehow they managed. The work that still needed to be done around the cabin was a welcome distraction, but it was a small place, and by the end of the third day, they had it in tip-top shape. Then the real torture began.

When Annie left him back in the summer, Joe thought he knew what hell was all about, but as the days dragged, he realized he was only just beginning to know the meaning of the word. They were literally living in each other's pocket and bumping into each other every time they turned around. There was no privacy, no space, no *room* to get away from each other. When she took a bath every night, he found himself listening for the sound of the running water and waiting for the subtle, enticing scent of her shampoo to drift under the bathroom door to tease his senses.

By the time she finished and left the bathroom in a cloud of fragrant steam, he was hard and aroused and frustrated. Every damn night.

Considering that, it was little wonder that he dreaded the setting of the sun. The nights were impossibly long, and when he did manage to fall asleep, which was only for short stretches at a time, Annie was waiting for him in his dreams.

He wasn't, he discovered, a man who handled celibacy well. He was short-tempered and edgy, with too much time on his hands. And the only distraction was Annie herself. Through half-closed eyes, he watched her every move and didn't care that she knew it. If Sam didn't call soon about a break in the case, they were going to have to go into Marathon or El Paso and see about getting Annie some maternity clothes, but for now, she still wore her jeans unsnapped. Just knowing her pants were only partially zipped under the long tail of her shirt drove him quietly out of his mind.

Once he might have found comfort in the fact that she was just as miserable as he was, but that only made him want her more. They were both waiting, fighting the inevitable, and the tension in the cabin was as sharp as shattered glass. By the morning of the fifth day, Joe couldn't take it anymore. He was going to blow the lid right off the place if he didn't do something about the hot energy crawling under his skin.

"Let's go for a walk," he said curtly as soon as they finished breakfast. "The doctor said you needed exercise, and we haven't been out of sight of the cabin since we got here."

"I'll pack some sandwiches," she said eagerly, as anxious as he to get out. "We can have a picnic."

At that point, Joe would have agreed to a full-scale barbecue cooked over an open campfire if it would get them out of the forced intimacy of the cabin. "Take whatever you want. I've got a backpack in the closet. I'll get it while you're getting the food together."

They were ready in five minutes and out the door in five and a half. It was a cool morning, but crystal clear, with the scent of pine heavy in the air. Wearing lightweight jackets they could later tie around their waists as the temperature rose, they took a path that meandered north of the cabin, walking single file at a leisurely rate as they struck off through the trees.

The forest was hushed and cool and bathed in shadows, the atmosphere almost churchlike, and neither felt the need to break the companionable silence. So, for long stretches at a time, the only sound was the whisper of the wind through the trees and the crunch of pine needles under their feet as they hiked farther and farther from the cabin. For the first time in days, they were both at peace.

They might not have spoken for hours, but, just as they stopped for a break, Annie spied a young deer standing fifty yards away in a small clearing off to their right. Still as a statue, it stood poised for flight and watched them with dark, liquid eyes. Instinctively, she reached for Joe's hand.

"Look," she whispered, and nodded toward the clearing.

His fingers closing around hers, he stood with his shoulder brushing hers, hardly daring to breathe. Then, just when it seemed as if time itself had stopped, the deer turned and bounded off into the trees, its white tail waving like a flag before it disappeared in the shadows.

That should have broken the hushed silence and the spell that had fallen over them. But when Joe looked down at Annie and found her looking up at him with shiny eyes, the intimacy that had pulled them together in the cabin was nothing compared to what they'd just shared there in the forest. He had to order himself to let her go, but even then, his fingers tightened around hers before he could bring himself to release her and step back.

"That was a surprise," he said in a voice as rough as a gravel road. "You don't see too many deer around here this time of year. Hunting season's right around the corner, so they're usually pretty skittish once the weather starts to cool off."

Her heart thumping in her chest, Annie could understand how the deer felt. Nothing had happened, but something in his gaze made her feel as if she'd just had a brush with a kind of danger that had nothing to do with fear. She wanted to run for the hills…and turn into his arms. Torn, she did neither, but followed his lead and acted instead as if nothing had happened. With her pulse skipping and her stomach jumping crazily, it wasn't easy.

"I could never shoot anything so beautiful," she said huskily, only to realize she didn't know if she'd ever done such a thing or not. "At least, I don't think I could. I'm not a hunter, am I?"

His lips twitched but didn't quite curl into a smile. "You? Hardly. Grant tried to give us some venison once, and you accused him of shooting Bambi."

She laughed, relieved. "Serves him right. If we need meat, that's what the grocery stores are for."

This time, he grinned, his brown eyes crinkling with amusement. "That's what you told him. He never made the mistake of doing that again." Still grinning, he said, "C'mon. Let's see if we can find Bambi's mother."

They hiked for the rest of the morning, then had lunch in a meadow that offered a breathtaking view. It was a quiet, tranquil spot, and though they were both more talkative than they had been all morning, Annie knew Joe wasn't any more relaxed than she was. In spite of the leisurely lunch they'd eaten, her heart rate hadn't slowed one iota from the moment she'd taken his hand when they'd spied the deer. And she doubted that his had, either. Though he was much better at concealing his emotions than she was, there was a tension in his jaw and a heat in his eyes that stirred a restlessness in her that made it nearly impossible for her to sit still.

So as soon as the remains of their lunch were repacked in the backpack, she jumped to her feet, eager to put some distance between the two of them before she did something stupid and reached for him again. If it happened a second time, she was afraid she might not be able to let him go. "Can we climb to the top?" she asked him as he, too, rose to his feet. "It doesn't look like it's that far."

"It's not," he replied, frowning. "But it's pretty rough."

"But the doctor said to get some exercise."

"Somehow I don't think he had mountain climbing in mind," he replied dryly. "And you're going to be sore enough tomorrow as it is. We haven't exactly been taking a walk in the park, you know. We're at least two miles from the cabin, and we've been climbing ever since we left."

"But it's such a wonderful day and I feel fine. We don't have to go all the way to the top if you don't want to. Just a little way up. Please? It'll be a downhill walk all the way home."

She wouldn't have figured herself for a finagler, but she looked up at him pleadingly and shamelessly batted her lashes and he never stood a chance. Oh, he knew she was blatantly working her wiles on him, but he laughed, and instead of teaching her a badly needed lesson about the dangers of flirting with her husband, he was willing to be amused.

"Okay," he chuckled, "but I don't want to hear a single

word of complaint out of you tonight when you're as stiff as a zombie and can't even get in bed without help.''

"Not a word,'' she promised solemnly, her blue eyes twinkling. "I swear. Let's go check out that rock. I bet it's got a great view of the valley.''

The *rock* she pointed to was actually a limestone out-cropping that formed half the side of the mountain three hundred feet above them. As far as distance went, it wasn't all that far, but the path wasn't the most stable one. A fire had taken out all the trees and vegetation several years ago, and since then, the path had been washed out by storms. Steep and rugged, there was nothing to hold on to but the crumbling rock itself. One wrong step and it was a long way to the bottom.

"If it does,'' he retorted, "you won't be seeing it today. It's too dangerous.''

"There must be another way to the top,'' she argued. "Look! There's a path that cuts through the trees. C'mon, let's check it out.''

She started around him before he could stop her, and in the process, stepped in a hole that was hidden from view by a layer of pine needles. Her ankle twisted, and with a startled cry, she pitched awkwardly to the side. Lightning quick, Joe reached for her, his curses ringing in her ears as he caught her just before she could hit the ground.

"Dammit, Annie, what the hell are you trying to do? Hurt yourself? If you fall up here, we're a long way from a doctor!''

"I know. I'm sorry. It was my mistake. I wasn't watching where I was going.''

It happened so fast, neither one of them had a chance to catch their breath or protect their hearts. One moment she was falling, and the next she was in his arms. Startled, she lifted her gaze to his, and all she could see was a need in his eyes that was as fierce as her own. Somewhere in the back of her head, the thought registered that she should move, slip free of his touch, laugh off the moment while she still could. But it was already too late for that. It had been from the moment his hands had caught her close.

"Joe…"

She couldn't manage more than that, just his name, but even she could hear the longing that turned her voice husky and deep. He stiffened, a muscle ticking along his hard jaw, and she almost cried out in protest. But then something in him seemed to snap, and with a muttered curse, his arms tightened around her. "Dammit, woman, I didn't bring you out here for this," he growled. "I swore I wasn't going to touch you again until you got your memory back. It's the only sane thing to do. We could both get hurt—"

"But I already hurt," she replied softly. Taking his hand, she pressed his fingers to her mouth. "Here. And here." Daringly, she moved his hand down to cover her wildly beating heart. "All I want you to do is kiss it and make it feel better. Just this once."

He shouldn't have. One of them had to keep a cool head, and if it wasn't going to be her, then it had to be him. But her breast was soft and warm in his palm, her heart hammering out an erotic rhythm that echoed in the throbbing of his own blood. He wanted her more than he wanted his next breath, and with a groan that came from the depth of his being, he knew he could no more resist her than a wolf could resist the call of the wild.

"Damn you, Annie," he muttered, drawing her closer, against his heart, "you don't play fair."

Covering her mouth with his, he gave in to the hunger that was knotted like a fist in his gut. His arms locked around her, his tongue dove deep, taking, wooing, seducing. Struggling to hang on to what was left of his control, he tried to give her tenderness, but he was too needy, too hard. His blood was hot in his veins, his arousal pressed against her belly, his mouth rough.

Intoxicated by the taste of her, he blindly fought at the buttons of her jacket, his fingers fumbling in his haste. He wanted, *needed*, to touch her—everywhere—to feel the softness of her skin, the delicateness of her bones under his hands, the sighs that rippled through her as he kissed his way down her body. Now. Right here on the side of the mountain.

Dizzy, delighted, Annie felt the rub of his tongue along hers, the touch of his fingers as he tugged her jacket from her and moved to help him. Reaching for the hem of the oversize sweatshirt she wore, her hands bumped into his. He cursed softly in frustration and she couldn't help but smile against his mouth. This was what she'd longed for since the last time he'd kissed her, what she'd dreamed of in the night and fantasized about during the day, this heat that jumped from his skin to hers, this fire that burned without a flame, deep inside her. Her heart quickened, and his answered. Seduced, she murmured his name and crowded closer.

Lost in the taste and feel and heat of each other, neither of them noticed that dark, angry clouds were gathering overhead and the temperature had started to drop until a cold wind danced across the exposed skin of Annie's chest and stomach as they fought to rid her of her sweatshirt.

Suddenly cold where only seconds before she'd been burning, she gasped. And only just then noticed the sky. "Oh, God! Look!"

Abruptly brought back to earth, his breathing ragged, Joe looked up and swore at the sight of the ominous clouds directly over their heads. "Damn, it looks like a norther's blowing in. We've got to get out of here!" The words came out harshly, but he couldn't help it. Not when his blood was boiling and he was so close to howling like a madman. Jerking her sweatshirt back down, he snatched up her jacket from where it had fallen to the ground and quickly helped her into it, as an icy wind picked up and started to swirl around them. Another glance at the sky had him reaching for her hand. "C'mon, honey," he shouted over the wind. "Just hang on to my hand."

The wind caught her hair, tugging it around her, blinding her. Muttering a curse, she grabbed it with her free hand and anchored it at the back of her neck. "Don't worry, you couldn't pry loose of me with a crowbar," she cried. "What's the shortest way back?"

"Straight down that path." They'd taken a circuitous route up the mountain, but now he nodded toward a rocky trail that didn't zigzag as most mountain trails did, but headed sharply down the hill in a straight line. "Just stay behind me and step everywhere I do." The words were hardly out of his mouth when it started to drizzle. Glaring at the sky, he cursed. "Damn, I should have seen this coming. C'mon. Let's go."

Anchoring her close, he plunged down the side of the mountain as fast as he dared, but they'd only gone a hundred yards when the skies just opened up and dropped an icy deluge on them. They were soaked to the skin in the time it took to gasp.

Annie's fingers caught tight in his, Joe slid on the wet ground and caught himself just seconds before he could drag them both down into the mud. "Dammit to hell! Hang on!" he yelled at her over the roar of the wind. "Once we get past these rocks, the going'll get a lot easier."

Annie didn't see anything that looked the least bit easy. In fact, the path he pulled her down looked like something out of her worst nightmare. Her heart in her throat, it took all her concentration just to nod and keep her feet. Then they reached the end of the rocks, the footing improved, and Joe picked up the pace just when she thought they couldn't possibly go any faster. Her wet hair streaming out behind her in the rain, she held on for dear life as they dodged trees and boulders in their mad rush down the mountain.

By the time they reached the cabin, the rain had the sting of sleet mixed in with it and an early darkness had fallen. Chilled to the bone, her tired muscles stiff from strain and the cold, Annie stumbled inside behind Joe and couldn't make herself go any farther. Shivering, she just stood there, hugging herself, right inside the door.

"Get your clothes off and get in the tub while I light a fire," Joe told her as he tore off his jacket and strode quickly to the fireplace. "Damn, I'm going to need more kindling. Hang on, while I get some from the porch."

Not bothering with his wet jacket, he hurried outside in his shirtsleeves and returned almost immediately with an armload of wood to find Annie standing right where he'd left her. Frowning, he stopped short. "Annie? C'mon, you need to get warm. Do you need some help getting out of your clothes?"

"N-no," she stuttered, shaking her head. "I don't think s-so. I'm just so c-cold." But as much as she needed to warm up, she couldn't make her arms unlock from around her body.

Joe waited, watching her through worried eyes, cursing himself for ever suggesting that damn walk in the first place. He should have checked the weather on the car radio—he knew how quickly fronts blew in out here—but all he'd been able to think about was getting out of the cabin and putting some space between them. If she got sick because of him—

He dismissed the thought before it could take hold and quickly turned to deposit the wood by the front door. Grabbing some towels from the bathroom, he took time only to light the gas wall heater in there before he returned to where Annie stood by the front door.

"All right, I've got the bathroom warming up. Now let's see about you."

Dropping a towel over her head, he rubbed her sodden hair briskly, then wrapped the towel turban-style around her head. Her teeth were still chattering, however, and his fingers quickly moved to the buttons of her jacket. "Okay, honey, drop your arms. That's it. No wonder you're freezing. This damn jacket's nearly frozen solid."

Without bothering to take his eyes from her, he threw the offending garment in the direction of the kitchen sink. "How's that? Think you can make it into the bathroom now and handle the rest while I start a bath for you? You really need to get in a warm tub and soak for a while."

"I may s-stay in there all n-night. Just give m-me a push in the right direction to get m-my legs going."

He did more than that. He swept her up in his arms, carried her into the now toasty bathroom, and set her on a stool next to the old-fashioned claw-foot tub so he could remove her shoes for her. Once he was sure she could manage her sweatshirt, he ran the water in the tub for her, adjusting it so that it wouldn't burn her chilled skin.

"Okay, it's all yours," he said finally. "Don't come out until you're good and warm."

"But you need to get out of your wet clothes, too," she protested.

"I'll change by the fire," he assured her, heading for the door. "Holler if you need anything."

He left her to her bath, shutting the door behind him as he stepped out into the main living area of the cabin. It was totally dark now and colder than the devil. Stripping off his shirt, he retrieved the firewood from where he'd left it by the front door and set about warming the place up.

After the fiery kisses they'd exchanged on the side of the mountain, the evening didn't end anywhere near the way Annie had thought it would. In spite of the chill that permeated her every pore, the desire Joe had stirred in her lingered in her system long after they returned to the cabin, rumbling like a thunderstorm that had moved out to sea and was still making its presence known. But for the first time, her mind was willing, but her body wasn't.

As Joe had predicted, their little hike, not to mention their dash through the rain, quickly caught up with her, and by the time she dragged herself out of the tub, she was a whipped puppy. Stiff and sore in spite of her long soak in the tub, she didn't have the energy to swat a fly, let alone think about making love to her husband.

Miserable, she tried to hide it and swore she didn't so much as wince when she joined Joe in front of the roaring fire he'd built in the fireplace. But he had eyes like an eagle and merely gave her an *I told you so* look that had her lifting her chin and claiming, "I'm fine."

"Sure you are," he snorted when she eased down onto the couch in slow motion. "I hate to tell you this, sweetheart, but if it came to a race between you and a snail, I'm not sure who'd win."

"That goes to show how much you know," she sniffed. "I could run a marathon if I wanted to."

"And maybe finish by the next millennium," he teased. Walking over to the stove, he dished her up a bowl of stew from the pot he had warming on the stove. "Here. It's just canned, but it should warm you up some. Tomorrow I'll make us some chili."

Dressed in dry jeans and a red cable-knit sweater he'd changed into while she was bathing, he took the seat next to her on the couch and made sure she ate every bite. As soon as she was finished, he scooped her up in his arms. "Okay, beddy-bye time for you."

"Joe! I can walk."

Flashing a grin at her, he strode over to the bed. "No kidding? Is that what you call it? It looked to me like you were just shuffling along." He already had the covers pulled back, and an instant later, he plopped her down right in the middle of the mattress.

Her heart thumping crazily, she expected him to join her, but he only pulled the comforter up to her neck and started tucking her in tight. Disappointed, she reached for his hand to stop him. "Aren't you—"

"No," he said quietly. A crooked grin tilting one corner of his mouth, he leaned down and kissed her on the cheek. "When I have you moaning in my arms, honey, I want it to be from pleasure, not pain. So go to sleep," he said gruffly. "You'll feel better tomorrow."

She didn't want to, but the down comforter and patchwork quilt he'd piled on the bed for her trapped in the heat, warming her all the way to her toes. By the time he doused the lights and stretched out on the couch with the one remaining cover he'd saved for himself, she was softly snoring.

The sleet stopped sometime before midnight, but the wind howled for hours, rattling the screens on the windows and causing the old cabin to moan and groan. Gradually, the logs in the fireplace burned down, slowly turning to embers that offered only marginal warmth against the cold that crept through every available crack and crevice.

Still asleep, Annie frowned and tugged the covers higher over her shoulders, unconsciously shifting to avoid the chill air that nipped at the back of her neck. The cold, however, followed her under the blankets that surrounded her like a cocoon, brushing at her exposed skin, refusing to be ignored as it cooled the sheets and persistently pulled her toward wakefulness.

Moaning softly, she pressed her face into her pillow, but then a log fell in the fireplace, sending a shower of sparks shooting up into the chimney. Startled, she came awake just in time to hear Joe damning the cold. "Joe? What's wrong?"

"Nothing," he said in a voice raspy with sleep. "The fire just died down and I'm putting more wood on it. Go back to sleep. It'll warm up in here in a few minutes."

He sounded more than a little put out. Frowning, Annie pulled the covers down just far enough to clear her nose and found him at the hearth, adding logs to the fire. Silhouetted by the flames, he was wearing the same jeans and sweater he'd changed into after their day in the great outdoors. As she watched, he tossed in another log, and in the flare of sparks that followed, she could see that his dark hair was tousled and his jaw was rough with the shadow of his beard. And he was shivering with cold in spite of the fact that he was standing so close to the fire.

Alarmed, she bolted up. "Why are you shivering? Did you catch a chill in the rain? Here, let me do that while you get under the covers. You look like you're freezing."

She started to throw off her own covers, but he stopped her with a hard look. "If you know what's good for you, you'll stay right there. I'll be fine once the fire catches good."

"But you've only got one quilt," she argued, suddenly realizing that he'd given her most of the covers when he'd tucked her into bed. "Dammit, Joe, why didn't you say something? No wonder you're cold. Here, take a couple of these—"

"No. I'm fine. And the couch is closer to the fire than the bed is. Just go back to sleep, will you? I'm fine."

"While you stand there shivering?" she retorted indignantly. "I don't think so. You never should have taken the couch on a night like tonight anyway," she scolded. "It must be thirty degrees in here. We should be sharing our body heat—"

The words died on her tongue when he shot her a glare hot enough to melt lead. "We'll be sharing a lot more than that if I crawl into bed with you, and you're in no shape for that tonight. So just leave it."

She should have. He was right. Her sore muscles had only tightened with sleep, and she had to be crazy to even think about inviting him into her bed. But helplessly caught in the heat of his eyes, she couldn't look away. He wanted her. She could see the need in the taut lines of his face, hear it in the rasp of his voice, feel it in her own body, in the steam that seeped through her like liquid heat. Making love would only complicate things between them, but logic had nothing to do with the need running rampant through her body. From the moment she'd awakened to find herself naked in his bed, it seemed they'd been circling each other in an elaborate dance of desire that had finally brought them to this moment in time. Yes, he could hurt her. But could anything hurt worse than denying them this one chance to love each other in spite of whatever the future might bring?

The decision made, she curled her shaking fingers into the covers and lifted them invitingly. "Come to bed and let me warm you," she whispered huskily. "The fire's hot enough."

Something flashed in his eyes, something dark and dangerous that made her heart trip over itself, and without a word he came to her, his tread slow and measured, his eyes trained unblinkingly on hers. She expected him to crawl right under the covers with her, clothes and all, but he stopped two feet from the bed and stripped his sweater over his head. In the firelight, his powerful shoulders and arms were sculpted and hard.

Deliberately, his hands dropped to the fastening of his jeans. "If you get scared or want me to stop, all you have to do is tell me," he said in a voice gritty with need. "I would never do anything to hurt you."

Her eyes locked on his fingers, she nodded mutely and suddenly felt as if there wasn't enough air in the room. Not sure if her reaction was a result of anticipation or fear, she told herself there was no need to be nervous. He was her husband—they'd made love countless times in the past. Just because she didn't remember a single one of those times didn't mean she had to tremble like a schoolgirl about to see a naked man for the first time. She was a grown woman, for heaven's sake!

Over the clamor of her own frantic thoughts, the rasp of his zipper being lowered was like a growl in the silence. Unable to stop herself, she glanced down...and promptly slammed her eyes shut.

He laughed, and she wanted to die. But then she heard his jeans hit the floor, and suddenly she ran out of time. A second later, the bed dipped as he slid in beside her. "You can open your eyes now," he said dryly. "I'm all covered up."

Mortified, she peeked through her lashes to find him lying on his side facing her, his head propped in his hand and his brown eyes glinting with amusement as he studied the red-hot tide of color that washed into her cheeks. "I'm sorry," she blurted out. "You must think I'm an idiot. It doesn't seem to matter that we've been married for five years or that I'm pregnant—I can't remember doing this before. I guess I'm a little nervous."

That was an understatement of gargantuan proportions, but he thankfully didn't tease her about it. "Then I'll just have to show you there's nothing to be nervous about," he said softly, smiling down into her eyes. "Just relax and leave everything to me."

She wanted to—God, how she needed to!—but her nerves were wound tight, her heart threatening to beat its way right out of her chest. She felt that she would shatter if he touched her, she desperately needed his hands on her, but she couldn't ask for that. Not yet. Her eyes swimming, she smiled tremulously. "Would you kiss me first? I always feel better when you kiss me."

With just that one simple admission, she destroyed him. He felt something crack, something near his heart, something that he would have sworn was stone hard. He lifted a hand to her hair and was stunned to find his fingers weren't quite steady. "So do I, sweetheart," he said thickly. "So do I."

He kissed her then the way he'd longed to, the way he'd dreamed of for longer than he could remember. Like it was the first time, the last time, and he only had one shot at it. With the patience of a man who knew exactly what he wanted and how to get it, he nibbled at her lips, then slowly deepened the kiss, easing her into it, until the only thought in her head was him and the magic he brought to her.

Seduced, she moaned and clutched at him, her fingers sinking into his shoulders and telling him without words that she wanted more. With a murmur of agreement, he made the kiss hotter, while his hands began a quiet, devastating seduction of their own. He never touched bare skin, but he didn't have to. With a skill that left her breathless, he rubbed the flannel of her gown over her breasts, her hips, until her sensitive skin all but cried out for the feel of his flesh against hers.

Gasping, she arched against him, her restless legs tangling with his. "Joe, please..."

She expected him to reach for the buttons of her gown then, but it was *her* hands he lifted to the buttons. "Take the gown off for me," he whispered. His brown eyes, glinting with playful humor, met hers. "I'll even close my eyes if you want me to."

She laughed, the sound hardly more than a gurgle of amusement. "Sure you will."

He pretended to look hurt. "Would I lie to you?"

He was teasing, but her expression was never more serious as she searched the rugged lines of his face in the light from the fire. "No, I don't think you would." Without another word, she started unbuttoning her gown.

Heat flashed in his eyes, warming her inside and out as his hand covered hers, and a grin propped up one corner of his mouth. "Does that mean I have to close my eyes? We're just getting to the good stuff, you know."

She grinned and pulled him down for a lingering kiss. When he finally eased back, they were both breathless and needy. "No, you don't have to close your eyes." With an easy, incredibly seductive movement of her thumb, she slipped the buttons free.

"There are already enough secrets between us as it is— I don't want any more. And it's not as if you haven't seen me before."

She was right, but as she sat up and slowly pulled the gown over her head, a pretty blush firing her cheeks, Joe felt as if time was spiraling backwards to when they were first married, when she was shy and eager and sweet and they couldn't get enough of each other. They'd laughed a lot in bed back then and thoroughly enjoyed each other.

The shyness couldn't last, of course, but she'd never lost her modesty, and somewhere along the way, he'd failed to even notice, let alone appreciate it. They'd both gotten caught up in their own careers, in life itself, and the laughter had died.

He wanted it back, he thought fiercely. He wanted back that wonderful something that they'd once had and let slip away. The Sunday mornings in bed with the comics. The shared bubble baths that had ended up flooding the bathroom floor. The strawberries and champagne at midnight. It was here now, so close it was almost in his grasp. All he had to do was find a way to hang on to it. And her.

Her gown landed on the floor beside his clothes, and his breath hissed out between his teeth. It always amazed him that she'd never thought of herself as pretty when she'd stopped him in his tracks the first time he'd laid eyes on her. Beauty had nothing to do with the world's definition of classical good looks, but with what came from the soul. And Annie's every emotion had always been right there in her face. She had a smile that was filled with warmth and laughter and eyes that spoke straight from the heart. She could sass with the best of them and cry over a lost puppy. If she was hurting, you knew it, and if she loved you, you knew that, too. And when she was at her most vulnerable, as she was now, she was breathtaking.

Her skin had always been flawless, but never more so than now, with pregnancy. She didn't try to hide herself from him, but the blush that slowly stole up from her breasts told him that she was fighting the need to cover herself. Needing to touch her, to hold her, he gently enfolded her in his arms, only to clench his teeth on a moan as her breasts, fuller now than they had been just days ago, settled against the hard wall of his chest.

"Honey, if you had a clue what you did to me, you could

make me do anything you wanted," he groaned. "You're killing me. You know that, don't you?"

Her bare hip nudging his, she moved against him, mischief dancing in her eyes. "Are your muscles hurting, too?"

"Witch," he laughed. "I believe you mentioned something earlier about me warming you up."

"No, *I* said I'd warm you," she corrected, grinning. "I believe I've done that."

"Oh, yeah, baby. I'm hot." And with no more warning than that, he rolled with her in his arms, dragging her under him.

At first, he thought he had gone too far, too fast. She stiffened instantly, her hands gripping at him as if to push him away, and he silently cursed himself for rushing her. But then she dragged in a shuddering breath, and he could almost feel the tension gradually drain out of her.

In the sudden stillness, her eyes lifted to his. "Okay?" he asked huskily.

She nodded, forcing her hands to release him, but only so she could loop her arms around his neck. "Make love to me," she whispered. "That's the only memory I want to have when you hold me like this."

She didn't have to ask him twice. Gathering her close, he kissed her hungrily, the patience he'd been so determined to give her quickly unraveling. "You want memories, sweetheart, I'll give you memories."

Giving in to the need that burned like a fire in his belly, he trailed his hands over her bare skin, warming her breasts, her stomach, the inside of her thighs, the very heart of her. Startled, she cried out and bucked against him, but he only recharted the same course with his mouth. She was still shuddering when he worked his way up her body to capture a pouting nipple in his mouth. Suckling her, he nearly lost it when she whimpered and clamped her hands around his head to hold him close.

"Joe!"

"I know, honey," he said raggedly, blowing softly on her sensitive nipple. "But it gets better." And to prove it, he twirled his tongue around that same damp nipple as if he was licking an ice-cream cone. Clutching at him, she nearly came up off the bed.

Fantasies. He gave her every fantasy she'd ever had and some she'd never dreamed of, teaching her things about her body that would have shocked her by the light of day. He loved every inch of her and she loved it. She sobbed and cried and wept with the beauty of it, and more often than not, she didn't know where her body ended and his began. And when she came apart in his arms for the third time before he took his own pleasure, the only memories in her head were those of Joe and his loving.

Chapter 9

Cuddled close in his arms, her head against his chest and the reassuring cadence of his heart pulsing in her ear, Annie stared dreamily out the cabin window and watched dawn slowly crack the darkness of the night. The blue norther that had raced through the previous afternoon was halfway to San Antonio by now and still blowing strong. The rain and sleet were gone, taking the clouds with them, and as she watched the morning sunshine creep across the land, the sky turned a beautiful deep blue.

The fire had long since burned itself out, and the air had a definite chill to it, but with Joe warming her like a blast furnace, she didn't need any other heat but his. Snuggling against him, she felt his arms tighten around her and smiled. He'd been awake nearly as long as she had and had been content to just hold her.

Dropping a soft kiss to his chest, she could have lain in his arms all morning, but after the night—and the loving—

they had shared, she knew they could no longer pretend that the rest of the world didn't exist.

"Joe?"

Nuzzling her neck, he buried his face in her hair. "Hmm?"

"We need to talk."

She felt him smile, then his hands began a slow exploration under the covers, warming her, making her muscles go weak one by one. "You talk and I'll listen," he growled. "Damn, you feel good in the morning, sweetheart. I've missed waking up with you like this."

The admission distracted her as nothing else could, and with a murmur of pleasure, she found his mouth and kissed him sweetly. When she would have pulled back, however, he groaned a protest and took the kiss deeper, his mouth avid and hungry on hers. Melting, she clung to him and tried to remember what was so important that she had to talk about it now.

She was breathless when he finally let her up for air, her blood warm in her veins. Her head slowly clearing, she stroked her hand down his back under the covers and said softly, "We have to talk about the baby, Joe."

He stiffened immediately. "No, we don't."

"But we can't ignore the situation. Not after last night—"

"Do you remember who the father is?"

"No, but—"

"Then there's nothing to talk about." Untangling himself from her arms, he slipped out of bed and drew the covers back over her before reaching for his clothes, his jaw rigid. "Stay in bed until I get a fire lit. I've got to get more wood."

He was gone before she could protest, shutting the front door sharply behind him as he stepped out on the porch.

When he returned a few minutes later, he didn't spare her a glance, but strode straight to the fireplace and knelt to rekindle the fire that had burned down to nothing but glowing ashes. His movements stiff and jerky, the set of his broad shoulders unyielding, he shut her out without saying a word.

Huddled against the headboard, her knees drawn up to her chest and the covers just barely reaching her bare shoulders, she shivered, but not from the cold. *Don't!* she wanted to cry. *We have to find a way to work this out. To decide what we're going to do if the baby turns out not to be yours. If last night meant anything at all—*

But no words of love had been spoken in the dark. No undying vows of everlasting devotion had been whispered in her ear. He'd promised her memories, nothing else, and he'd delivered. Until she remembered the past, they were likely to be the only ones she had.

In no time at all, he had the fire blazing again, with enough firewood neatly stacked at one end of the hearth to keep it burning for hours. There was no reason for him to go back outside, but when he turned away from the fireplace, he headed for the front door.

Surprised, Annie sat up straighter, clutching the covers to her breasts. "Where are you going?"

"For a walk," he retorted, jerking open the door. "Don't wait breakfast for me. I don't know when I'll be back."

He didn't ask her if she wanted to go with him, or give her time to make the suggestion herself. The door shut with a snap behind him and he was gone. Staring after him, her eyes stinging with unexpected tears, Annie told herself that he just needed some time to himself. And who could blame him? She wasn't the only one who suffered because of her amnesia. He didn't know if he was going to be a father or a duped husband, and there was no answer she could give him, nothing she could say that would end the turmoil he had to be feeling. All she could do was leave him alone and let him come to grips with it in his own way.

Determinedly dragging her gaze away from the door, she grabbed her clothes and escaped to the bathroom for a shower. Twenty minutes later, she still had the cabin to herself. Tempted to glance out one of the front windows to see if she could spot Joe, she did no such thing, but started breakfast instead in the hope that he would back any minute. And when he walked through the front door, she didn't want him to find her pacing the floor and worrying just because they'd had a little disagreement. She did, after all, have some pride.

Whistling with a forced cheerfulness, she laid slab bacon in an iron skillet and set it on the front burner of the stove, then pulled a carton of eggs from the refrigerator. She'd cooked the same breakfast any number of times since she'd come home—the simple chore should have been a snap.

But she was distracted, and twenty minutes later, she had a disaster on her hands. She burned the bacon and kept breaking yolks when she tried to fry eggs over easy, the way Joe liked them. By the time she finally admitted to herself that she was having a bad day, she'd gone through half a dozen eggs and had to end up scrambling them. If Joe had been there, he would have teased her unmercifully. But he was nowhere in sight—she checked.

Frustrated, not sure if she was going to laugh or cry, she set the cooked food on the table and shook her head in disgust. It was a pretty sorry sight. The toast was cold and the eggs runny, but it was all edible, nonetheless. And there was enough for an army. The only problem was there was no one there to eat it but her, and she only had to feel her stomach rumble once to know that she wasn't going to be able to force down a single bite.

Tossing down a pot holder, she grabbed an old sweater from the closet and headed for the door. She wasn't chasing after the man, she assured herself. She was just going to tell him breakfast was ready. Then she'd leave him alone.

Calling his name, she struck off into the trees, following his footsteps in the damp ground. Within seconds she'd left the cabin behind, but his tracks were still clear, and she forged ahead. Then his tracks just gave out. Frowning, she was searching the pine needles underfoot for some sign that he had been that way when suddenly the images underfoot and those in her head shifted and changed....

The trees were thick as thieves in the night, surrounding her, hiding her from view, and if she hadn't known better, she would have sworn she was miles from civilization. But there was a small shopping center a mile down the road and Interstate 10 just beyond that. Holding her breath, she listened for the sound of a motor, a car, but it was late— most people were at home in bed by now. And those that weren't wouldn't come anywhere near where she was. There was a creek at her back, and it was raging with water from the storm that had flooded the city earlier in the evening.

"Oh, God!"

Recognition hit her then, draining every drop of blood from her face as broken images flashed before her eyes and the pieces fell together like a child's puzzle. And just that easily, she could see the spot where she'd buried Robert Freeman. It was on the Driscoe Ranch, just north of the city limits, where the new Forest Park subdivision was scheduled to be built next spring.

"No," she whimpered, burying her face in her hands. But terror, as fresh as when she'd knelt beside the open grave *she* had dug and covered that poor man's face with dirt, clawed at her, ripping away chunks of the darkness that shrouded her memory, giving her no choice but to re-member. "No!" She didn't want to remember that—it was just a dream! But the image persisted, as real as her hands in front of her face, and suddenly she was running, scream-ing for Joe.

Locked in her worst nightmare, her eyes wide and des-perate, the thunder of her heart loud in her ears, she never heard him frantically call her name as he searched the woods for her. She burst through the trees into the cabin clearing, and suddenly he was there, reaching for her, and with a sob, she went into his arms. "We have to go back!" she cried, clinging to him as tears streamed down her face. "I remember where I buried the banker."

Joe took the news like a blow to the chin. No, dammit! They needed more time together before they went back to the real world. Before she remembered everything and he lost her again. Just a few more days, another week, just long enough for her to fall in love with him again, so she wouldn't just walk out the door when she remembered that he hadn't wanted her to have a baby right now.

But they'd just run out of time and there wasn't a damn thing he could do about it. She was right. They had to go back.

Swearing silently, damning the Fates, he murmured soothingly, "It's okay, honey. Everything's going to be all right. Nothing's going to hurt you."

"You have to call Sam."

"I know. I will," he promised. "Just as soon as you're calmer. You're still shaking like a leaf."

Her eyes welling with tears all over again, she buried her face against his chest. "It w-was horrible," she said thickly. "I could see m-myself b-burying him, and sud-denly I—I knew where I dug the grave. It wasn't a dream, Joe. I really did it."

He winced at the horror in her voice and knew there was nothing he could do to take away her fear. And he hated it. He hated his own helplessness, his inability to do anything when she needed him most.

Tightening his arms around her, wishing he could draw her right inside him and protect her from the world, he said, "We're not going to jump to any conclusions until we get back to town and get some answers. You hear me? Promise me, Annie. Just because we haven't thought of a logical explanation for this doesn't mean there isn't one."

"But—"

"No buts. Promise me."

He was whistling in the dark and they both knew it, but she gave him the promise he needed. "All right. I'll try not to jump to any conclusions."

"Good." Turning her toward the cabin, he urged her up on the porch. "Why don't you start packing while I call Sam? It looks like we're going home."

They drove all day, stopping only for gas, a quick bite to eat, and bathroom breaks, but an hour after the sun had set, they were still on the road. It had been a long, exhausting day and it wasn't even close to being over with. Each dreading what was to come, they stared straight ahead at the dark ribbon of the highway and hardly spoke.

Twenty minutes before they reached the outskirts of San Antonio, Joe called Sam on his cellular to give him their estimated time of arrival. Casting a quick frown of concern at Annie, who sat stiffly at his side, her hands tightly gripped in her lap, he told his friend, "We'll meet you at the entrance to the ranch."

"I'm already there," Sam told him. "The evidence boys have been there most of the day, ever since you called. We set up lights when it got dark, but we haven't found any-

thing yet. I had to bring in the dogs, Joe," he warned him.
"I hate like hell for Annie to see them, but this old ranch
is at least three thousand acres and covered with cedar. One
part of it looks pretty much like another, and Annie was
scared and probably confused the night she buried the body.
If she can just get us close to where she thinks she dug the
grave, the dogs'll find it."

"You're just doing your job, Sam," he replied grimly.
"Nobody can find fault with you for that. We'll be there
as quick as we can."

Pushing the end button, he set down the phone and
reached over to cover Annie's hands in the dark. "I know
this isn't going to be easy for you," he said quietly, "but
there's nothing for you to be frightened of. I'm not leaving
your side, and knowing Sam, half the police department
will be there to make sure you're safe and nothing goes
wrong. Whatever happens, just remember that you're the
victim in this. You haven't done anything wrong, honey."

"Not unless you count burying a dead man without no-
tifying the police." Her hand turning in his, she grasped at
his fingers. "I'm trying to be objective, Joe, but I've got
to tell you that right now, I'm not getting anything but bad
vibes about this."

"Just hang in there, honey. It will be over soon, and
you'll be fine."

She wanted desperately to believe him, but as they drew
closer and closer to the turnoff that would take them to the
old Driscoe Ranch, tension knotted in her stomach like a
hot, hard ball. Then they were exiting the interstate, and
she thought she was going to be sick. The feeling only got
worse when they reached the ranch entrance, where Sam
was waiting for them, as promised.

His expression more somber than she'd ever seen it, he
greeted her with a nod as she and Joe stepped from the car.

"I hate like hell that you have to be a part of this," he told her, "but we've searched the area that matched the description you gave us and haven't found anything."

"He's there," she said hoarsely, hunching her shoulders against a cold that had nothing to do with the chilly weather. "I know he's there. Did you check along the creek?"

He nodded, grimacing. "There are creeks all over this damn ranch, but they're seasonal and it hasn't rained in weeks. They're all dry."

Staring past him at the lights that flickered in the darkness among the trees, signaling where the police were concentrating the search, Annie could see the grave again as clearly as if she stood before it. "It's way back in the back," she said hollowly. "In the northwest corner. I'll have to show you."

No! Joe almost roared. He didn't want her to so much as set foot on the property, let alone hunt down a shallow grave, but the nightmare would never be over until she did. His face carved in harsh lines, he slipped his arm around her waist. "Why don't you drive, Sam? We'll ride with you."

There was nothing to mark where the grave was, not even a pile of fresh dirt, but Annie gave Sam directions to it without making a single mistake. When he braked to a stop facing a dry creek bed, she pointed to where his headlights cut through a thin stand of cedars. "There," she said flatly. "I buried him at the base of that big cedar."

Not convinced, Sam frowned. "Are you sure you've got the right place? There are a million cedar trees around here, and that dirt doesn't look like it's been moved in a hundred years."

"That's it," she retorted. "Trust me."

"All right, then," he sighed. "Let's check it out."

Within ten minutes, he had the lights and a portable generator there, as well as the evidence team. Then the dogs were brought in. If Sam needed proof that Annie had the right spot, he got it. The second one of the handlers led a bloodhound to the spot where Annie had indicated, the dog let out a howl that could have curdled blood.

Standing next to one of the powerful lights that stripped away the night for fifty yards in every direction, Joe's arm a comforting weight around her shoulders, Annie shivered as a second, then a third dog took up the howl, like some kind of eerie twilight bark. Fighting the need to squeeze her eyes shut like a frightened child, she stood straight as an arrow and faced what was to come.

The dogs were taken away, and for the sake of preserving evidence, the grave was exhumed by four officers with shovels rather than heavy machinery. In the tense silence that had fallen with the silencing of the dogs, the sound of the first shovel striking dirt was like the blow of a hammer. Annie flinched, then forced herself to stand still, waiting, like the others, for the first sign of the body. It seemed to take forever.

Although she'd only dreamed of the dead man once, his image was so fixed in her mind that she could have picked him out of a crowd of thousands. She'd thought she'd known what to expect, but the body the four policemen finally uncovered was discolored and cold and starting to decompose. Covered in dirt, the shock of dark hair and the banker's pinstripe suit clearly visible in the bright light, it was and wasn't the man she'd buried. The features looked different, like something out of a horror movie. If it hadn't been for the telltale scar near the mouth, she might not have recognized it at all.

"Oh, God, the scar!" Gagging, she pressed her hand to

her mouth and, for the first time, turned away. Shaking, she pressed her face into Joe's shoulder. "It's him. It's him!"

Standing next to her and Joe, Sam motioned for one of the men to bag the body. "Come on," he told Joe. "Let's get her away from this circus and back to the car. It's colder than hell out here."

Murmuring to her, Joe steered her toward the car, and within seconds, the three of them were headed back to the ranch entrance. Numb with cold, Annie sat in the back seat with Joe and couldn't get warm in spite of the fact that Sam had the heater turned up to high. She could feel the warmth wrapping around her ankles, but it didn't seem to help.

His angular face harsh in the meager light that came from the lit dash, Sam parked next to Joe's car and left the motor running. His arm resting against the top of the back seat, he turned sideways in the seat to face his passengers. "I've got to ask you some questions, Annie," he said carefully, quietly. "I know you probably wish I'd do this another time, but your memories are probably never going to be fresher than they are right now."

He looked so miserable that she couldn't help leaning forward to pat his arm. "It's okay, Sam. I know you're just doing your job."

His mouth quirked into a rueful smile. "Yeah. But sometimes it's the pits. So tell me about that night and how you remembered where the body was."

"I was walking in the woods looking for Joe and it just came to me," she replied. "I could see the creek and knew there was a strip center down the road, close to Interstate 10. And suddenly, I just knew."

"You knew what?"

"That the land I was seeing was on the old Driscoe

Ranch. It was like a veil lifted for just a second and everything fell into place."

"Do you remember how you got here that night? Who you were with? What kind of vehicle you transported the body in? We know someone else had to be with you, Annie. Who was it? Give me a name, a description, anything."

Closing her eyes, she tried to force the memory past the wall that was once again in place, but all she remembered was the fear. "I was scared," she said shakily. "Terrified. That's all I remember—just being scared out of my wits the whole time I was digging the grave."

"Scared of what?" Joe asked. "Of who?"

"I don't know. I don't remember anyone else being there." Suddenly realizing what she had just said, she blanched. "Oh, God, maybe I really did kill him and was afraid of getting caught—"

"Stop it!" Joe ordered harshly. "Do you hear me? We've already been through all this, and I don't want to hear another word about you killing anyone. For God's sake, we left town because someone was trying to terrorize you! He's the son of a bitch who probably did this. He's the one you should be looking for," he told Sam angrily. "He's been to our apartment, dammit! Surely someone must have seen him."

"We're working on that," Sam said. "We still don't know how he got inside the mansion to leave that delivery on your doorstep, but we think someone visiting one of the tenants was probably on the way out and let him in. With so little to go on, it hasn't been easy. But we got a break tonight, thanks to Annie. We won't know how big a one until the lab boys do their thing."

That was all Joe needed to hear. "Then you don't need us any more. I'm taking her home."

"Not without a uniform, you're not," he said, and

reached for his radio. "From now on, you're under twenty-four-hour surveillance until whoever's after Annie is safely under lock and key."

Nothing could have pleased Joe more. "You won't hear any complaint out of me. Let us know if you find out anything." Opening his door, he pulled Annie out after him. "C'mon, honey, let's go home."

News of the discovery of Robert Freeman's body hit the streets the next morning, and Annie awoke from a troubled sleep to find her face, along with that of the dead man's, splashed across the front page of the paper. Horrified, she stared down at the picture of herself and told herself this couldn't be happening, but the constant ringing of the telephone told her the nightmare was all too real. Newspaper and television reporters from as far away as Houston and Dallas called, wanting exclusive interviews. And those who didn't call were camped out on the front porch of the Lone Star Social Club, just waiting for her to stick her nose out the door so they could bombard her with questions.

Agitated, her stomach clenching with nerves, she hated being the focus of their attention. A man had died a horrible death, and she had buried him. There was nothing else she could tell them. Why couldn't they leave it at that? Didn't they know that if she remembered *anything,* she'd go to the police immediately?

Feeling as if she were trapped in a dark, bottomless prison with no way out, she forced down breakfast because the baby needed her to eat, but the French toast tasted like cardboard and tended to stick in her throat. Halfway through, she pushed it away and rose to her feet to prowl around the kitchen.

Joe didn't say a word, but she felt his eyes on her and turned to find him watching her in concern. "I'm sorry," she said, waving helplessly at her abandoned plate. "That's all I can manage."

The phone rang—again. Unable to stop herself, she flinched. After the first five or six calls, Joe had let the answering machine take over, but it was the constant ringing that grated against her nerve endings. Would it never stop?

Watching her jump like a startled cat when the phone rang for the third time in as many minutes, Joe swore viciously. She was pale as a ghost, with dark circles under her eyes, and she had to be exhausted. He'd held her in his arms all night long, and he knew better than anyone just how little she'd slept. She was on the edge, dammit, and too damn thin! She needed to eat, to rest, but as long as reporters were hounding her and she thought she was somehow responsible for Robert Freeman's death, he knew there was little chance of her doing either.

Making a snap decision, he pushed back from the table. "I don't know about you, but if I have to listen to that damn phone ring all day, I'm going to go crazy," he said tersely. "Get dressed, honey. We're getting out of here for a while."

He took her out the back way so that the reporters camped out on the front porch of the old Victorian wouldn't see them, then spirited her down to the Riverwalk. Turning the opposite way from Joe's Place, he strolled hand in hand with her like they were lovers on a holiday and made her laugh at least a half-dozen times. And although there was a plainclothes policeman only three steps behind them every step of the way, they were, for a little while at least, able to forget last night and the decomposing face of a man Annie had apparently been the last one to see alive.

Even on the Riverwalk, however, they couldn't escape the real world for too long. With Annie's picture boldly splashed across the front page of every paper in the city, it wasn't long before she was recognized. Joe caught more than one startled glance thrown their way and knew if he had seen them, Annie had, too. He felt her stiffen beside him, her steps falter, as a bald-headed man with a beer belly hanging over his belt openly stared at her with a suspicion he made no attempt to hide. For two cents, Joe would have decked him. But that would only have caused a scene, and that was the last thing Annie needed. So he just shot the jerk a go-to-hell look and turned Annie back the way they had come.

"I need to check in with Drake at the restaurant," he told her when she gave him a puzzled look. "And you need to put your feet up for a while. If you want, you can even take a nap in my office."

It was a good idea, but the second they stepped into the restaurant, Joe knew he'd made a mistake. The place was unusually packed for a weekday morning, and it wasn't hard to figure out why. There was a friend or business acquaintance at just about every table, all of them no doubt wanting to reassure themselves that Annie was okay since they hadn't been able to get her on the phone. And she didn't know any of them from a stranger in the street.

When she got her memory back, she was going to be overwhelmed. Now, however, she had to greet and chat with people she didn't remember, which was bound to be stressful for her. But there wasn't much he could do about it. When friends went out of their way to check on you, you couldn't just brush them off.

Forcing a smile, he nodded in greeting and tightened his fingers around hers. "I hate to tell you this, sweetheart," he said in an aside that carried no farther than her ears, "but it looks like all our friends have shown up at the same time to make sure you're okay."

Startled, she looked around. "Friends? Where?"

"At every table. Lord, it looks like our wedding reception." Grinning ruefully, his eyes met hers. "I know this is the last thing you want to do today, but I don't think that we've got much choice. They're here because they're concerned about you, sweetheart. You're going to have to talk to them."

After all that she had been through, he wouldn't have blamed her if she balked, but she had always had class. Squaring her shoulders, she dragged on a smile that wasn't just for show but actually reached her eyes. "Then you'll have to introduce me," she said simply. "Let's start with the couple at the table by the fountain. They look really worried."

"They're my godparents," he told her. "And they're crazy about you."

The next two hours were a blur that Annie never quite remembered later. Feeling as if she and Joe had stumbled upon a surprise party in their honor, she smiled and laughed and charmingly apologized for her faulty memory just about every time she turned around. People whose faces didn't look the least bit familiar hugged her and kissed her, and she could do nothing but return the affection and wonder who they were. Joe, bless him, stayed faithfully by her side and, when he got the chance, tried to drop hints in her ear about who everyone was so she could keep track. After the twentieth introduction, she stopped trying to keep the names straight and struggled instead just to keep smiling. When everyone was satisfied that she was okay, she promised herself, she was going to go home and go to bed.

But just when part of the crowd left, others, including Phoebe and Alice Truelove, arrived, and the process started all over again. Exhausted, her head throbbing and her back starting to ache, she reinforced her smile and thought of the nap she was going to take when this was all over. Then she started to cramp.

At first, she told herself it was her imagination. She was just tired and had been on her feet too long as she and Joe circulated among their friends. But the small twinge that caught her in mid-sentence quickly turned into a very real cramp that ripped through her abdomen like a rusty knife. Ashen, she gasped and clutched at Joe's arm with one hand while the other protectively covered her belly.

Caught in mid-sentence, he glanced down at her with a distracted smile that vanished the second he saw her distress. "What is it? You're pale as a ghost."

"The baby," she said faintly, only to wince as another cramp caught her. "Oh, Joe, I think something's wrong!"

"Excuse us," he said curtly to a restaurant-supply buddy, who had stopped by just to offer them his support. Without another word, he swept Annie up in his arms and quickly carried her to his office. Setting her down in his big office chair, he knelt next to her and cupped her face in his hand. "Are you in pain? Where does it hurt? Should I take you to the hospital? Dammit, sweetheart, talk to me! What do you want me to do?"

Helpless tears welled in her eyes. "I don't know," she cried, clinging to his hand. "I'm so scared! I know you can't be as happy about it as I am—not yet, anyway—but I don't think I could take losing it. Not on top of everything else. Please…"

"Hush," he ordered with gruff sternness and pressed a quick kiss to her mouth. "You're not going to lose the baby. Just hang on while I call Dr. Sawyer."

His hands were steady as he turned to his desk and quickly found the phone book, his voice even as he called Annie's obstetrician to relay the problem to her. But on the inside, his gut was churning, and he silently admitted to himself that he was scared out of his mind. Could a woman die these days from a miscarriage? God, he couldn't lose her! Not now. Not when he was just finding her again.

The doctor wanted to talk to Annie directly, so Joe quickly put her on the line, then stood at her side and listened to her end of the conversation with growing misgivings. He didn't know much about the aches and pains of a normal pregnancy, but even he could tell that things didn't sound good.

When she finally handed him back the phone to hang it up, she was paler than before, her eyes stricken. "She said to get to the hospital as fast as we can. She'll meet us there."

Two hours later, Joe was prowling the hospital corridor outside the emergency room, ready to tear the place apart if he didn't get some answers soon. When Annie's doctor stepped out in the hall, he reached her in two long strides. "How is she?" he demanded. "Is she okay? She hasn't lost the baby, has she? When can I see her?"

The older woman smiled and patted him on the shoulder. "She's going to be fine, Joe. And so is the baby. You can see her just as soon as we get her transferred upstairs to a room."

"A room? You're keeping her?"

"Just overnight," she assured him. "Just to make sure." Her smile fading, she warned, "You're going to have to see that she takes better care of herself. She's not eating right or getting enough rest. I know there's not a lot anyone can do about her memory, but all this stress isn't good for the baby, Joe. Or Annie. She's too thin. But it's her blood pressure I'm really worried about."

Joe stiffened, alarmed. "Her blood pressure! What's wrong with it?"

"It's through the roof, that's what's wrong with it! And that's nothing for a pregnant woman to play around with, Joe. If something isn't done to get it down, she and the baby could be in real trouble."

Staggered, he took the news like a blow to the head. "It's this damn murder! I guess you saw this morning's paper?"

Elizabeth Sawyer nodded. "It must have been hell for her."

"It was. She hardly slept last night, and today, we haven't been able to turn around without running into a reporter or friend. She's trying to rest, but how can she when the only thing people in this town are talking about is her?"

"Then a short stay in the hospital will at least get her away from the gossip and notoriety for a while. Maybe things'll die down by tomorrow."

Joe hoped so, but he wasn't holding his breath. "Can I stay with her awhile?"

"A half hour now and another half hour tonight," the doctor replied. "I'm sorry, Joe, but it's the only way she's going to get some rest." Glancing at her watch, she smiled. "Why don't you go on up to the fourth floor? She should be in her room by now. Someone at the nurses' station will tell you which one."

She was lying in bed, trying to keep her eyes open, when Joe finally found her room and walked in. She was still pale, but the color was starting to seep back into her cheeks, and the panic had faded from her eyes. When she smiled sleepily at the sight of him, he felt his heart expand like it had taken a breath.

Crossing to the bed, he took her hand and pressed a kiss

to the back of it. "Hi, sleepyhead," he said huskily. "The doc said I could stay for a little while, but you look like you're out on your feet."

He started to pull his hand back, but she stopped him simply by tightening her fingers around his. Her heavy eyelids drifting down, she murmured, "Don't go yet. I want to know what Dr. Sawyer said. Just let me rest my eyes for a moment."

"Rest them as long as you want, sweetheart. That's why you're in here. To rest and take it easy." His hand still held in hers, he pulled up a chair next to the bed and sat down to wait for her to open her eyes again. But her breathing slowed, the grip of her fingers relaxed, and he suddenly realized that she was asleep.

He should have left then, but he stayed the full thirty minutes, sitting by her bed, holding her hand while she slept. A nurse peeked in once, then left them alone, and still he sat there. He could have lost her. And the baby. All this time, he'd thought he was doing so well keeping his heart on a leash. Determined not to let himself care too much until he knew who the baby's father was, he would have sworn that the concern he'd felt was nothing more than what he would have felt for any other unborn child. He'd been wrong.

Chapter 10

"I'm going to let her go home," Dr. Sawyer told him the next morning when she caught up with him right outside Annie's hospital room. "Her blood pressure's much better, but she's not out of the woods. She just can't take any more stress."

"I know," Joe said, guilt stabbing him. He should never have let her stand around talking to people yesterday. She hadn't had enough time to recover from the long drive from the mountains, let alone the nightmare at the Driscoe Ranch. When he'd walked into the restaurant and seen the crowd waiting for them, he should have thanked everyone for coming, then insisted that Annie get the nap she needed. That wouldn't happen again.

"I'm going to unplug the phone and TV and discontinue the paper for a while," he promised. "I should have done it already, but it all happened so fast."

The doctor nodded approvingly. "Good, but you can't stop there. I'm talking no arguments, no discussions that'll push her blood pressure up or start her stomach churning, no situations that'll strain her already frazzled nerves. If she's going to carry the baby to term and deliver it safely, she has to be kept happy and calm. So if you're having any marital problems," she warned sternly, "you're going to have to wait until both Annie and the baby are out of danger to work them out. Do I make myself clear?"

Joe nodded. "Perfectly. But just for the record, the only problem we're having right now is Annie's memory. It's coming back in bits and pieces, and none of it's been pleasant for her."

"No, I don't imagine it has," Elizabeth Sawyer said sympathetically. "But knowing you're there for her has to be a comfort to her. Just stay close, Joe."

He planned to do just that, but as he stepped into her room as she was finishing her breakfast, Annie's lost memories chafed him more than she could possibly know. She looked up at him with a bright smile of welcome and all he could think about was taking her in his arms and telling her everything. She needed to know about the argument that they had had the night before she'd left him, how much he'd regretted it ever since. They'd both been unhappy and upset and the situation had just blown up in their faces. He needed to tell her that he hadn't meant any of it, and if he could go back and unsay the words, he would, in a heartbeat. She might not remember any of it, but he did, and the things they'd said were festering like a boil under the skin. Until they could discuss it and clear the air between them, they were never going to be able to put the past behind them and go on with their marriage.

But he couldn't tell her that. Frustrated, wishing he could whisk her back to the cabin and have her all to himself again, he could do nothing but growl, "Good morning,

Mrs. Taylor,'' then lean down and brush a tender kiss across her mouth.

He'd meant to keep it light and teasing, just a playful nip that would make her laugh and her eyes sparkle. But the second his lips touched hers, he felt her start of surprise, the way her breath hitched in her throat and her mouth opened shyly to his, and the desire that was never far from the surface whenever she was near flooded through him in a hot rush. With a murmur of pleasure, he gathered her close and kissed her with a sweet tenderness that left them both weak with need.

Her heart thundering a thousand beats a second, Annie stared up at him with dazed eyes as he slowly, reluctantly, raised his head. "Well," she laughed shakily, "I guess I don't have to ask if you missed me. That was some kiss, Mr. Taylor."

Trailing a finger over the blush stealing into her cheek, he drawled, "I aim to please, Mrs. Taylor. How's my favorite wife this morning?"

"Excuse me, but did you say your *favorite* wife?" Her blue eyes, bright with mischief, sparkled up at him. "I know I've forgotten a lot of things, but surely I would have remembered if you were a bigamist."

He chuckled, grinning. "No, I haven't been holding out on you—you're the one and only Mrs. in my life. So how are you and that baby of mine feeling? Dr. Sawyer said you had a good night."

Caught off guard, she blinked, sure she must have misunderstood him. But his steady gaze met hers head-on, and there was no doubt that he'd just claimed the baby as his. Confused, she stared up at him searchingly. "We did. *I* did. But Joe, I still don't know who the baby's father is. Did Dr. Sawyer say something that led you to believe—"

"Shh." He cut her off simply by pressing his fingers

gently to her lips. "We didn't even discuss the baby's paternity, sweetheart. As far as I'm concerned, there's nothing to discuss. The baby's mine."

He meant it. She looked in his eyes and felt as if he'd reached right inside her and touched her heart. He really didn't care if she remembered later that someone else had fathered her baby—he was claiming it as his. He would love it and care for it and give it his name, no questions asked.

"Oh, Joe."

She started to cry, she couldn't help it, but before she could do much more than sniff, he replaced his fingers with his mouth, gave her a quick kiss, then straightened, grinning, and presented her with a sack he'd been hiding behind his back. "No tears, honey—you'll get your new clothes all wet. And then what will you wear home?"

Distracted, she glanced down at the plastic shopping bag he'd shoved into her hands, then back up again to where he stood watching her expectantly. "You bought me clothes? Maternity clothes?"

"Well, I could hardly let you parade around town with your jeans unsnapped, could I?" he teased.

"But it's barely nine o'clock in the morning. How—"

"I went shopping after I left here last night," he explained. "The maternity shop in the mall was already closing, but when I told the lady I needed to buy you a complete wardrobe, she opened right up. I hope I got the right size."

He'd bought her a red corduroy jumper and a long-sleeved white cotton blouse that she could also wear with pants, and she loved them on sight. Rushing into the bathroom to try them on, she emerged a few minutes later, dressed in her new clothes and barefooted, a pretty blush tinging her cheeks and a smile stretching from ear to ear.

Spreading her arms wide, she twirled in front of him. "What do you think? Is it me?"

Joe took one look and felt the punch of desire all the way to his toes. She gave the old saying *barefoot and pregnant* a whole new meaning. There was nothing the least bit fancy or seductive about the outfit, but somehow, she made it look like silk. He'd always liked her best in red, and that hadn't changed. With her dark hair and creamy complexion, her skin took on a rosy glow and her eyes a sparkle that was bewitchingly lovely. She looked the way she had when they were first married...happy and carefree and in love...and all he wanted to do was sweep her into his arms and carry her home to bed.

But as much as he wanted to, he couldn't. She needed to rest, and that's the last thing he would let her do if he got his hands on her anytime soon. "Oh, it's you, darlin'," he drawled, grinning. "If I'd known I was going to get a private fashion show, I wouldn't have had the rest of the stuff delivered to the apartment. Why don't we go home and you can try it all on for me?"

"Go home?" she echoed, startled. "I can go home?"

"Just as soon as you get your shoes and jacket on and I sign a few forms for insurance. Of course, I guess I could arrange with Dr. Sawyer for you to stay a few more days if you like," he added teasingly. "You do look more rested—"

"Oh, no, you don't, Joe Taylor!" she warned as she hurriedly stepped into her loafers and grabbed her jacket from the small closet near the bed. "You're not leaving me here a second longer than you already have. See? I'm ready. I'll meet you at the car."

She didn't even know where he'd parked, but she was already out the door and heading toward the elevators. Laughing, Joe hurried to catch up with her. "Slow down, sweetheart. You're not going anywhere without me, remember? I've got the keys.''

Over the course of the next three days, Joe totally abandoned the restaurant, leaving it and the arrangements for the grand opening of the new one in Drake's capable hands while he stayed home with Annie and took care of her. Hardly letting her out of bed except to go to the bathroom or lie on the couch with her feet up, he took Dr. Sawyer's order literally and saw that she rested around the clock and ate like it was going out of style. He cooked tempting dishes for her, all but hand-fed her, and made sure she cleaned her plate. When she grew tired of lying around reading, he entertained her with funny stories and even brushed her hair for her until she fell asleep. If she'd been the least bit self-centered, she would have been spoiled rotten.

Instead, she was enchanted.

For three days and nights, he made it impossible for her to think of anything but him. He babied her and pampered her, and made her heart sing every time he stepped into the room where she was. And she couldn't keep her eyes off him. She watched him because she couldn't help herself, because she longed for the feeling of his arms around her again, because there was no question that she was falling in love with him all over again. And she no longer had the strength to fight it.

By the afternoon of the third day, she only had to look at him to know that it was his baby that she carried. She couldn't remember its conception or prove anything until she got her memory back or the baby was born, but she knew, she just knew, that it was his child she carried. It had to be. Even if they had been having problems before she'd left him, she couldn't imagine herself letting any other man touch her, let alone make love to her. Not after loving Joe.

Knowing that she hadn't been unfaithful to him lifted a load from her shoulders she hadn't even known was there until it was gone. And just that easily, she was free. Free of the pain of self-doubt, of questioning her own integrity. She still didn't know why she had left him or what she had done during the two months they were separated, but at least she hadn't crawled into bed with another man while she still had her husband's wedding ring on her finger.

She had to tell him, of course. Whether he believed her or not, he had to know that *she* believed that she'd never turned her back on their marriage vows.

So that night after supper when she insisted on helping him with the dishes, she struggled to find the words. Rinsing dishes for him to load in the dishwasher, she cleared her throat, searching for an easy way to begin, but there wasn't one. He'd never once mentioned the future or voiced an opinion on whether he thought their marriage had a ghost of a chance after everything that had happened, and she didn't want him to think that she was bringing up the subject because she expected anything from him. But he had to know that she'd never given him any right not to trust her.

And there was no way to say it but just blurt it out. "I didn't fool around on you when I was gone, Joe," she said with quiet confidence, shattering the comfortable silence between them. "There was no other man. The baby really is yours."

In the process of reaching for the plate she held out to him, he sent her a sharp look. "You remembered something?"

"No," she said with quiet dignity. "I just know."

Staring down at her, he wished like hell he could believe

her, but unlike her, he remembered every moment of that last month before she'd left him. And they'd only made love once. And while it wasn't impossible that she could have gotten pregnant then, the chances were slim. And no one regretted that more than he did.

Taking the plate from her, he turned to add it to those already in the dishwasher. "It doesn't matter. I'll love it no matter whose it is."

He meant to reassure her, but when he turned back to her, her eyes were swimming in tears that, even as he watched, spilled over her lashes and slid silently down her face. Alarmed, he reached for her. "What is it, honey? I thought you'd be pleased."

"I am!" she sniffed. "But I want you to believe me."

Did she think he didn't want that, too? In spite of everything that had happened, he still loved her. But love and trust, he was discovering, didn't necessarily go hand in hand. Once, she could have told him the moon was turning cartwheels in the sky and he would have found a way to believe her, but those days were gone, apparently forever. And no one regretted that more than he did.

"I didn't say I didn't believe you," he pointed out huskily. "Just that I would love the baby no matter what. I'm trying, Annie. The last couple of weeks haven't been easy on either one of us, and all we can do is take things slow and give ourselves some time. Everything will work out the way it's supposed to."

"I know. It's just so hard sometimes." Giving him a watery smile, she dashed impatiently at her wet cheeks. "I'm sorry. I didn't mean to cry all over you, but I don't seem to have any control over it. I guess it's because I'm pregnant. It's supposed to make you weepy or something."

He laughed and gathered her back against his chest. "Are you kidding? Sweetheart, you've been able to cry at the least little thing every since I've known you. We went to a Super Bowl party at Grant's house on our first date, and you cried when the Cowboys won—and when the losers congratulated them. You get teary-eyed over 'The Star-Spangled Banner,' for God's sake! Why do you think I carry a handkerchief with me everywhere we go? Nine times out of ten, you're going to get sentimental about something before we get home.''

''Stop!'' she cried, laughing. ''I couldn't possibly be that bad!''

''Wanna bet? I can have you in tears—and I don't mean unhappy ones—in about thirty seconds flat, and I don't even have to turn on a sappy movie to do it.''

''You can not!''

''Watch me,'' he growled, and swept her up in his arms.

''Joe! What are you doing? Where are you taking me? Put me down. You don't have to carry me like I'm some kind of invalid.''

Chuckling, he ignored her and carried her into the living room, where, one by one, he turned out all the lights until only one was left burning. Sinking down onto the couch, he settled her comfortably on his lap. ''Now,'' he said with a wicked grin, ''watch the clock.''

He just meant to tease her, to nuzzle her neck and tell her how she knocked him out of his shoes with just her smile the first time he laid eyes on her, but she felt so good in his arms, so trusting, that it wasn't that first meeting he found himself remembering, but the night they'd first made love. His heart did a slow, lazy turn, and suddenly it was vitally important that she remember, too.

With fingers that were suddenly unsteady, he captured her face in his hands and stared down at her with eyes that were dark with emotion. ''The first time we made love, you were still a virgin,'' he told her in a low, rumbling voice that had turned as deep as the night. "You were so beautiful, so sweet, and I was terrified of hurting you. We'd waited so long, and I wanted it to be perfect for you, but I felt like a raw kid who'd never been alone with a woman before. My hands were shaking," he admitted ruefully. "Do you remember?"

Mutely she shook her head, and just that easily, he won their bet. Tears welled in her eyes, but he took no joy in the victory. He wanted, *needed,* her to remember. Not just their first time together, but their love. *Him,* dammit! They'd had something that should have transcended decades, lifetimes, and they'd foolishly let it slip through their fingers. Somehow, they had to get it back.

"Then you smiled at me and kissed me," he said softly, "and I knew that I'd move heaven and hell before I'd hurt you. If you remember nothing else, remember that, sweetheart."

A single tear spilled over her lashes. "Oh, Joe, I want to. I want to remember everything!"

"You will, honey. Just give yourself time."

He kissed her then because he couldn't help himself, because it seemed like weeks instead of days since he'd held her like this, because he didn't want to think about the things she might remember that could take her away from him. As long as he was holding her, kissing her, loving her, he couldn't lose her. Not again.

But he hadn't forgotten Dr. Sawyer's warning. Reluctantly, he dragged his mouth from hers, but only to trail slow kisses over the curve of her cheek. "We've got to stop this, sweetheart," he breathed into her ear. "It's getting late and you need to go to bed. The doctor said you were supposed to rest, remember? That means eight hours of uninterrupted sleep a night."

She moaned softly and clung to him. "Only if you come

with me.'' Turning her head to capture his mouth with hers, she kissed him sweetly, hotly. "I don't like sleeping without you. I keep reaching for you.''

He groaned at that admission and tried to remember all the reasons he'd stubbornly slept in the guest room ever since he'd brought her home from the hospital. But she was so soft in his arms, so damn seductive, that he could hardly think straight. He was already hard for her, his body crying out for the feel of her under him, surrounding him. And the doctor hadn't specifically said no sex.

He never remembered making a decision, but suddenly he was pushing up from the couch with her in his arms and heading for their bedroom. The lights were still on, the stereo softly playing, the dishwasher grumbling as it went through its cycles. He didn't care. The rest of the world could have been racing past their front door like a herd of elephants, and he never would have noticed. Not with Annie in his arms.

He walked straight to their bedroom and laid her in a patch of moonlight on their bed, then came down beside her without ever taking his mouth from hers. Somewhere down on the Riverwalk, music drifted faintly on the cool night air, but he never heard anything but Annie. The whisper of her clothes, then his, as he undressed them both, the music of her sighs, the thunder of her heart. Her skin was like marble in the moonlight, her hair a dark tempting cloud across the pillow. Impossibly moved, he murmured to her, kissing his way down her body and back up again. Under his mouth, he felt her breathing change, her heart quicken. Smiling against her belly, he pressed his ear to her rounding belly and wondered if he imagined the slight murmur that could have been his child's heart. Sweetness rippling through him, he traveled up to her breasts and knew that he wasn't imagining the increased fullness there. Or her sensitivity. He kissed a tightly puckered nipple, and she moaned, arching into his mouth as her hands blindly flew to his head to cradle him close.

Tenderness. She'd never known such tenderness. Tears rose to her eyes, horrifying her because she was afraid he would misunderstand, but before she could blink them away, he was rising above her to kiss them away. His voice rough in the darkness, he told her how she delighted him, the pleasure that she brought him with just the light in her eyes. With every word, every touch, he slowly, inexorably drove her from one sensual peak to another. And all the while, tears streamed silently down her cheeks.

She knew he must have loved her a thousand times before, but she couldn't believe that any of those times had been like this. So sweet. So overwhelming. So incredibly beautiful. He knew just where to touch her to make her shudder, just how to kiss her to make her melt. He made her throb; and God help her, with maddening patience, he made her want until she burned.

And that was when she turned into a woman she didn't know. Sobbing, aching for release, she clutched at him, scratched at him, demanding everything. And he laughed. The monster laughed!

"Yes," he growled, kissing her fiercely as his fingers twined with hers and trapped them against the mattress. "I want you wild, sweetheart. Hungry for me. Show me what you want."

Loving her, urging her on, he destroyed her inhibitions and taught her that she was a sensuous woman who knew how to get what she wanted. She teased, she seduced, she rubbed and flirted and drove him crazy with fingers that were quick as lightning at one moment and slow as a winter dawn the next. And he never stood a chance. She had the satisfaction of making him groan and thought she had him right where she wanted him. He was hers and she meant to claim him. She was still contemplating ways she could drive him out of his mind with pleasure when he parted her thighs and surged into her. Before she could even gasp, she shattered, his name a startled cry upon her lips.

Long after she'd drifted off to sleep in his arms, Joe held her close, his body sated and exhausted, bittersweet emotions churning in his gut, keeping him awake. He hadn't lied when he'd told her that he would love the baby no matter what, but looking back with a clearer head than he'd had in months, he knew now that if the baby turned out not to be his, he had no one to blame but himself. He'd wanted security for them in a world where there really was none and had ended up sacrificing the most important person in the world to him to get it. God, what a fool he'd been!

He'd been so focused on what he wanted that he hadn't been able to see what she needed. All she'd wanted was more of his time and attention, a baby, the type of home life that she'd always dreamed of. Hardly unreasonable requests of a wife from her husband. But at the end of an eighteen-hour day that had held nothing but one headache after another, he hadn't been happy about coming home to what had sounded like demands, just because he was tired. They'd fought and argued and grown further and further apart. Instead of giving their marriage first priority, he'd given all his attention to the restaurant, and they had come apart at the seams. Over and over again, she'd tried to tell him how unhappy she was, but the words just hadn't registered. And now that he was listening, it might be too late. She slept contentedly enough in his arms tonight, but how long would that last once she remembered that for the last six months of their marriage, he'd seldom been there for her when she needed him?

He could lose her again, he thought, shaken. At any moment of the day or night, time could run out and the shadows clouding her memory could lift. He'd hurt her once; she might not want to chance that kind of heartache again, especially now that there was a baby to protect. She could walk out the door, and it would all be over. Forever. Because if she left him a second time, she wouldn't be back.

No, dammit! he thought fiercely. He wouldn't lose her. Not again. Instinctively, he tightened his arms around her, only to have her murmur in protest. Easing his hold, he quietly soothed her with his hands and voice until she drifted back to sleep, but deep in his gut, worry gnawed at him. It was a long time before he slept.

The man standing in the shadow of the building across the street watched the last of the lights in Apartment 2B of the old Victorian mansion go out, his expression as cold and bitter as the night. The bitch was starting to remember. She'd already led the police to the body—it was only a matter of time before she remembered the rest and had the cops hunting him down like some kind of rabid dog.

Damn her, he should have gotten rid of her when he had the chance! he thought furiously. But the conniving little witch had tricked him. She'd acted like she was half out of her mind with fear and had all but crawled to do his bidding. Then, when he'd dropped his guard, she'd brained him with the shovel. By the time he'd come to his senses, she'd been halfway back to town. If he could have gotten his hands on her then, he would have taught her just what real fear was.

But her time was coming, he promised himself. Oh, yes! And then he was going to make her suffer for all the hell she'd put him through. He just had to get to her before she remembered and eliminate her. Ten minutes, that's all he needed. Ten minutes alone with her and Annie Taylor would never bother him or anyone else again.

He knew it wasn't going to be easy. He'd been tailing her ever since she'd come out of hiding to lead the police to Freeman's body, laying back out of sight, watching her, studying her. But that damn husband of hers hadn't let her out of his sight for a second, let alone ten minutes. He'd watched her like a hawk protecting its own, and the few times he hadn't been hovering close, the pig in street clothes hovering outside their apartment was always there, always watching. It was damn frustrating.

A lesser man might have given up and run for Mexico while he still could. But trouble was what he was good at. And he wanted Mrs. Taylor. He wanted her bad. And he was going to get her. He already had it all worked out.

Far back in his subconscious, Joe heard the sirens echoing through the canyons of downtown, but it was the shrill ringing of the phone that woke him just before dawn. Mumbling a sleepy curse, he kept one arm snug around Annie and fumbled for the phone on the nightstand with the other. "'Lo?"

"Mr. Taylor?"

"Yeah?"

"This is the 911 operator, sir. I'm sorry to disturb you at this hour, but we just got a call that your restaurant at 3257 Navarro is on fire."

"What!" Coming abruptly awake, he bolted straight up in the bed. "Has anyone called the fire department? What started it? How bad's the damage?"

Already reaching for his pants, he barked the questions into the phone, but the operator was as cool as a cucumber.

Her voice professional and steady, she replied, "We have no way of knowing that at this time, but two fire trucks have been sent to the scene. They should be arriving shortly."

Only then did the sirens that seemed to be screaming to a halt right outside their bedroom window register. "I hear them now. Thanks for calling. I'll be right there."

He slammed down the phone and quickly strode over to the closet for a shirt. When he turned back to the bed, it was to find Annie pulling on a forest green sweater and jeans, her face pale in the predawn light. "It's the restaurant," he told her grimly. "There's a fire. I've got to get over there."

Annie didn't bother asking questions that would be answered soon enough. She simply sat on the side of the bed and quickly tugged on thick socks and her shoes. "I'm going with you."

"The hell you are," he growled. "It's too dangerous."

"I'll stay out of the way," she promised, "but I'm not letting you go down there alone." The matter settled as far as she was concerned, she tied her shoes and pushed to her feet. "Let's go."

"Dammit, Annie, will you listen to me?" Hurrying after her, he caught up with her just as she pulled her jacket from the closet by the front door. Grabbing her arm, he whirled her to face him. "You are *not* going with me! You got that?"

It was the wrong tone to use with her. Her chin came up, her blue eyes flashing fire as she stood nose to nose with him. "I don't remember asking your permission."

He swore, but he couldn't get angry with her when she was ready to fight him and anyone else for what she believed in. His Annie was coming back to him slowly but surely, and even though there was a chance that all their newfound closeness would vanish with the return of her memory, he couldn't regret it.

Sighing, he released her, but only for a moment. Before she could even begin to sputter a protest, he leaned down to give her a quick, hard kiss. "You're right," he said, surprising her. "I can't stop you from going. But it's probably already a madhouse down there, and a fire's no place for a pregnant woman. I don't want you to get hurt, honey," he said bluntly. "I know you don't want me to face this alone, but I'd much rather do that than take a chance on something happening to you or the baby. If you stay here, at least I'll know you're safe."

He had a point, the dog, one that she didn't have a single argument for. But everything inside her rebelled at the thought of letting him walk out the door alone. For all they knew, the restaurant could even now be burning to the ground. She wanted to be with him, to be at his side and offer what comfort she could. But he was right. She had to think of what was best for the baby.

"Promise you'll call me as soon as you see how bad it is," she insisted. "If I don't hear from you within fifteen minutes after you walk out the door, I'm coming down there. I mean it, Joe—"

"I'll call," he promised, giving her another quick kiss, "just as soon as I see what's going on."

He was gone before she could tell him to be careful, leaving behind a silence that was thick and heavy and cloying. The sirens had finally stopped wailing outside, but she could hear the broken, staticky transmission of the fire trucks' radios on the morning air, the sound of shouting a hundred yards downstream where Joe's Place sat nestled in the bend of the river, the wicked crackle of flames burning white-hot.

Chilled, sick to her stomach, she slipped on her jacket

and hurried out onto the balcony off the kitchen. The restaurant was blocked from her view by a thick stand of magnolia trees, but nothing could block the smoke that rose from the fire. Thick and black, it lifted into the morning sky like a thunderhead until it dwarfed the surrounding skyscrapers of downtown.

"Oh, God." Hugging herself, she stared at it and felt her heart sink. She'd hoped that the fire was nothing more than a simple kitchen fire, smoldering grease that put out a lot of smoke and not much else. But that kind of smoke didn't come from anything minor.

She should have gone with him, she thought, stricken. Even if he didn't want her to. Joe's Place was more than just a business to him—he'd put his heart and soul into every inch of that restaurant—and losing it would devastate him. She could just see him, standing back out of the way of the firemen, watching it burn and knowing there was nothing he could do to stop it.

Restless, her heart breaking for him, she went back inside so she wouldn't miss his call and anxiously paced the confines of the living room. She knew he had to be there by now—it only took a matter of minutes, and he'd been running when he went out the door. But five minutes passed, then ten, and she grew more and more agitated. Why didn't he call? He knew she was worried—

She jumped at the sudden, sharp jangling of the phone and snatched it up before the first ring was completed. "Joe? What took so long—"

"Mrs. Taylor?"

The male voice at the other end of the line wasn't Joe's but it sounded vaguely familiar. Wondering if it was someone from the restaurant, she clenched the phone tighter. "Yes? Who is this? Please, I can't tie up the line. I'm waiting for a call from my husband—"

"I know," the caller cut in grimly. "I'm sorry to be the one to inform you of this, but Mr. Taylor was injured in the fire."

"What! How? Is he all right? Where is he? I'm coming down there—"

"No! He's not at the fire. He's already being transported to the hospital."

"What hospital? I'll meet him there."

"The Methodist."

Tears welling in her eyes, she choked, "Thank you so much for calling me! I'm leaving right now."

Before she even slammed the phone down, she was running for the door, her feet barely touching the floor. He was hurt. Fear squeezed her heart. What could have happened? she wondered wildly. Was he burned? She whimpered, tears gathering in her eyes at the thought. No! He couldn't be! The firemen wouldn't have let him get anywhere near the flames.

She was halfway down the stairs when she remembered that she hadn't driven since the morning she woke up in his bed with no memory of who she was. Joe had had her car moved to the parking garage down the street from the apartment, but she hadn't a clue where her keys were and there wasn't time to look for them. The morning shift had to be arriving at the restaurant by now—they couldn't have heard of the fire yet. If she couldn't grab a cab, she'd get one of the waitresses to drive her to the hospital.

Her thoughts already jumping ahead to what she would find when she got there, she never saw the man waiting for her on the mansion's wraparound porch until she came running out the front door and almost ran over him. "Oh! I'm sorry! I didn't see—"

She glanced up, intending to offer an explanation for nearly flattening him, but the words died on a strangled gasp. Recognition slapped her in the face, and between one frantic heartbeat and the next, she remembered. Everything. "Oh, God!"

"Well, well, well," he sneered, watching in satisfaction as horror flared in her eyes. "I see you remember me. That'll make things easier, won't it?"

"No!" she lied. "I don't remember anything. I swear!"

"Then maybe I should remind you," he taunted, his smile ugly. "The last time we saw each other, you brained me with a shovel right before I was about to—"

She clamped her hands over her ears, horror rippling through her as one terrible memory after another slapped at her. The murder in the garage she'd stumbled across just by dumb luck. The dead man's blood soaking her clothes as she was forced to help lift the corpse into the murderer's van. And the grave. The smell of dirt and death and fear. And then that awful moment when this monster had her down in the dirt, his breath hot and foul on her face as he fumbled with his zipper.

He'd tried to rape her.

"No!" she screamed, and turned to run.

One step. That's all she was able to take before he grabbed her with the speed of a striking rattler and sank his fingers into the tender skin of her arm. "Oh, no, you don't. You're not going anywhere but with me. We've got a little unfinished business, lady."

Frantic, she looked around for the policeman that she only just then noticed was nowhere in sight. Smug, her tormentor only laughed. "Don't bother searching for your watchdog. He's taking a nice long nap thanks to a little konk on the head. C'mon, let's get out of here."

"I can't. My husband's hurt—"

He laughed, the sinister sound sliding over her nerve endings like ground glass on an open wound. "Stupid bitch! *I'm sorry to be the one to inform you of this, but Mr. Taylor was injured in the fire,*" he mocked.

Horrified, she gasped. "You made that call?!"

Grinning evilly, he nodded. "I thought about setting that fire while he was cooking in that fancy restaurant of his, but this is better. He's off putting out fires, and I've got you. He won't know anything's wrong until it's too late."

"I'll scream!" she cried, tugging wildly against his hold. "Let me go or I swear I'll scream so loud they'll hear me all the way down at the restaurant!"

"Over the sound of those damn sirens?" he taunted as another fire truck, sirens screaming, rushed right past them on the street. "I don't think so. Anyway, I've got this."

Moving in what seemed like slow motion, he pulled a small, deadly pistol from behind his back and pointed it right between her eyes. Frozen, her heart stopping dead in her chest, Annie didn't have to ask him what his intentions were. She could see the murder in his eyes. He was going to kill her.

Chapter 11

"Now that we have that settled," he snarled, "I suggest you get in the van." Nodding toward the faded red van that was illegally parked at the curb, he smiled evilly. "We're going for a little ride."

"No! Please—"

"Oh, you're going to please me, all right. This time I'm going to make sure of it. You shouldn't have gone to the cops." His eyes dark and flat and cold as hell, he tightened his grip on the gun. "You know what I do to people who don't know how to keep their mouths shut? I put a bullet between their eyes and it takes care of the problem every time. And just think—you even know where you'll be spending eternity. Thanks to your loose tongue, you've already got your own grave dug. Oh, the cops filled it in, but you shouldn't have any trouble digging it out again. I've got the shovel all ready for you in the back of the van."

Her eyes locked in revulsion on the gun, Annie felt a whimper squeeze its way through her tight throat and hastily, painfully, swallowed it. No! she thought furiously, stiffening. She wouldn't show this monster weakness—he thrived on it. And she damn well wouldn't drive herself to her own execution without putting up a hell of a fight. He was going to kill her anyway. Why should she make it easy for him?

Standing her ground, praying he couldn't hear the knocking of her knees, she said flatly, "If you're going to kill me, you're going to have to do it here. I'm not going anywhere."

It was the wrong thing to say to a man who had nothing to lose. His eyes narrowing dangerously, he edged closer and snapped the gun under her chin, grinding it into the hollow below her ear. "Don't tempt me, lady," he ground out softly between his teeth. "Killing gets easier every time you do it, and with all the sirens around here, I can take care of you and anyone else who gets in my way and be halfway to Mexico before anyone finds the bodies. You want to do it here? Fine. I'm ready when you are."

"Annie! Hello, dear. I just heard the fire engines and came outside to see what was going on. Did you see all the smoke coming from the Riverwalk? It looks like it's coming from the bend of the river—"

Stiffening at the first sound of Alice Truelove's worried voice, Annie whirled just in time to see the Lone Star Social Club's elderly manager hurrying up the steps to the porch. Her heart stopping in her breast, she wanted to cry out at her to run, but she never had a chance. In the blink of an eye, the man at her side stepped close and jabbed the gun in her ribs so the old woman couldn't see it. One look at the hard glint in his eyes and Annie knew that if she so much as breathed wrong, he'd kill them both.

Forcing a stiff smile, she said, "Hi, Alice. I saw the smoke, too, but I don't think we have anything to worry about.'' The fib stuck in her throat and she had to swallow before she could go on. "You haven't met my…brother, have you? This is…Mike. Mike, this is Alice Truelove. She manages the Lone Star.''

"Great,'' he muttered, pushing the gun harder against her side. "Now let's get out of here.''

Startled, Alice looked back and forth between the two of them. A blind woman couldn't have missed the tension between them, and Alice Truelove had the eyes of a twenty-year-old. Her gaze narrowing slightly, she greeted the man at Annie's side cautiously, then turned to Annie. "You're leaving? But what if the fire's near Joe's Place? Maybe you should wait—''

"I can't.'' Stumbling for an explanation, she blurted out the first bald-faced lie she could come up with. "I'm sure it's coming from farther downriver—Joe's down there and he would have called if there was a problem. And M-Mike and I h-have plans. He's in town for just a short time and wanted to visit our father's grave.''

Bewildered, the older woman blinked in confusion. "And you're going there *now?*''

"I have to,'' she said quickly when the devil at her side nudged her toward the steps. "When Joe gets back, will you tell him that I had to go but I'll be back as soon as I can? I didn't have time to leave him a note.''

"Of course, dear. I'll watch for him and catch him the second he walks through the front door.'' Trailing after them, she frowned worriedly at the top of the steps as they hurried down the sidewalk. "It was nice meeting you, Mike!'' she called after them. "Drive carefully.''

Not sparing her a glance, he only muttered nasty curses in Annie's ear and hustled her around to the passenger door of his van. Jerking it open, he pushed her across the seat so he could follow her inside. "You drive,'' he told her coldly, and forced her into the driver's seat. "And don't even think of trying anything funny or I'll come back later and pop off granny and your old man just for the hell of it."

Annie shuddered, not doubting him for a second. She'd already seen him kill once, and he hadn't even blinked. Nausea swelling in her throat, her heart thudding, she started the van and slowly pulled away from the curb. Joe would come for her. He had to. Clinging to the thought, she scanned the rearview mirror for him expectantly. But the only person in sight was Alice. Still standing on the porch, a frown etching her brow, she watched them drive all the way down the street until they turned the corner and they disappeared from view.

Alice Truelove considered herself a discreet woman who knew how to mind her own business. Oh, she enjoyed playing matchmaker now and again, but she wasn't one of those nosy landladies who was always pushing her nose into the lives of her tenants. That just wasn't her way. The Lone Star Social Club was more like a boardinghouse than an apartment building and while the eight apartments were spacious, they were all within what had once been a single home. And when you were living right on top of people, all you had to do was stand back and listen to find out what was going on.

Unlike most of the other tenants, she'd known Annie and Joe Taylor were in trouble long before most of their other neighbors had. For months, they'd spent too much time apart, and whenever Alice had seen the two of them together, their smiles had been forced, the unhappiness in their eyes plainly visible. As much as she'd hated it, Alice hadn't really been surprised when Annie had left.

But, Lord, she'd been sad for them. And the longer Annie had been gone, the more Alice had worried. No one knew better than she how the Lone Star could draw lovers together, but no amount of charm had seemed to help Annie and Joe.

But she was back now, and Alice had only had to see them together to know that the Taylors were well on their way to finding each other again. She couldn't have been happier for them if they'd been her own kin, but as she stared down the street where Annie had disappeared in a van that Alice had never seen before, she couldn't shake the feeling that something wasn't quite right. If that fire wasn't at Joe's Place, it was too close for comfort, and Annie should have been down there with Joe. And what was the all-fired hurry to get to the cemetery, anyway? Surely they could have waited until later to do that?

Troubled, she started to turn back into the house, telling herself that it was none of her business if Annie and her brother chose to run off when her husband's restaurant could be burning to the ground. She wasn't a busybody and if she wanted to steer clear of earning that tacky title, she would go into her own apartment and not worry about what the Taylors were doing.

But she hadn't known that Annie even had a brother. And she really hadn't liked the looks of him. Or the look of fear in Annie's eyes. If Mike really was her brother as she'd claimed, what could Annie possibly be scared of? And if he wasn't, then who was he and why had Annie gone with him? Busybody or not, Alice knew a bad smell when she smelled one, and she was going to get some answers. Hurrying inside, she headed for the phone.

When she dialed the restaurant, however, all she got was a stilted, recorded message from the phone company that said the number was not in working order. And outside, another fire engine screamed down the street. Worried, she hung up the phone, grabbed the key to her front door, and headed for the Riverwalk and Joe's Place.

Ashes. What had once been one of the most popular restaurants on the Riverwalk was now nothing but a burned-out shell. A black skeleton of charred, still-smoking beams that looked like they would fall in on themselves any second. The last of the flames had been put out, but the firemen who had been called to the scene were taking no chances. Decked out in yellow rubber coats and boots, they kept the water coming, soaking everything in sight.

It was still early yet, but the sound of sirens had brought people running. They stood on both banks of the river, silent, solemn spectators, tourists and locals alike, and watched the scene as grimly as if the loss were their own. Only a few knew that the gray-faced man who stood alone on the fringes of the crowd was the one who had really just lost his life's work.

The smell of burned wood sharp in his nostrils, Joe felt nothing but numbness. Gone, he thought dully. In the time it took to strike a match, it was all gone.

"It looks like it was arson, Mr. Taylor," the fire inspector said grimly as he stomped through the ashes to join him. "It went up too fast and was too hot to be an electrical fire. If I had to guess, I'd say it was gasoline, but it'll be a while before we can pin down what accelerant was used. I've already notified the police. They're going to want to talk to you."

Nodding, Joe stared blindly at the disaster before him and tried to make sense of it. But how could anyone explain an arsonist? He readily admitted he wasn't a saint—he hadn't gone through life without making an enemy or two. But this wasn't the act of a business competitor who might be hacked at him for lowering the price of his lunch special.

Oh, no. This was vicious, without conscience, the work of a bastard who had wanted to strike a low blow. He had.

And Joe didn't know a soul who fit that description. Not one. Anyone who knew him knew that he was a reasonable man—if they had a beef with him, all they had to do was discuss the problem with him. Not burn his restaurant to the ground.

"We also have a witness who claims he saw the arsonist," the fire inspector continued. "The only problem is, we don't know how reliable he is. He's a homeless man, a laid-off construction worker who promised to tell us everything we wanted to hear if we'd just buy him breakfast. He might just be looking for a free meal."

Only half listening at first, Joe snapped to attention. "He saw the bastard set the fire? Where is he? I want to talk to him."

"I thought you might," the other man replied, his mouth curling in a tight smile. "C'mon, he's over here."

Joe followed him over to the spot that had been the Riverwalk entrance of the restaurant. Now it was nothing but a pile of blackened bricks. Beside it waited a gaunt, middle-aged man with a grizzled jaw and bloodshot eyes. His clothes were wrinkled but clean, his canvas tennis shoes worn and holey. Not the least bit intimidated, he held out his hand to Joe and introduced himself. "How do you do, sir? I'm Seth Bishop. You're the owner?"

Joe nodded and gave his hand a firm shake. "Joe Taylor. I understand that you saw the slime who did this. Can you describe him for me?"

"It was right before sunup," the older man replied, "so the light wasn't real good, but I could tell he was a tall fella—at least six-two or three. But he wasn't real heavy, maybe around two hundred at the most. He was dressed all in black, so he sort of blended in with the shadows."

There was a commotion by the barriers the police had put up to keep the crowd back, and Joe looked up to see Alice Truelove hurrying over to him. "Joe! Thank God," she sighed. "I've been worried sick—"

"I'm fine, Alice," he assured her quickly. "Just a minute and I'll be right with you." Turning back to Seth Bishop, he asked, "What about this jerk's face? Would you recognize him again if you saw him?"

"Oh, yeah. He was an ugly son of a bitch...." Suddenly aware of what he'd said, he cast a quick look at Alice and mumbled, "Sorry, ma'am. I didn't mean no disrespect," before turning his attention back to Joe. "He was sort of shifty-looking, Mr. Taylor, with a square jaw and a big nose, and one of those marine haircuts. I think his hair was brown, but it was so short, it was hard to tell. And he had one of those little red cans of gasoline with him. That's why I noticed him in the first place. He kept looking around real nervous-like, then disappeared into the bushes on the side of your building. Next thing I knew, the place was going up like a bonfire and he was racing up the stairs to street level down there by the Commerce Street Bridge."

Startled, Alice gasped. "Why, that sounds like Annie's brother!"

Distracted, Joe frowned in confusion. "What are you talking about? Annie doesn't have a brother."

Her worst fears confirmed, the old lady blanched. "Oh, dear, I was afraid of that. But Annie insisted he was her brother and they were going to their father's grave. I thought it was odd. The fire trucks were screaming and the smoke was coming from this direction, but she insisted that she and her brother had to go to the cemetery right away—"

"Cemetery? What cemetery?" Alarmed, Joe grabbed her

by the arm. "Start at the beginning, Alice. Where did you see Annie and this man?"

"On the front porch of the house." Her beautifully lined cheeks as pale as parchment, she told him everything she could remember about the odd conversation with Annie and the man she'd introduced as her brother. "She said his name was Mike and he was only in town for a short while," she concluded. "They were going to their father's grave, but they wouldn't be gone long. Since you were gone, she wanted me to be sure and tell you where she'd gone when you got back. Then they left in a red van. Annie was driving." Distressed, she looked up at him with tears in her eyes. "She's in trouble, isn't she? I shouldn't have let her go. If something happens to her because of me…"

She couldn't finish the thought. His face carved in harsh lines, Joe told himself there was no reason to panic. Annie was still leery of men she didn't know—she never would have gone off with anyone she wasn't comfortable with. Alice must have misunderstood. After all, she was pushing eighty, and sometimes her hearing wasn't very good. Annie could have said this Mike character was a friend's brother or something like that, and Alice just missed it.

It was the only logical explanation, but it did nothing to ease the jumble of nerves that coiled in his gut. No one knew better than he did just how sharp Alice Truelove was. She'd been managing the Lone Star Social Club for longer than anyone could remember and could tell you the name of every tenant who had ever lived there. She didn't make mistakes about anything to do with her renters.

So who had Annie gone off with? And why was she driving some strange man's van? She hadn't driven since she'd lost her memory, and in the past, she'd never liked to drive other people's vehicles. What the hell was going on?

Questions pulling at him, doubts churning like acid in his stomach, he slipped an arm around Alice's shoulders and gave her a reassuring squeeze. "Let's don't go jumping to any conclusions. We don't actually know that she's in trouble. What about the cop that was assigned to watch over her?"

"He was nowhere in sight," she said worriedly. "And she looked scared, Joe. She tried to pretend that everything was okay, but she had that same look in her eyes that she had when she first came back to you. You know—that terrified, hurt look that just made you want to wrap your arms around her and promise her she was safe."

His jaw clenching, Joe nodded stiffly. Oh, yes, he remembered, all right. It was a look he'd hoped to never see in her eyes again. Dropping his arm from her shoulders, he dug in his pocket for his wallet and pulled out a twenty dollar bill. "This doesn't come close to showing my appreciation, Mr. Bishop," he said quietly as he pressed it into the other man's hands. "But it should get you a good meal. If I can ever do anything for you, you'll find me right here, rebuilding this place. Now, if you'll excuse me, I've got to see about my wife."

With Alice at his side, he hurried back to the apartment, hoping against hope that Annie had returned while he was gone. But the apartment was empty and looked perfectly normal. She'd even locked the door when she'd left. There was no note, nothing to show why she had walked out of their apartment with a stranger looking scared to death.

The silence and a worry he couldn't control tearing at him, he turned back from a quick inspection of the apartment to find Alice standing just inside the front door, twisting her hands. "I think we need to talk to Sam," he said flatly, and headed next door.

* * *

Sam had a rare day off, but that only meant one thing. Instead of working down at the police station, he worked at home. A cup of coffee growing cold at his side, he grabbed one of the unsolved case files he'd brought home from the office with him and spread it out on the kitchen table in front of him. Concentrating on its contents, he didn't hear the knock at the door. Then the doorbell rang.

He almost ignored it. He had a hell of a lot of work to do, and if that was Alice, she'd want to chat, and he just didn't have the time. She was a sweet old lady, but she didn't like to see anyone unhappy, and she'd been trying to find him a nice woman ever since he and his wife had divorced a month and a half ago. So far, he hadn't had the heart to tell her she was wasting her time.

The doorbell rang again and he gave up in defeat. "Hold your horses. I'm coming."

He strode into the living room, promising himself he was going to get rid of his visitor just as soon as he could. But the second he jerked open the front door and saw Joe and Alice standing there, their faces drawn and grave, he immediately motioned them inside. "What is it? What's wrong?"

"We're not sure anything is," Joe told him as Alice preceded him into the apartment. "The restaurant burned to the ground this morning—"

"What! I heard the sirens, but I didn't realize it was the restaurant."

"It was set," he said flatly. "But that's not the worst of it. While I was down there taking care of things, Annie left the apartment with a man she introduced to Alice as her brother. Supposedly, they were going to visit their father's grave."

Surprised, Sam frowned. "I didn't know Annie had a brother."

"She doesn't. Whoever this jerk was, he matched a witness's description of the man who set the fire at the restaurant."

Swearing, Sam shut the door and motioned them both to sit down. "What the hell happened to the uniform I had assigned to your place?"

"I don't know. He was there when I left—that's the last time I saw him. Maybe he got called away because of the fire. Things were pretty intense there for a while. The fire department was afraid the fire was going to spread to the buildings on either side of the restaurant, and they were calling in all the help they could get to evacuate everyone."

"That's no excuse," Sam growled. "He was ordered not to leave his post no matter what. He should have known the fire was a possible distraction. Damn rookies!"

"Don't blame him," Joe said bitterly. "I should have seen it, too, but I got a call that it was the restaurant, and I never even thought that Annie was the real target."

"We'll get her back, Joe. How long as she been gone? Give me a description of this man she was with. Did anyone see what kind of vehicle they were in?"

"I did." Her mouth twisting with distaste, Alice gave him a detailed description of Annie's companion. "They left in a faded red GMC van and turned west onto Commerce. Annie was driving. I'm not sure what year the van was, but it wasn't one of those fancy new ones."

"Did you get a glance at the license plate?"

Regretfully, she shook her head. "I was so upset that Annie would go off with that man when Joe's restaurant might be burning that I didn't notice." Worried, she said, "You are going to catch him, aren't you?"

"We're damn sure going to try," he growled. "But I can tell you right now, folks, we haven't got a hell of a lot to go on. Why would Annie say they were going to her father's grave? Is he buried here in town?''

"No, he's buried in Oklahoma.'' A thought hit Joe then and chilled his blood. His eyes flew to Sam's. "A grave. She said she was going to a grave. Do you think she was trying to tell me the bastard was taking her to where she buried Freeman?''

The words were hardly out of his mouth before Sam was quickly striding to the phone. "You may be right. It would be a smart move on his part since we've already exhumed the body and investigated the scene. He wouldn't be expecting us to go back there and probably figures he's a regular Einstein for thinking of it.''

Snatching up the phone, he called the police station and spoke to another detective. Quickly and concisely, he gave him a description of the van and Annie's companion. "When last seen, the van was going west on Commerce. The suspect had Annie Taylor with him, and I believe they're headed north on I10 to the Driscoe Ranch. No weapons were seen, but we have to assume that Mrs. Taylor is with him under duress and the suspect is armed and dangerous. Get backup out there to where Freeman's body was found. I'll meet them there.''

When he hung up, his only thought was to grab his gun and car keys and run for the door. The only problem was Joe was standing right in front of the front door, blocking it. "I'm going with you.''

His tone was hard and curt and would brook no argument. Sam gave him one anyone. "You know you can't go, Joe. This is a police matter. Let us handle it.''

"She's my wife.''

"You could get hurt.''

"She's my wife.''

It was an argument Sam had no response for. Swearing,

he scowled at his friend and gave serious consideration to cuffing him to the nearest solid piece of furniture. But if it was his wife in the hands of a piece of scum, he wouldn't be able to stand on the sidelines and watch someone else try to save her, either.

"Dammit, Joe, I know that and I don't blame you for being worried. But you can't help Annie now. If anything, you'll be in the way..." Seeing the granite set of Joe's chin, he gave up with a muttered curse. "I could arrest you for interfering with a police investigation. You know that, don't you?"

Joe only shrugged. "Do what you have to do, but hurry up and make up your mind. Annie needs me."

"For all we know, she could come back any second. You should be here."

Eager to help, Alice said, "I'll watch for her. If she comes in, I'll call the station and they'll notify you."

Trapped, Sam could do nothing but give in. Sighing in defeat, he scribbled his cellular number on a pad by the phone. "Just call me direct, Alice, if you see Annie or hear from her. C'mon, Joe. Let's go."

She couldn't lose control now. Joe was coming for her.

Annie knew it as surely as she knew that she had never been more miserable in her life than she had in the two months that they'd been separated. Tears threatened then, hot, scalding tears that thickened in her throat and burned her eyes, making it nearly impossible to see, let alone drive. No, she told herself fiercely. She couldn't think about that right now, couldn't remember the things they'd said to each other, the way they'd hurt each other. If she did, she'd fall apart, and she'd be damned if she'd give her captor the satisfaction. She'd rather eat worms.

Dashing at her wet cheeks, she forced down the lump of

emotion in her throat and stiffened her spine. Her heart slamming against her ribs, her voice carefully expressionless, she asked, "Where do you want me to go?"

Smug now that he had her right where he wanted her, he leaned back in his seat and eyed her with cool deliberation, the gun he still held on her not wavering so much as a centimeter. "Turn right at the next intersection and stay on San Pedro until I tell you to turn."

Following his instructions, Annie almost wilted in relief. He hadn't been serious about taking her back to the Driscoe Ranch. He'd just been pulling her chain, trying to frighten her to death. But that was okay because this was better. Much better. San Pedro was one of the city's major thoroughfares and ran for miles through one neighborhood after another. It went right past San Antonio College, where there were almost always people about. If she kept her eyes open and she was lucky, she just might be able to spot someone, *anyone,* she could signal to for help.

Her hands damp on the steering wheel, she checked the rearview mirror and the side ones, then glanced ahead, her eyes constantly searching for the light bars of a patrol car. But the traffic was disappointingly normal, and as they drove past the college, there wasn't so much as a security guard in sight.

Watching her through narrow, beady eyes that missed little, her companion warned coldly, "Don't even think about trying something, you little bitch. You hear me? I've got no reason to keep you alive, so don't push me." Signaling with the gun, he motioned for her to change to the left lane. "Get over. We're turning left on Hildebrand."

Her heart froze in her breast. If they drove far enough west, Hildebrand led right to Interstate 10. From there, it was only ten miles to the Driscoe Ranch. No! she cried silently. This was all just a cruel joke. He couldn't really be taking her back there. He wouldn't! He couldn't be that sadistic.

But this was the same man who had looked Robert Freeman right in the eyes and put a bullet in his head.

Nausea curling into her stomach, she slowed down for the turn onto Hildebrand and silently ordered herself to get a grip. Panicking now wasn't going to do anything but get her killed. She had to stay calm and keep her wits about her and stall as long as she could to give Joe and the police a chance to find her. Because they would come for her. Going as slow as she dared, she turned at the next intersection like an old woman who had a carton of eggs on the front seat and was afraid of jostling them.

"Get on with it," he ordered tersely. "Now!"

"There's a school zone—"

"The hell there is!" Uncaring that someone in a passing car might see, he held the gun so she could see him caress the trigger. "I said drive and I meant it."

Her heart in her throat, she had no choice but to pick up her speed to the posted speed limit. Then, all too soon, she could see the interstate in the distance. Her fingers gripped the wheel until her knuckles turned white. *Act normal,* a voice whispered in her ear. *Don't let him see that you're afraid.*

But the monster thrived on fear—he could smell it in the air. His mouth curling into a sinister smile, he said, "Go north on I10."

"No!"

Wicked laughter whispered over her, making her skin crawl. "Oh, yes," he purred. "You know the way."

She turned because she didn't have any choice. Because he was going to kill her no matter what she did, and the longer she could put it off, the more time she had to think up some kind of way out of this nightmare. She had a baby to think of, to protect, a husband who would blame himself the rest of his life if something happened to her. She had to do something!

But short of running the van into another car and chance hurting herself and the baby, not to mention a total innocent in the other vehicle, there was nothing she could do while she was driving. So she drove, reluctantly following his roughly growled directions, every muscle in her body slowly, painfully, tightening as they drew closer and closer to the spot where he'd forced her to bury Freeman after he'd killed him in cold blood in the Transit Tower parking garage.

Then, before she was ready for it, she was leaving the road behind and taking the van over a rough path carved out of ranch land that was thick with cedar and cactus. Within minutes, the city, civilization, *help,* was left behind. She braked to a stop and felt her breath lock in her throat as her eyes fell on the mound of dirt under a cedar tree fifty yards in front of the van.

It looked like exactly what it was—a grave. Once Freeman's body had been removed, the police had pushed the dirt back over the shallow pit, but she didn't fool herself into thinking it would be empty for long. Once before, he'd intended this to be her final resting place, and she'd outsmarted him. He wouldn't let her do it again.

"Get out," he said coldly, shattering the silence. "You've got some work to do."

Her hands starting to shake, she climbed out of the van and looked around wildly for a way out. But she was trapped as surely as if he had her backed up against the wrong end of a dead-end alley. Last time, after she'd knocked him cold with the shovel, the dark shadows of the night had covered her like a shroud and he hadn't been able to follow her. But it was broad daylight now, and there was nowhere to run, nowhere to hide. The second she tried to make a break for it, he'd shoot her.

Trapped, she stood quivering by the van, her heart jerking out a frantic rhythm as he came around to join her. Now, she thought, swallowing a sob. He would do it now. And there was nothing she could do to stop him!

But instead of shooting her, he grabbed her by the arm, startling a gasp from her, and hauled her over to the pile of dirt. Forcing her down on her knees, he aimed the gun right at her head. "Dig!"

Stunned, she stuttered, "I—I can't. I h-haven't got a shovel."

He laughed, truly amused, but there was nothing funny about the hate that glistened in his eyes. "You think I'm stupid enough to give you a shovel after what you did the last time? Not on your life, bitch. Use your hands."

She couldn't. She couldn't put her hands in the same dirt she'd dropped by shovelfuls on Robert Freeman's pasty face. Not without gagging. With no amnesia to protect her now, time spiraled backward in a dizzying rush, and all too easily she was sucked back into the nightmare of the fateful night she'd watched the banker die. She could feel the chilly slap of the wind against her skin, the terror that burned her throat and stomach, the bile that rose to her mouth every time her eyes inadvertently found the small, deadly bullet hole in the center of his forehead.

And now it was her own grave she had to dig.

Trembling, her fingers curled into fists. This wasn't the end. She couldn't let it be. She'd always been an optimist, the one who fought against all odds when people all around her were giving up and wimping out. Even when she'd left Joe, she hadn't given up on their marriage, though there'd been a lot of people who had been quick to accuse her of doing just that. She'd just loved him so much that she'd had to resort to drastic measures or risk losing him forever.

She had to do the same thing now. She couldn't give up just because things had gotten a little sticky. The fiend standing over her had made a mistake with her the night he'd killed Freeman—there was a good chance he would do so again. All she had to do was be ready.

But it was hard. God, it was hard! She couldn't seem to stop shaking or draw a deep breath. Dizzy, the gun like an obscenity just inches from her head, she raised up on her knees and bent over the pile of dirt, forcing herself not to cringe. Scooping it up in her trembling hands, she turned and tossed it aside, then bent to the task again. And again. Time ceased to exist. There was only the feel of the dirt on her hands, the smell of it and cedar in her nose, and the bitter taste of fear on her tongue.

Working in rhythm to the frantic pounding of her heart, she zoned out and couldn't have said when she first noticed that the man at her side had become almost hypnotized by the repetition of her movements. The hand pointing the gun at her head was steady as a rock, but the finger that had mockingly played with the trigger when she'd first started to dig had relaxed and now barely touched it. Slanting a look at her tormentor beneath her lashes without once breaking her rhythm, she caught a quick glimpse of slightly glazed eyes and bored features.

For the first time in what seemed like hours, hope stirred in her breast. She was more than halfway through hollowing out the grave. Whenever he decided it was deep enough, he wouldn't say a word—he'd just pull the trigger. If she was ever going to do anything, she had to do it now.

There was no time to plan, no time to do anything but act. Her fingers scooping up two handfuls of dirt, she turned just as she had every other time…and tossed it in his face.

Chapter 12

"**Y**ou bitch!"

Snarling, he dropped the gun and grabbed at his eyes, and that was all the opening Annie needed. She whirled, a sob lodging into her throat, and darted into the trees.

"Damn you, come back here! Do you hear me?" he screamed as he dropped to his knees and scrambled for the gun. "You come back here or I swear to God you'll beg me to kill you when I finally catch up with you!"

He cursed her to hell and back, but she never looked back. She didn't dare. Her lungs straining, the pounding of her heart booming like thunder in her head, she ran, dodging trees and bushes, whimpering as cedar branches slapped at her face and grabbed at her clothes. From nowhere, a vine reached out to snag at her foot. She stumbled, crying out in surprise.

And her tormentor heard her. Lifting his head like the devil scenting a sinner, he blinked the last of the dirt from his eyes and spied her thirty feet to his right, half hidden among the trees. A nasty grin stretched across his thin-lipped mouth as his fingers closed around the gun. Straightening, he took aim.

The roar of the gun going off sounded like an exploding cannon amid the thick stand of cedars. Annie screamed and dived for cover, knowing as she did so that it was too late. He'd had a clear shot and she'd been a sitting duck. Her breathing ragged, she cowered in the dirt, waiting for the pain to register.

But the only place she hurt was where she'd scraped her knee against a rock and ripped the skin away. Not questioning her good fortune, she was up and running in a heartbeat, tearing through the trees like a madwoman, her only thought to get away.

Caught up in the terror that shrouded her brain, she never saw her kidnapper curse and take aim again, never saw Sam Kelly step out of the trees and shoot the gun from his hand. All she heard was the report of the gun. Sobbing, her lungs burning, she ran blindly, without a thought to where she was going, tripping over rocks and cacti, hurting herself and too scared to care.

Sweat trickling into her eyes, she didn't see the man who stepped out of the bushes in front of her until it was too late. She plowed into him, and, lightning quick, his arms closed around her like a trap.

"No!" Screaming, she pounded at him with her fists, striking out at his head and shoulders and connecting with every blow. "Let go, damn you!"

Joe flinched and tightened his hold on her. "It's all right, honey. You're okay. I've got you now. You're safe."

Panic choking her, she didn't hear. She fought him wildly, scratching and biting at him, fear for her unborn baby giving her added strength. "No! I won't let you hurt me again! Do you hear me, you slimeball? I'll kill you—"

Joe grunted at a particularly well-aimed blow to his middle and grabbed her hands, trapping them against his chest. "Annie, it's me. Joe. I'm not going to hurt you, sweetheart. *Look at me!*"

The softly grated words penetrated the terror gripping her, and with a start of surprise, she glanced up. Her eyes, wide and unfocused, abruptly cleared. "J-Joe?"

If he lived to be a hundred, Joe didn't think he would ever forget the broken sound of his name on her lips. His throat tight, tenderness flooding his heart, he had to swallow twice before he could say thickly, "Sam got him, honey. He's never going to hurt you again."

Dazed, she glanced around. "Sam? Sam's here? Where—"

"Over there in the trees," he said, nodding back behind her where Sam and a half dozen uniformed officers already had her kidnapper in cuffs. "Alice rushed down to the restaurant just as soon as you left and gave me your message. Thank God, she ran into you or we never would have figured out where he'd taken you."

Emotion clutching his heart, the need to touch her almost more than he could bear, he gently swept her hair back from her face with fingers that were still far from steady. Close, he thought, shaken. They'd come so damn close to not reaching her in time. With backup behind him, Sam had broken every speed limit, but then as they neared the Driscoe Ranch, he'd had to cut the sirens and slow to a crawl as they made their way through the cedars to the creek at the back of the property. To do anything else would have tipped Annie's kidnapper off to their presence and probably have gotten her killed, but the silent, careful drive through the ranch had taken ten years off Joe's life.

Then, as they'd approached on foot the site where Freeman's body had been found, he'd seen Annie running through the trees like a wild woman, falling, and a bastard with a gun take aim. At her, the woman he loved more than life itself. His heart had literally stopped in his chest.

He could have lost her right there. Just that easily, he could have lost her forever. Sick to his soul at the thought, he couldn't stop touching her and assuring himself that she was really all right. "It's over, sweetheart. The son of a bitch is in custody and we all saw him try to kill you. Even if you never remember what he did to you that night in the parking garage, he's going to jail. He'll never come near you again."

Desperate to believe him, she stared up at him searchingly. Behind her, she heard Sam reading her tormentor his rights, but it was the rock-solid steadiness in Joe's eyes and the feel of his hands on her that convinced her more than anything that the nightmare was finally over. She was safe.

Terror drained from her in a rush. Light-headed, her knees threatening to buckle, she started to tremble and couldn't stop. She felt Joe stiffen in alarm and tried to tell him she was okay, but her throat was hot and tight. "Oh, J-Joe," she choked, and threw herself into his arms. Bursting into tears, she clung to him as if she would never let him go.

Later, she never knew how long she cried. It seemed like forever. Her eyes burning, her throat raw, she cried because she was safe, because nothing could hurt her while Joe had his arms around her, because she'd been so afraid that she would die and he would never know what had happened to her. But most of all, she cried because she remembered. And it hurt.

Sweeping her up off her feet, Joe carried her to Sam's car, murmuring to her all the time. "Go ahead and cry, sweetheart. That's it, let it all out. After everything you've been through, you're entitled."

"I remember," she cried, pressing her face against his throat, soaking his shirt. "I finally remembered."

Joe's heart constricted, missed a beat, then stumbled back into rhythm. Instinctively, his arms tightened around her, denial instantly rising to his tongue. He knew she needed to remember—he wanted her to—but not yet, dammit! Not until they'd had more time together. Not until he'd won her love back and she'd at least give him a chance to work things out between them before she walked out on him again.

"We'll deal with that later, honey," he said, shushing her. "Right now it's more important that you're okay. Did he hurt you? You're white as a sheet. Maybe we should have a doctor take a look at you..."

She sniffed, wiping at her cheeks. "No, I'm all right. Really. I'm just a little shaky. I'll be fine once I get away from here."

The sound of a siren drowned out the last of her words, and they both looked up in time to see an ambulance race through the cedars and brake to a stop in a cloud of dust. A shout from Sam drew the paramedics, who burst from the vehicle to the spot where his men had the suspect handcuffed and surrounded. Sitting on a fallen log, his mouth twisted with bitterness and blood dripping from the makeshift bandage wrapped around his forearm, the wounded man stared stonily ahead, ignoring them all.

Leaving the suspect to the uniformed officers and the paramedics, Sam strode over to Annie and Joe, his eyes narrowing as they took in Annie's pale face and tearful eyes. "What did he do to you, Annie? If he so much as laid a finger on you, I need to know."

"Nothing...this time," she assured him. "But on the night Freeman was killed, he tried to rape me."

The scowl darkening his brow didn't ease so much as a

fraction, but there was a definite glint of satisfaction in his eyes. "You got your memory back."

She nodded. "After Joe left to check out the fire at the restaurant, I got a call that he'd been hurt in the fire—"

"What?!"

"That's how he got me out of the apartment," she told Joe, wincing at his roar. "I thought his voice sounded familiar, but as soon as he said you were hurt, all I could think about was getting to you. I rushed out of the house, and there he was, waiting for me on the front porch. The second I saw him, it all just came rushing back."

Her mouth flattening into a grim line, she turned hard eyes on the man who had put her through hell twice. "He and Freeman were partners and were supposed to skip the country that night that I came across them by accident in the Transit Tower parking garage."

Remembering, she felt her blood run cold and buried her hands in her jacket pockets. "When Mr. Larkin didn't make our appointment at eight, I figured he'd had some trouble coming in from Houston. So I waited another hour just in case, then headed back to the parking garage."

Disgust, self-directed, twisted her mouth. "I should have been paying more attention—I know that now—but I was ticked that Larkin hadn't had the courtesy to at least call me and cancel, and I didn't even notice how deserted the garage was. Then when I was almost back to my car, I heard Freeman and that scumbag over there arguing about how they were going to split up the money. That's when I realized they'd robbed the bank. Freeman claimed he'd taken most of the risk, so he should get a larger percentage. That's when he shot him," she said, distaste twisting her mouth as she stared at her kidnapper. "He didn't even try to reason with him. He just pulled out a gun and shot him."

Her eyes stark with the horror of it, she blinked up at

Joe and Sam. "It all happened so fast, I didn't have time to try to hide. Not that it would have done any good," she added. "There were only two cars on that floor—my Volvo and the van—so there was no place to hide. I don't remember making any noise, but the next thing I knew, he was holding the gun on me."

"He made you help him load the body in the van, didn't he?" Sam guessed. "That's why you had blood all over your clothes."

She nodded, shivering. "He told me if I didn't do what he said, he was going to kill me right there. I had no reason not to believe him."

Joe swore long and hard. "Goddamn his filthy soul, I hope he burns in hell."

"After the body was in the van, he forced me in the back with it and drove out here," she continued. "The whole time I dug the grave, he was holding the gun on me, just daring me to give him a reason to pull the trigger." Her voice cracked then, and she had to swallow before she could continue. "I kept telling myself that if I just went along with him, he wouldn't hurt me. But then after I finished burying the body, he…h-he grabbed me a-and—"

"That's enough," Joe growled. "Dammit, Sam, she's pregnant! She's been through enough. I'm taking her home!"

She would have liked nothing better, but the truth had been locked up inside her for too long, and she had to get it out. "No, I have to finish this now," she insisted. Lifting her chin, her eyes met his unflinchingly. "He didn't rape me, but it wasn't from lack of trying. When I fought him, he told me he was going to put a bullet in my head when he was through with me, then bury me on top of Freeman. That's when I hit him in the head with the shovel."

"You should have aimed a hell of a lot lower and cut

him off at the…knees," Sam amended grimly. "Knocking him senseless was a good start, though. So how'd you get home?"

"I walked," she said simply. "All night."

"Why didn't you call me?" Joe demanded. "You know I would have come for you."

He didn't so much as mention their separation, but she heard the hurt in his voice and knew what he was really asking. Even though they'd been separated, surely she must have known that she could call on him for help. Why hadn't she?

"I was terrified." Just thinking about it again made her want to fold in on herself and cry. "There are some houses a couple of miles down the road, but I was so scared, I wouldn't go anywhere near them. All I could think about was getting away. And getting home."

To him.

At the time, she hadn't realized that she was instinctively making her way to him. Her brain had been on automatic pilot; her feet had had a will of their own. But deep down inside, her heart had led her to the one person who could make her feel safe.

"I was so afraid that he was following me that I didn't even turn on a light once I got in the apartment," she continued huskily. "I took a shower in the dark, then went to bed. When I woke up in the morning, I didn't remember anything."

"Did he say anything about the money?" Sam asked. "Freeman took half a million from the bank. That's not exactly the kind of change you carry around in your pocket."

"They packaged it up and sent it to an apartment they'd already rented in Acapulco," she said promptly. "The son of a bitch was real smug about that, especially after he killed Freeman. The whole time he made me dig the grave, he kept bragging about how he'd get to keep all the cash now. All he had to do was fly down there and pick it up, and he could live the rest of his life like a king.''

Sam snorted. ''Now I guess he's going to have to eat those words, huh? Idiot. If he'd run for the border instead of trying to scare you to death, he might have gotten away with it. Now, all he's got to look forward to is a nice long stretch in Huntsville with the rest of the pond scum.'' Relieved, he shot Annie a broad grin. ''You just made my job a whole lot simpler. If he was stupid enough to put that money in the mail, then we can bring the feds in. They can find out where he sent it, and when, and get it back.''

Turning to Joe, he tossed him his keys. ''Take her home, man. I'm going to be tied up at the station for a while, so you might as well take the Jeep. If I need a ride later, I'll give you a call.''

Joe didn't have to be told twice. Bundling her into the Wagoneer, he climbed behind the wheel and headed home. He tried to tell himself they could relax now—it was over—but he only had to look at Annie's face to know that it was a long way from that. Pale and silent, her eyes not quite meeting his, she sat beside him, well within touching distance but somehow out of his reach.

Had she remembered the baby wasn't his? he wondered, only to immediately reject the idea. No! She was his and so was the baby. He loved her, dammit, and somehow he had to find a way to convince her that they belonged together, no matter what. Because he wasn't going to lose her. Not after they'd just found each other again. Somehow they'd find a way to work it out. But first he had to show her how much she meant to him.

He hadn't forgotten how she'd reacted when she'd first started to remember the nightmare she'd been through, and the second they got back to the apartment, he walked her straight back to their bathroom and turned on the shower. Without a word, he turned back to her and reached for the hem of her sweater.

"Joe!"

"Shh," he soothed. "I smell like smoke and I know you want to get the feel of that bastard's hands off you. Let me take care of you. We'll both feel better after a nice hot shower."

He needed to pamper her, to wrap her close and take the shadows from her eyes. They would have to talk—he knew that as well as she did—but not yet. Not until he had a chance to touch her and hold her. If he lost her after that, at least he would have these minutes—and the last few weeks—to remember.

Slowly, piece by piece, he gently peeled her clothes from her, then tore off his own and urged her under the warm spray of the shower. In the time it took to draw in a sharp breath, they were both soaked. Without a word, he reached for the soap and worked up a thick, cleansing lather between his hands.

Steam swirled around them, encasing them in a world of misty heat and tenderness. The pounding of his heart slow and heavy in his chest, he washed her gently, running his hands over her long after the soap had slid from her body and washed down the drain. A sigh rippled through her; her breathing changed ever so slightly—he heard it, felt it. And still he stroked her, warming her, heating her until her eyes grew languorous, the muscles of her neck weak. With a soundless moan, she leaned her head against his chest and groaned.

A smile pulled at the corners of his mouth. "That's it, baby," he rasped softly. "Just relax."

He washed her all over, until she was flushed and

boneless and came apart in his hands. Her knees had long since deserted her, and with a murmur for her to hang on, he shut off the water, propped her against the wall, and reached for a towel. His body hard and tight with need, he dried them both, then scooped her up and carried her to bed.

He ached to make love to her, but he only settled her against him and pulled the covers over them. When he had her where he wanted her, her head against his shoulder, her body snug against his, he sighed. Now, with nothing between them, they could talk.

"Before you say anything," he said quietly, "I want you to know that I love you. I fell in love with you the first time I ever laid eyes on you and that hasn't changed. It never will. The whole time you were gone, I was miserable."

"Joe—"

Taking the hand she pressed to his mouth to stop his confession, he dropped a kiss to her knuckles, then trapped her fingers against his heart and held them there. "No, I need to say this," he insisted. "Now that you've got your memory back, you know who the baby's father is. If you were so unhappy when you left me that you turned to somebody else like you threatened to, then I've got to take the blame for part of that. I should have listened to you."

Tears pooled in her eyes. "Oh, Joe, there wasn't another man," she was finally able to tell him without a doubt. "I just said that to shake you up. I was pregnant when I left you."

The announcement fell between them like a lit firecracker. She saw shock, then hurt flare in his eyes and would have given anything to take the admission back, but she couldn't. For too long, they had avoided talking to each other about anything important, and on the rare occasions when they hadn't been able to sidestep a discussion about the pitiful state of their marriage, they'd done nothing but argue and cast blame. But now they had a baby to consider, and it had to stop.

"You knew you were pregnant when you left?"

"That's *why* I left."

He took the news like a slap to the face, and she ached for him. God, they'd made each other so unhappy! "I didn't know what else to do," she confessed huskily. Scrambling up, the sheet pressed to her breasts, she sat facing him and tried to make him understand. "You weren't ready to be a father—you kept finding excuses to put it off—but we were going to have a baby, anyway. All your time was wrapped up in the restaurant, and then when I found out you were going to open a second one without even discussing it with me, it just seemed like we were going in two different directions."

His shoulders propped against the headboard, he had to admit she was right. "That was my fault. I should have told you. I was going to, but I knew you'd hate the idea, and I kept putting it off, hoping to find the perfect time. But it just never came up. You were always so touchy about the time I spent working—"

"Because you were spending seventy hours a week at the restaurant and I never saw you! I was afraid you were turning into my father right before my eyes, and I was turning into my mother. I could see myself raising our child alone while you made more and more money, and it scared me to death."

Still afraid of that, she said soberly, "I can count on the fingers of one hand the times my father did things with me and my mother when I was growing up. For most of my childhood, he was a stranger to me. I didn't—I *don't*—want that for our baby. So I left." She tried to smile, but could only manage a weak grimace of pain. "Looking back now, I can see it was a stupid thing to do, but I thought I could shake you up and make you realize that I was more important to you than your restaurant. But you worked harder than ever while I was gone. I checked."

He didn't deny it—he couldn't. It was true. He'd spent every waking moment at the restaurant during the two months she was gone. And there'd been a lot of nights he'd slept on his office couch rather than go home to an empty apartment, an empty bed.

"I couldn't face this apartment without you," he said bluntly. "So I buried myself in work. I had to or I would have come after you even though I promised to give you some space."

When she only looked at him, unconvinced, it was all he could do not to snatch her back into his arms. They'd always communicated better in bed than anywhere else, and all he had to do was hold her, kiss her, and they'd both forget that there'd ever been a cross word between them.

But making love wouldn't solve this problem. Their whole future lay in the balance, and unless he could find a way to convince her that he was nothing like her father, he was going to lose her. This time for good.

Taking her hand, he rubbed his thumb in slow circles across her knuckles. "I understand your fears, honey, but put yourself in my shoes for a minute. You know what my childhood was like. While your daddy was devoting all his time to working, mine couldn't keep a job. Half the time, birthdays and Christmas were just another day of the week. Oh, he always had an excuse, and according to him, it was never his fault. But it was, dammit!" he said resentfully. "He was just flat out irresponsible. I swore when I had a wife and kids, I would never do to them what my old man did to me and my mother. That's why I worked like a fiend.

It was never just about making money. You wanted a baby and so did I, but it was important to me to make sure we were financially secure first. Anything else would have been unacceptable.''

Her eyes, dark with despair, lifted to his. "But no one ever thinks they're really financially secure. Especially when they have children. You'll want to make sure you have enough put away to take care of me and the baby if something happens to you. Then if we have another baby, you'll need to put more away. Don't you see? It's a vicious circle that never ends. The next thing you know, our children will be grown and you won't even know them. Or me.''

"You really think I would let that happen? Where was I when Sam thought you needed to get out of town for a while?''

"With me at the cabin, but—''

"That right," he cut in. "And we weren't just there a day or two, either. I was prepared to stay weeks, even months, if that's what it took to keep you safe. And then today, when the restaurant went up in flames, I didn't even think twice about it once Alice told me you were in trouble. Yes, the restaurant is important to me, but I *love* you. None of it means a damn without you.''

He saw the doubt in her eyes, the desperate need to believe.

Aching to kiss her, to draw her into his arms and show her that the trials they had been through had only strengthened their love, he couldn't do anything but tighten his hold on her hand. If she didn't know in her heart that he was sincere, all the kisses in the world wouldn't do any good.

"If I learned anything over the last couple of months, honey, it's how precious our time is together," he said huskily. "We don't know when it's going to be snatched away from us, and I don't want to lose any more of it than we already have. If that means compromise, then I'm all for doing whatever's necessary. We'll work it out together. Because I want to be there to hold you when you're sick and rub your back when it hurts. Our baby's going to need a brother and a sister and a full-time daddy who's crazy about her mother. Nobody else can do that like I can. Give me a chance, sweetheart. Give *us* a chance.''

Her blue eyes searching his earnest brown ones, Annie didn't doubt that he meant every word. Deep inside, her heart expanded. God, she loved this man! More now than the day she'd married him. She'd known when she left him that she was gambling everything. A successful, married man, alone and lonely, was an easy mark for any number of unscrupulous women with dollar signs in their eyes. But he was and always had been a chance worth taking.

She could trust him, she realized as a slow smile broke out on her face. With her heart, with their baby, with a future that looked more beautiful with every passing second. Her eyes shining with love, she lifted an impish eyebrow at him. "A brother *and* a sister, hmm? Three kids? You think you're ready for that?"

His own grin wicked, he drawled, "Honey, as long as you're their mama, I'm ready when you are. So are you giving us a chance or what?"

Surprised that he even had to ask, she laughed happily and launched herself into his arms. "What do you think?"

Epilogue

Five and a half months later

Twins. They had twins.

Standing at the side of his daughters' crib on their first night home from the hospital, Joe gazed down at the impossibly small babies and couldn't seem to stop smiling. Lord, they were so tiny! And unbelievably beautiful. Just like their mother. And they were all his. He still couldn't believe it. How could he have known that this was what it was like to be a daddy?

Glancing toward the bed, his heart turned over at the sight of Annie sound asleep on his pillow. Her labor hadn't been easy, but she'd pulled through it without a word of complaint. He'd been so proud of her. She'd been in so much pain, but her only concern had been for the babies. And him. He'd been a basket case. Every time a pain had ripped through her, he was the one who'd winced. By the time he'd held his daughters for the first time, he knew why they called it labor. He'd felt like he'd been caught in the wringer of an old washing machine. Annie, on the other hand, had been as fresh as a daisy once the hard part was over with.

God, he loved her! He didn't know if he'd ever be able to show her how much. The last six months had been like something out of a dream, but if he was dreaming, he didn't want to ever wake up. While they'd waited for the birth of their babies, they'd made some drastic, but much needed, changes in their life. They'd opened the second Joe's Place as planned, then rebuilt the original, but only after some structural changes in the original design. It was larger now, and included not only a nursery, but a real estate office for Annie and Phoebe. He only had to walk across the non-smoking area to see his wife whenever he wanted. A man couldn't ask for much more than that.

Annie was on maternity leave right now, of course, but later, she intended to put in ten or so hours a week, just to keep her hand in things until the kids were older. When she did, Joe would keep the babies. He couldn't wait.

Providing financial security for Annie and their children would always be important to him, and doing so in a way that both he and Annie could live with had been his one big concern. But things had a way of working out in the most unexpected ways, and no one had been more surprised than he when Drake had approached him soon after the restaurant had burned about buying into the business. He'd already proven himself to be a great manager, but he wanted something more permanent than that, more lasting, something he could help build and have the satisfaction of knowing that at least a piece of it was his.

After discussing it with Annie, they'd agreed to sell Drake twenty percent, and that had turned out to be the smartest business move he and Annie had ever made. With the money that Drake brought into the business, they were able to set up trust funds for the kids that would be worth a fortune by the time they reached adulthood. A second manager had been hired, freeing Joe from the hands-on running of either restaurant, so he spent his days overseeing everything and his evenings and nights at home. Just that easily, he and Annie had everything they'd ever wanted.

Satisfied that his children were safe and sleeping soundly, he made his way across the room in the dark and carefully climbed into bed, trying not to wake Annie as he lifted her slightly and settled her against his chest. But the second he was horizontal and holding her close to his heart, she stirred against him and pressed a kiss to his chest. "Hi, daddy," she murmured teasingly. "How're the kids?"

"Sleeping like angels," he replied softly. "Which is what their mama should be doing."

"Later," she promised. "Right now, I'm too happy. How about you?"

"Oh, I'll sleep later, too. Right now, there's this beautiful woman in my arms who's keeping me awake."

Chuckling softly, she playfully punched him in the shoulder. "You know what I mean. Are you happy?"

The old Joe would have given her a quick, positive answer without thinking about it, but he was a far cry from the Joe Taylor who had once taken happiness and love for granted. He'd been blessed and he knew it. "I've got you and the kids and this funny feeling in my heart whenever I think about the three of you," he murmured, tightening his arms around her. "I walk around with a goofy smile on my face all the time and I can't seem to stop humming. If that's not happiness, then I don't know what it is."

Love flooded Annie's heart and brought the sting of tears to her eyes. Drawing back just far enough to see his beloved face, she gave him a watery smile. "Me, either, but I'm suffering from the same thing and it feels wonderful. Do you think it could possibly get any better than this?"

"I don't know," he said with a grin, tenderly wiping the tears from her cheeks. "But we've got the next forty or fifty years to find out. Ask me again, then."

"You can count on it," she promised, laughing, and kissed him like there was no tomorrow. They had decades ahead of them, where once she wouldn't have given them weeks. Just thinking about it made her light-headed with joy. How had she gotten so lucky?

*   *   *   *   *

Bestselling author

JOAN JOHNSTON

continues her wildly popular miniseries with an
all-new, longer-length novel

The Virgin Groom

HAWK'S WAY

One minute, Mac Macready was a living legend in
Texas—every kid's idol, every man's envy, every
woman's fantasy. The next, his fiancée dumped him,
his career was hanging in the balance and his future
was looking mighty uncertain. Then there was the
matter of his scandalous secret, which didn't stand a
chance of staying a secret. So would he succumb to
Jewel Whitelaw's shocking proposal—or take cold
showers for the rest of the long, hot summer…?

Available August 1997
wherever Silhouette books are sold.

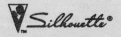

TRINITY STREET WEST

where danger lies around every corner—
and the biggest danger of all
is falling in love.

Meet the men and women of Trinity Street West
in the compelling miniseries by

Justine Davis
continuing in September 1997 with

A MAN TO TRUST
(Intimate Moments #805)

Kelsey Hall was hiding secrets and needed
someone to trust, and Cruz Gregerson, the one man
she desperately wanted to trust with her secrets *and*
her heart, was the one kind of man she knew she
couldn't—a by-the-book cop. But this time, he wasn't
thinking with his badge....

INTIMATE MOMENTS®
Silhouette®

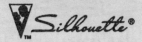

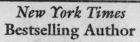

Share in the joy of yuletide romance with brand-new stories by two of the genre's most beloved writers

DIANA PALMER
and
JOAN JOHNSTON
in

LONE STAR CHRISTMAS

Diana Palmer and Joan Johnston share their favorite Christmas anecdotes and personal stories in this *special hardbound edition.*

Diana Palmer delivers an irresistible spin-off of her **LONG, TALL TEXANS** series and Joan Johnston crafts an unforgettable new chapter to **HAWK'S WAY** in this wonderful keepsake edition celebrating the holiday season. So perfect for gift giving, you'll want one for yourself...and one to give to a special friend!

Available in November at your favorite retail outlet!

Only from

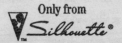